I0663147

It's a Kink Thing

KINKS AND CROSSHAIRS

M.C. ROTH

Kinks and Crosshairs
ISBN # 978-1-80250-995-3
©Copyright M.C. Roth 2022
Cover Art by Kelly Martin ©Copyright November 2022
Interior text design by Claire Siemaszkiewicz
Pride Publishing

Published in 2022 by Pride Publishing, United Kingdom.

Pride Publishing is an imprint of Totally Entwined Group Limited.

KINKS AND CROSSHAIRS

Dedication

For Q

Chapter One

Henley

The only thing worse than undercover work was babysitting. At least when he was undercover, Henley could give himself a cool superhero name and occupation like 'Mr. Duncan Peters, high school superintendent and nighttime vigilante'.

But babysitting?

Some agents loved it, but they were the ones who called it 'bodyguard duty' and got thrills at the idea of taking a bullet for someone whose middle name was 'rich boy'. Sure, there were some good cases out there, but for the most part, it was that rich boy in front of him.

He cast his gaze around the club, trying to ignore the way the lights made his temples throb every time they caught his eyes. The entrances were clear, with the same bouncers who had been standing guard all night. Only one had slipped away briefly and had returned red-faced with a hickey on his neck and lipstick smeared against the corner of his lips. *Lucky guy.*

The ceiling was solid drywall, only interspersed with two vents and the constant flashing lights. No one was getting the jump on him from above. And luckily, there was a single door, which made his job a hell of a lot easier but had him worrying about fire hazards.

The gig wasn't *terrible,* but it got old fast when his charge was some spoiled brat who was high on blow and had fucked seven different chicks in the last three days.

He kinda envied the kid's stamina, though.

Somebody didn't. Someone had put a death threat out on the kid after Henley's boss had apparently fucked with the wrong people. *Didn't see that one coming.* Henley rolled his eyes. He'd never seen so much drama in his life.

The kid's father had enough money and pull to get three more bodyguards assigned, along with his regular squad of four goons. The other two additional bodyguards were nothing more than glorified mercs with a bit of a conscience, but Henley?

He chuckled, shaking his head as he spied his 'colleague' along the far wall. He was checking the exits, same as Henley was, with his beefy arms crossed and his tattoos on display, much to the ladies' delight.

Henley hadn't actually been a mercenary for a long time, even if almost nobody in the world knew that. But even while in that department, people treated him as a bit of a joke. He didn't have the size or the tattoos for anyone to take him seriously.

Nodding along with the beat, he did a little twirl, bumping hips with a lady who gave him a *whoop* and a smile. She was rocking six-inch heels like they didn't even hurt, dancing with him for a minute before he gave her a wink and melted away from the crowd.

The view was decent from where he leaned against the wall, the beat shivering against his back. Tattoo guy was pretty hot, but one dropped suggestion for a hookup in the bathroom and that ship had sailed. And as nice as the ladies were, they didn't exactly have the equipment Henley was after.

Sigh. Sometimes it was like guys didn't expect him to be gay. It wasn't his fault that he missed more than he hit when trying to spot a fellow nut fan.

He *tried.* There was a rainbow sticker on the butt of his gun and a matching pin on his fanny pack that gave him away, if anyone cared to be observant. As for the fanny pack, he was bringing the trend back, and it was a great place to store extra clips for his lethal baby.

His knife was pink — and fabulous, too — although it was tucked away where no one could see it. And he was drinking a strawberry daiquiri — a little more strawberry, a little less daiquiri...because he *was* working, after all.

How could I not be gay? The male body and all its intricacies was where the party was at. It was a true shame that some straight men never indulged in the pure wonder that was the prostate.

Sighing, he tried giving the goon one last look from across the room, standing on his tiptoes to see over the writhing mass. *I need a fucking stool.* It was like trying to spot someone in a corn field.

His phone buzzed from within his fanny pack, humming against his belly and sending the strange sensation of vibrating bullets against his skin. Tapping the line hooked over his ear, he turned away from his charge, marching to the exit and easing through the first layer of doors to where the music volume was more reasonable.

"Rosco." He used his mercenary name to answer.

"Is he safe?" asked Mr. Martinez, his kinda-sorta boss on the other end of the line. Henley let out a huffing breath as he peered at a few flyers that had been pinned to the wall separating the club entrance from the outside world. *Are 'high' and 'drunk' still considered safe?*

"He has a full squad with him at all times. No one is getting to your son unless he goes through every one of us first." He pressed the speaker farther into his ear, trying to catch Martinez's reply over the music.

"My sources tell me that the hit will be taking place tomorrow. I don't think I need to tell you what will happen if you fail me."

Always such a chipper guy. There was a reason that his body count was nearly as high as Henley's — which happened to be the main reason for Henley's undercover assignment to the case.

"He's not making it easy. He should be underground, not in a club," said Henley, ripping the number off one of the advertisements for car cleaning and stuffing it into his pocket. He was between vehicles at the moment, but he never knew when he would need a bit of remains scrubbed out of his back seat.

The bar was packed, and of course, the little dipshit he was trying to protect had dragged them to the same club again for the third night in a row. One more night and he would have to look up to see if his benefits covered hearing damage.

The music was so loud that it couldn't have been legal, thrumming against his chest in a monotonous beat that made him feel way too old. He knew music and a good beat, but that shit coming out of the speakers? *Gah.* He'd heard the same whispered line after a siren over thirty times that night alone.

The lighting was the second issue. It was hard to tell a purse from a weapon, and he had to squint to try to catch a glimpse of his Romeo across the club. The swirling lights helped visibility a bit, unless they were shining directly into his eyes. If someone smuggled in a shotgun, he wouldn't know until it was pressed to the back of the kid's head.

It really didn't explain why Henley was looking at close to forty female booties without a single interesting dangly between them. The kid's father had cleared the bar of all male clientele after a quick phone call. They were certain that a man had sent the threat, so bring on the ladies, right?

"I've banned every possible assassin from that club, and, as you said, you have a full detail on him. How is that hard?" asked Mr. Martinez, his voice dropping into a growl. "Keep him safe, or you'll wish you were dead."

Because apparently chicks couldn't kill.

Henley begged to disagree. The woman who'd trained him was the most terrifying person he had ever met, and she could probably still kick his ass, even though she was in her late forties and had popped out three screaming munchkins in the last five years.

"Hello?" Henley tapped his ear, but the line had already gone dead. *Just what I need…another death threat.* Some people collected stamps or classic dinky cars, but Henley had always liked to stay on the wilder side of things.

But death threats weren't worth much, and he couldn't exactly leave them for his family if he did wind up getting shot.

He popped back through the club door, shaking his head as he eyed his charge, who had a different woman in his arms and another grinding against his back. Looking off to the windows that lined the entire side of the club, he stared into the night, letting the music roll over him.

"You gonna head out soon?" asked his sexy goon as he moved closer, shouting into Henley's ear over the music. His breath was tinted with bitter alcohol and his shirt reeked of cigarettes. Maybe Henley had dodged a cancerous bullet.

What time is it? Oh, shit. Henley glared at his watch, hoping that the numbers were wrong. There were so many exposed women on the dance floor that he must've retreated into himself to try to save his sexuality. Women could be beautiful, but not when they were stumbling drunk and groping the only guy on the dance floor as if he were the last dick on the planet. Henley had seen that dick unfortunately, and it was not worth the effort.

He shook out his hand, his watch shifting on his wrist but not resetting like it was supposed to. He'd been standing there for the last half hour, not even getting fucking paid. *Babysitting blows.*

"Yeah, and the offer still stands. Come by my place if you want a good time later," said Henley, pulling the bodyguard down to him to whisper into his ear. The guy went tense, jerking back with narrowed eyes.

Nope, no interest at all. Couldn't blame him for trying. He hadn't bothered to ask the goon's name, so his hopes hadn't been that high, anyway.

The bodyguard shouted something, but Henley didn't bother trying to decipher it over the thrumming beat. He'd struck out...nine times in the last week?

Maybe it had been more. Either way, everyone must've gone straight or moved to Colorado, because it was a fucking desert out there right now.

Pushing his way through the sea of sweaty, horny and drugged bodies, he headed for the exit and the promise sweet night air. Sweat beaded over his temples as he nodded to one of the bouncers before pushing his way out of the door. The touch of fresh air was better than a power nap on a Sunday afternoon and twice as refreshing.

Taking a breath, he slammed the door behind him, cutting off the plaguing sound of yet another siren. Whoever was making club music these days needed a muse or something because that shit had been pathetic.

Or maybe it's because anything remotely pop-like gives me hives?

The club door led directly to the street, a few streetlamps spotted over the empty plane of asphalt and concrete. The closest one flickered, giving off the same sound as a humming cricket as the bulb flashed. The smooth road was barely three steps away, the thin sidewalk the only thing separating the club from the rest of the world.

Old brick buildings surrounded him on all sides, with so many spots to hide that it was nearly impossible to cover them all. Three were multi-leveled stores, some with apartments above. The one across the road with the pale brick and the flashing sign was where he'd set up his temporary apartment when he'd taken the assignment.

Usually he didn't like to eat so close to where he worked, but the apartment window offered a perfect view of the place, and he could see inside the club with the stretch of windows that surrounded it from floor to ceiling. He was technically on point for the assignment, so he didn't want to let the kid out of his sight for too long.

He'd chosen that particular apartment because he'd heard a rumor that the club was a kink club of sorts, too. He didn't care if it hosted a munch or a full-blown party, because some fresh faces were exactly what he needed, even if they weren't the feral pups he was looking for.

Unfortunately, he had yet to see a single hint of leather making its way through the doors as he'd watched from his perch on the couch.

Henley slowed his pace as the thump of the music started to dim, pulling the sleeves of his shirt down over his wrists. The air had started to grow crisper as winter approached, although the days were still somewhat warm. If he held his breath long enough, he could almost see the steam of it under the lamp light as he exhaled.

When he'd moved to Canada, he had done it because everything he'd known about the country had told him it was supposed to be cold, with igloo houses and dog sleds and shit.

Three years earlier, during his first summer near the southern tip of the country, the air had been so thick and hot that his ice-cream cone had melted in thirty seconds flat. He'd spent most of the summers half naked by a pool since, only venturing out when he could get away with his long-sleeved T.

He had half considered moving back to... No, he was never going back, no matter how hot it got.

Luckily, the winters were ball-freezing cold, which was exactly the way he wanted them. And the kink community was thriving, even if they were more on the down-low than where he was from.

Nonchalantly reaching for his gun, he clicked the safety off, dropping his hands a moment later. There was someone standing outside of his apartment building, leaning down and inspecting the lock. The place was a little run-down, but it had decent security, and the guy didn't look like anyone he'd seen in the video feeds he'd hacked.

He had an entire wall covered in labeled pictures with every person who had come and gone in the building since he'd set up there. He didn't bother with their actual names on the photographs because *'lady with nine cats'* and *'guy who is always high'* were way easier to remember.

But the guy at the door was nowhere on his wall. In fact, it looked like the guy was either unsuccessfully trying to pick the lock, or...

Henley slowed, flexing his biceps to make sure that his knife was still securely strapped there. He couldn't feel the one at his ankle through his sock, but he had checked on it the last time he'd taken a bathroom break. The one at his back along his waistband shifted with every move, comforting him with its weight.

Something caught the light as the man at the door dropped to his knees, leaning closer to the lock. His long hair looked nearly as dark as the night that wrapped around them, falling past his shoulders to hide most of his face from Henley's view.

"It works better with the right equipment," said Henley as he ducked into the security lights at the door, taking a quick glance at his ankle as he took another step. A tiny sliver of a pink handle looked back at him. It was a specialized ceramic that was sharp as fuck and tricked most metal detectors. Unfortunately, it came with the cost of single-use-only sometimes, as it would shatter if he slammed it into someone's spine.

He'd been eyeing up a baby blue one just like it online a few days prior, and he hadn't decided if it was going to be his birthday gift to himself or not. Then there was the gun with pink bullets, of course. *Do they make pink bullets? Nah, it doesn't matter.* He would just make them himself.

The guy at the door snapped up to his feet, looking over his shoulder in surprise. "What?"

Very nice. The lock picker was taller than Henley had thought, and probably around six-one, which was just the type of challenge he usually looked for. He was thinner than he had looked from afar, packed into a thick coat that was too warm for the weather and dark gloves that hid his presumably pale skin from view. His long hair scraped against his coat as he moved, whooshing as if a breeze had picked up in the middle of the city.

The way the security lights caught his eyes made them appear almost black, highlighting the pale skin of his cheek bones and accentuating his jaw that looked strong enough to be a nutcracker.

"I just..." The lock picker trailed off as he gave Henley a once-over, flickering his gaze from the toes of Henley's rainbow runners and pausing on his fanny pack for a moment.

One look spoke more than a thousand words. It was the same look that Henley had been seeking for weeks. *Yes! There are still gays out there. Play this right.*

"You were *just* trying to pick the lock. Let's see what you've got, because it obviously isn't working," said Henley, crossing his arms so he could touch the blade at his wrist. It was rigid under his fingertips as he slipped down his sleeve to the handle, ready to pull it from its holster. The gun at his waist seemed to throb, exposed and visible to anyone who cared to look.

It was on display for a reason. Bad guys always seemed to wait to act until he grabbed for his gun. Watching their surprise as he pulled a knife on them instead was half the fun.

"I'm not." The lock picker shook his head, his eyes going wide as he caught sight of Henley's gun. Taking a step back, he let one a whooshing breath, condensation steaming against his lips. "I just... My key won't work."

Ah shit. Henley blinked, squinting at the guy's hand in the low light. Maybe it was time for him to give up his stubbornness and wear the glasses his optometrist had insisted on. He hadn't missed a target yet, but it was only a matter of time.

The guy didn't have any equipment on him at all. No pins or picks—just a ring and a couple of funky-looking key chains attached to an array of colorful keys. If he wasn't mistaken, the guy had gone to three different Mexican resorts and had gotten a sandal keychain at each one.

I'm getting way too paranoid for my own good.

"Heh." Henley scrubbed the back of his head, widening his stance *just in case*. He'd been fooled before by guys that were half as cute. One had even managed to get a jump on him when he'd reached for his dick, leaving a scar the size of a nickel right next to the prize.

But this guy wasn't *cute*, he was beautiful, with a smooth face that looked like it had never had a five o'clock shadow. *Lucky bastard*. Henley had a shadow fifteen minutes after he shaved, and by the end of the day, he looked like he'd been roughing it in the woods for a week. It was too bad that a beard didn't suit him.

"I'm Henley," he said, holding out his hand like an absolute dork. He flushed, ready to draw his hand back, before the guy clasped it, shaking twice.

Taking a moment to enjoy, Henley smiled up at the stranger. His grip was good, his wrist relaxed, so he was probably a successful interview candidate and definitely didn't have any weapons concealed there. And his legs were too close together to have enough balance to start a fight that he would have any chance of winning.

That left two options — civilian or amateur.

"You're supposed to tell me your name, too," said Henley, sliding his thumb over the back of the amateur's gloved knuckles. The leather was soft, like it had just been dipped in body butter.

"Li."

Interesting. The guy didn't look like a 'Li'. He looked more like a 'Damien', or 'Grey', or 'Marius' — with a little less vampirism. There was a chance it was a fake name, though.

"Can you help me get in?" asked Li, handing his keys over to Henley. "I just moved in, and the key the superintendent gave me doesn't work. I've been trying for five minutes, but no luck."

"There is no superintendent, and you look like you could save your time and kick the door down instead," said Henley, playing with the keys in his hand. None of them felt heavier than they should have…or lighter. Companies were getting better, though, and things could be hidden in the most innocent of places. One of the keychains looked pretty suspect. No one actually kept a smiley face on their keychain, did they?

"Um, Mr. Richty? Does he have a different title? Landlord maybe? And I can't *kick* the door down. That just sounds painful and expensive." Li reached for his keys, and Henley dropped them into his outstretched palm.

"I'm just fucking with you, kid. Try the blue one, and wiggle it a little," said Henley, leaning up against the door and crossing his arms. Li's hand trembled as he searched for the right key, almost dropping the entire bundle before he found it at last. A flush bloomed across his cheeks, and he looked to Henley every few seconds.

Civilian it was. *Booooring*, unless they were kinky. Normally, Henley had no problem asking someone outright. It was a conversation starter.

"Can I put a collar around your throat and plug your ass with a tail before I chase you around my apartment?"

There could be a reason that he was striking out so often. The last goon had looked like he was about to pass out when Henley had run that by him.

"Oh," said Li, slipping the blue key into the lock. It turned on the first try, the door clicking open with a low clunk. "Thanks, but I'm not a kid."

Henley grinned to himself, shuddering in the cool air. Of *course*, Li wasn't a kid. He was definitely legal, hence fair game. He did look a bit skittish, though.

"Sorry, Li. You said you just moved in?" asked Henley, slipping through the door as Li held it open for him like a gentleman. "You know what? I can't call you Li. It just doesn't suit you, and it's just going to bother me all night." He grinned at Li, waiting for the telltale flush that would spark any second. *Fuck*, he loved being right.

Li looked good to begin with, but with the beginnings of a blush, he turned downright fuckable. Henley was going to climb him like a tree…then trip him and take him the fuck down.

On that thought, maybe there was more than one reason he was striking out.

"All night?" asked Li, his voice catching with an adorable stutter that would have been cute if it hadn't been so sexy. The breeze of the closing door caught his dark hair, throwing it over his shoulder until his pale neck was on display. It looked like it would hold his marks for days.

"Yeah," said Henley, pulling the door shut behind him and leaning against it. The night air hadn't done Li justice. His skin was flawless perfection, everything hard and soft in just the right way. He belonged in a penthouse suite, not a run-down apartment building with neglected flyers bursting out of the busted rectangular mailboxes.

"This is the part where you ask me to show you around, and I show you my favorite spot. I'm a gentleman like that." Henley eyed Li up, wishing that he could see right through his thick jacket. Was he soft there, too, or hard and thick like his long legs? "Then I'll show you *your* new favorite spot." Henley leaned in, rocking up on his toes so he could get close enough to whisper into Li's ear. It was a bigger stretch than he'd expected. "I'll give you a hint. It's your prostate."

Chapter Two

Henley

"Um." Li flushed deeper, going from cute to a glorified tomato in seconds. His wide eyes were blue, not dark like Henley had originally thought, with flecks of brown. Li's breathing picked up, his chest heaving as Henley hovered close.

Virgin, maybe? Henley took a step back to give Li some space. He loved to play the predator, but he wasn't actually one.

"I mean, I would really appreciate it if you showed me around the place, but maybe just that? I'm not really comfortable with anything else. I'm not...like that," said Li, clenching his gloved hands.

Like what? Gay? Kinky? Horny? The possibilities were endless. It all boiled down to the same thing...a big fat no.

Sighing, Henley ran his hand through his hair before starting up the stairs. "Yeah, sure, kid. Just let me tell my cock to back off, because he's been striking out all month." Henley poked at his crotch. He was still soft, but if Li had said yes, he would've been ready in a second. "Down, boy."

Li snorted, his quiet steps barely making a sound as he followed Henley up the stairs. For a big guy, he was really quiet. Not that he was *that* big. He looked thick through his jacket, but there was no way that that could all be muscle.

"My floor, in case you change your mind. I'm number seven, but I always have music going, so you'll have to knock really loud," said Henley, shooting Li a wink. He was actually in number eight, but that would be his little secret.

Li was right behind him instead of two steps back like Henley had thought he'd be. The skin prickled on the back of his neck, and he paused, looking down the stairs as he touched his gun. Li took up most of the stairway, his breathing low and soft. It was too quiet.

One look at Li's innocent blush, and the feeling passed.

He really, *really* needed some stress relief. But it sounded like it was going to be him and his hand again. He was working on a record, although Guinness didn't seem to keep track of solo masturbation stats.

"I'm the next floor up," said Li as they kept working their way up the spiral. Henley's lungs were starting to burn, but he kept his breaths even. He was a sprinter, not a long-distance runner, but he was not about to pant in front of a civilian. "I'm number twenty-six, in case you need any sugar. You won't have to knock loud because my cat will hear you coming and meow like crazy."

"I love cats," said Henley, grinning at Li, who felt even closer, his breath tickling the back of Henley's neck. "Just walk beside me, kid. You're so close it's making my neck hurt."

He would rather Li was above him, cause the bigger they were, the more cock he got when they fell. *Down boy. Damn cock.*

"Not a kid, *old man*," Li growled back, his polite shyness falling away for the first time.

So it *was* an act. *A slightly more interesting civilian, then.*

"I like it," said Henley, puffing out his chest and gut in an attempt at looking anything over his one-hundred and sixty pounds. "Makes me feel distinguished. I gotta work on my dadbod, though. Do you have any nachos and beer? But only light beer, please, otherwise my ass gets big." He let the air out in a rush, chuckling as Li grinned back at him.

And *that* had Li looking at his ass, which was perfect. Henley chuckled again. It was like he was a secret agent or something. Babysitting aside, he loved his frickin' job.

"'Kid' makes me sound like I'll get ID'd at a strip club," said Li, skimming his hand along the banister as he moved up beside Henley, their arms brushing.

"They don't card the strippers, kid, so I think you'll be fine." They were almost at the top of the stairs, and he was officially out of breath. Their footsteps echoed just a touch louder than his breath as they approached the fire exit.

"Ouch," said Li, grinning through his fake-hurt. His eyes lit up, sparkling as they paused at the 'Fire Exit Only' sign at the top of the stairs.

"It's a compliment," said Henley. "Exotic dancers are hot as hell, and they are very athletic. Some of them could probably dislocate your dick with how flexible they are."

Li snorted, shaking his head. "You're an interesting guy, Henley. You know what? I'm not gonna call you that, because I'm never going to remember your name all night. You'll be 'old man' from now on."

Henley laughed as his own words were thrown back in his face. It had been a while since anyone had caught him off guard like that.

"Well, here it is, kid," said Henley, sliding a card from his pocket to trick the motion sensor he had installed, before he slipped through the door. The sensor was simple but effective for those who weren't expecting it. He waited for Li to get all the way through before he let the door close. Once it thunked shut, the lock clicking in place, he pulled his card away, alarm-free.

The night air felt even cooler ten floors up, with the breeze buffeting against the flat roof and kicking up tiny pieces of dust destined for Henley's eyes. He blinked the grit away, looking straight up to the stars. Even with the city's glow, they were still magnificent.

"It's beautiful," said Li, taking a few steps away from the door. Henley hummed in agreement, taking another deep breath of fall air. Crisp leaves mixed with the hollow echo of a recent rain filled his lungs to the brim.

"Careful near the edges, 'cause there are no railings," said Henley, glancing over the shallow lip at the edge of the tar. He could see straight into a couple of apartments and had caught the occasional hint of nudity as he'd passed time there.

Unfortunately, he could see straight into the club as well, which was why he had installed similar door sensors on every building in sight. It was the perfect place for a shooter to set up if they wanted to take his charge out. The little shit was in clear view of the window, even as one of the goons tried to beckon him away.

The rich idiot had a death wish. No matter how many times Henley had told him, he had gone back to doing whatever the hell he wanted. Shaking his head, he turned away from the club. He was done thinking about work for the night.

"You like it?" asked Henley, turning to Li. Li had stalked off to the side of the roof and was looking down into the alley that had been riddled with dozens of garbage bags the last time Henley had seen it. The flush on his cheeks was barely visible under the bright security lights as he hurried back to Henley's side.

"There are people down there," said Li, his voice barely above a whisper as he pulled his jacket tighter, a shiver traveling down his frame

Henley chuckled. The kid was unreal. He couldn't remember the last time he had seen someone that was so ripe with naïve innocence. He'd seen four people fuck in that exact alley in the last two days. The worst experience had been when he'd stood guard at the entrance while his charge fumbled with his dick and a woman fake-moaned for thirty seconds.

Waiting until Li was in range, Henley reached for him, moving slowly so Li would have the opportunity to pull away. Smirking, he clasped Li's warm hand in his, threading their fingers together before hauling him closer. Li had removed his gloves and his hands were even softer than Henley had suspected, the zinging touch going straight to his gut.

That's it. A thrill shot up his spine as Li stumbled, probably taken off guard by Henley's strength. Henley would admit — to no one but himself — that he was on the shorter and thinner side, but underneath his baggy clothes, he was fucking mighty.

"What were they doing?" asked Henley, tugging Li until their chests were nearly touching. Li was breathing fast, his pupils wide in the low light. A few strands of hair caught the breeze, dragging over Li's lips in a caress that Henley longed to repeat.

It's been a long time. He couldn't remember the name of the last sub he'd played with, fucked, then held until the sun came up. Even if he could remember, he wouldn't have gone back for seconds.

Henley caught the sound of a faint feminine moan over the wind, followed by a much deeper one. *Shit.* It sounded like his tattooed goon was trying to reaffirm his manhood after Henley had hit on him.

"Um…stuff. Something they shouldn't d-do in p-public," said Li, his shy stutter back with a vengeance. The playful attitude had disappeared again, leaving a dreadful act in its place.

Henley squeezed his hand until Li gasped and tried to pull away. He didn't want the shy kid act. He wanted fun. He touched their chests together, suppressing the shudder at the warmth of Li, even through his jacket. The kid felt jacked through all that padding, and his height made for an excellent wind block. "Don't be like that. Tell me what they were doing."

"She's blowing him," said Li, the waver in his voice almost gone. "And he's whining like a little bitch." He let out a stuttering breath, and Henley could feel his chest pounding through the layers.

Grinning, Henley slid his hand through Li's hair, groaning at the silky strands. The kid must've had one hell of a two-in-one shampoo to have hair that soft — or maybe it was just natural, like the smoothness of his face. "If you were the one down there, what position would you be in? I can't picture you whining like a bitch, but I can see you on your knees."

Sliding his knee between Li's legs, he eased forward until he could barely feel the outline of Li's cock. He was hard, not quite throbbing, but interested, which was a relief. "Tell me to stop, and I'll stop. You say no, and I'll stop. Now, which position would you be in?"

"I'm not... I mean, I've never..." Li trailed off as Henley moved his knee to press harder against his groin.

It felt nice — thick, heavy and downright huge. If he had his guess, the dick against his thigh was going to rearrange his top ten.

"I can go slow, kid. If you answer my question, I'll be nice, but if you don't, then you might not enjoy the consequences." Henley laid it right out, hoping that the kid caught on so they could get to the fucking. Reward and punishment were where Henley thrived.

Li furrowed his forehead and his eyes went wide as his blush turned rosy. Henley wondered if the kid had ever seen another cock up close, let alone a handcuff or two.

It wasn't so much the size of the kink as the way he played with it that counted. It didn't matter to him if his partners *thought* they were kinky or not, because by the time he was done with them, they would *know*.

Henley leaned in, breathing against Li's neck before placing a single open-mouthed kiss. Li swallowed under him, his throat bobbing as Henley scraped his teeth over the smooth skin that only had the barest hint of a prickle.

"I don't want it slow," said Li, his voice going deeper as Henley nibbled on his chin and neck. Li's skin was hot under his tongue, his mouth tingling with every touch. Unfortunately, the fucker was too tall for him to reach his lips, and strong enough to resist Henley's grip on his hair. *So far.*

"You're good at avoiding questions," said Henley, sucking the spot until it bloomed burgundy. Li tasted of citrus and something dark that laced over his tongue and made him *want.* He dropped one hand to Li's jacket zipper, easing it down one click at a time.

"You're good at asking questions that I don't want to answer," said Li, letting out a small gasp as Henley dipped inside his jacket and smoothed a palm over the plane of his chest. He moved his hands to Henley's hips, rocking into his thigh.

Biting down until Li whimpered, he tugged the jacket zipper the rest of the way down, sliding his hand over the thin cotton T-shirt he found underneath. Li was solid and cut under the plush coat, his nipples pebbling into tiny points that tented the fabric. It was a shame that he had bothered to cover himself up with the coat at all. A body like Li's was meant to be seen. *By me.*

"Answer." Henley's voice went dark, and he bit down again until he knew he would leave bruises behind. Adjusting his hand in Li's hair, he tugged him back until Li arched his neck and he swallowed. Li's cock throbbed as he responded to the mix of pain and pleasure, leaving no doubt as to whether he was kinky.

Henley smirked, licking his lips and humming at the taste.

"I'd be standing, but I wouldn't be whimpering. You would be the one crying as I fed you my cock," said Li, growling as Henley kept tugging until his neck had to be aching from the position. He moved his hands to Henley's wrists, digging in until Henley moaned.

Fucking A. It was always the shy ones who ended up having the dirtiest mouths. They usually had the best moves in bed, too.

Li was powerful, that much was obvious from what he could see through the tight T-shirt, but he wasn't pushing Henley away. If anything, he was holding him close, the grip on Henley's wrists unrelenting. That much power could break him and overwhelm him in a way that was too dangerous, even for him.

Shuddering, Henley took a deep breath, pressing his forehead to Li's chest before breathing him in. Was it a full moon or was he just that lucky?

"Why the virgin act, kid? Or maybe it's the bravery that's an act and you're really just a scared pup." He scratched deep into Li's scalp, tangling the soft strands between his fingers as he eased his grip.

Li growled, the sound sending a surge of blood straight to Henley's cock. Henley looked up a moment before the guy's lips smashed against his own, taking his breath and the last of his hesitation.

His hold on Li's hair was forgotten as he was momentarily swept away, going boneless, even as he fought to keep control. Grabbing the back of Li's neck instead, Henley pulled him close, tipping up on his toes to devour the sweetness pressed to him.

Blood surged south until he was hard enough that he could probably use his dick as a rolling pin for pastry. Li's lips were innocence and brute force, all wrapped up into one. He was tentative, probing with his tongue and shrinking away from Henley's touch as he plunged inside, but he was also unyielding, his jaw tense as he pushed back against Henley's lips. His power alone was enough to make Henley's head swim.

"I'll choke on your cock if you can get me on my knees," said Henley, biting on Li's ear lobe as he took gasping breaths to try to combat his swimming head. Li went tense against him, grabbing Henley's hips hard enough to bruise. "How hard can it be for a big guy like you to take down little old me?"

"You asked for it, old man."

As Li lifted him by the hips, Henley hooked his feet behind Li's knees, folding them like a stack of cards. He cradled Li's head as they fell, using their momentum to roll them over until he was straddling Li's lap. Moving to grip his wrists, Henley pinned them above Li's head as they settled on the unforgiving surface. Li restrained between him and rough asphalt against his skin was better than cocaine.

Li let out a gasp as Henley ground down, bringing their lips together to swallow Li's groan with his mouth. Somehow, he tasted even better with his heart pounding and hair splayed over the rooftop, already tangled and mussed. Henley wanted to make it look so much worse, until there was no question as to what Li had been doing.

His quiet moans were perfection as Li fluttered his eyes shut, giving in to Henley completely with one slick kiss. His mouth was sin, and his cock was like an iron bar through his slacks. It really was too bad that Henley didn't bottom often, because that was one cock that he would be willing to experience.

For a man who had said he was a virgin, he gave in easily. Henley hummed, slipping his tongue between

Li's lips and toying with him as he loosened his hold. There was so much more fun to be had.

"You're fast," said Li as he leaned back, rucking up Henley's shirt and resting a hand over his belly. It wasn't slow and exploratory like Henley had expected, but his fingers still lit up a path of fire, leaving goosebumps in their wake. He avoided Henley's gun, which was definitely a good thing. Touching his gun was a one-way ticket to a never-wake-up nap.

"And you're strong, exactly how I like my pups," said Henley, biting at Li's lower lip until he tasted blood. The coppery hint flooded his mouth and nose, sending him higher.

"Do you accost a lot of strangers on rooftops?" asked Li, palming at Henley's ass. He thrust up a few times before taking Henley off guard as he surged to one side.

With a dull thud, and maybe a mild concussion, Henley hit the flat-top roof, his ears ringing from the blow. *Ow, but still hot.* His breath stained the air as Li hovered over him, his hair hanging down like a privacy drape. A few strands tickled his cheek and he broke out in a shiver. "Only when I'm horny as fuck."

"Christ," Li cursed, moving one hand to Henley's throat before resting lightly against his pulse. His eyes were wide as he wet his lips. "You're like the wet dream I never knew I had." He let out a laugh, shaking his head. "I never thought..." Li curled his lips into a smirk. "Too bad you'll be fulfilling my fantasy and not your own." He tightened his grip on Henley's neck, scooping Henley's wrists and pinning them with one large hand.

A pebble dug into Henley's back, and he arched to try to escape the inevitable bruise. Perhaps he had underestimated Li—or perhaps he was finally having a smidge of luck.

Should I struggle? He didn't want to freak Li out, but at the same time, he wanted to resist so Li would pin him harder. It wasn't often that someone managed to get him on his back, and it felt better than expected. Still, he was *not* choking on cock, no matter how hot Li was.

In a move that would make Matt Damon proud, Henley freed one arm before hooking it around Li's throat. He cocked his hips, tangling their feet together, before using every bit of strength he possessed to try to flip Li over.

There was a second of absolute powerlessness when Li's body resisted him like a solid wall of muscle, before it finally started to budge. Henley made it almost halfway before Li tightened his hand and slammed his hips down, pushing Henley hard into the asphalt. The sensation of their cocks meeting in a brutal kiss only separated by a few measly layers pushed a groan through Henley's lips at the same time Li went slack.

Henley took every advantage, twisting and flailing until Li fell to the side with a grunt. Scrambling, he launched himself on Li's back, forcing Li's cheek into the dirt and gravel as he brought his hands behind his back. Their chests heaved as Henley planted himself on Li's back, grinding into his ass like it was bought and paid for.

He couldn't remember the last time he had been so hard, energy zipping through his limbs as he throbbed. Most subs gave him a cursory struggle when they found out what he liked, but it was rare that his heart rate was ever jacked.

It was rare that it was so *real.*

"Tell me to stop," said Henley, panting into Li's ear as he attempted to struggle. Cranking Li's arms higher on his back, Henley moved one hand to grab both wrists, kissing the back of Li's neck as he went still.

"Don't stop," said Li, letting out a long groan as Henley rutted harder, sliding his covered cock between Li's cheeks. He shuddered, a full-bodied thing that Henley felt in every cell.

"Nervous?"

Li shook his head, swallowing with a click. "No, but I've never…"

He trailed off and Henley had to roll his eyes. There was no way that Li hadn't rolled someone in the hay in his lifetime. The guy was smoking, and despite his acting skills, the virgin card was so beyond unbelievable at this point that he wasn't sure why Li was even trying.

"I've never fucked a guy."

Oh. *Oh.* Henley licked his lips, cheering internally at his great luck. The only thing better than fucking a guy was breaking one in.

"And you want this old man to show you the ropes?" asked Henley, dropping his free hand to Li's hip and tugging him to his knees. There was just enough room for Henley to slip his hand into the front of Li's pants, and fumble with the button and zipper until there was only a thin stretch of boxers between Li's cock and his palm. One more pull, and the boxers were gone, too.

Shivering, Henley trailed a finger down Li's cock, stopping at the head to smear the drop of pre-cum around until it dried in the chilled air. Li hissed and tried to hump his hand, shuffling his knees until more of his weight was on his cheek.

I guess my little pup likes a bit of pain, too. Perfect.
"No."

Henley froze, Li's body burning against him at that simple word. He swallowed the sudden guilt that whirled up, ready to release Li at the slightest bit of resistance. "You want me to stop?"

"No, don't stop. I just...just get it over with and fuck me already. You don't have to show me the ropes," said Li, his voice coming out a bit muffled as his hair stuck to his lips. There were so many tangles already that Henley imagined him brushing it out for hours after they were done, reliving every moment as the brush tugged his hair.

Most anal virgins were impatient until their pants were down—then they hit the brakes. But Li was the exact opposite. Henley was going to have to steal Li's driver's license so he could send him a freakin' thank you card.

"I can do that, if you're good," said Henley, leaning back so he got the first real look at the prize beneath him. Creamy, pale skin and ass muscles from the gods had his mouth watering. "When's the last time you were tested?"

"Six weeks ago. I get tested routinely for work because I get exposed to...bodily fluids sometimes," said Li, trying to shuffle out of his pants and boxers that were still wrapped around his legs at the level of his knees.

Henley kneeled on the crotch of Li's slacks, immobilizing him with a simple touch. "I was tested two months ago, and I haven't fucked anyone since, unfortunately. I'm still gonna use a condom, if that's okay. I don't really trust strangers who try to accost me on rooftops."

Li snorted, tugging at his arms uselessly and hissing when Henley moved them higher up his back. "Do you usually keep condoms on you if you've been celibate for two months?"

"Absolutely," said Henley, fishing open the zipper of his fanny pack. It was slightly squashed from the struggle, but luckily, he didn't keep grenades in it anymore. He'd learned that one the hard way.

"Did you think my fanny pack was a fashion statement? Because it definitely is. It's just a practical one." He rifled through the contents. It was always full, no matter how many times he cleaned it out.

That's where my favorite clip went. Oh, and a piece of gum. He shoved the gum into his mouth, pulling out a condom and a single-use packet of lube before placing them both on Li's back beneath his restrained hands.

"I thought you were wearing it because you're an old man. Pretty sure my mom still has hers in her closet from the eighties."

Grinning, Henley ripped open the lube packet with his teeth, grimacing when a bit got into his mouth. He should have gone with the flavored stuff, but it just wasn't as nice as the long-lasting. He hoped Li was still laughing at him in a minute.

With zero ceremony, Henley lined up three lubed fingers, holding them tight together so he would have a chance of breaching Li's virgin ring. He waited until Li was halfway through a breath before he pushed through the furl, sinking them all the way to the base.

"Ah, fuck." Li shouted, arching his back as he uselessly tried to tug his arms free. He gasped as Henley moved, searching for that little spot that would blow Li's mind through the pain.

"You like it?" asked Henley, biting his lower lip to keep his own groan behind his teeth. Li was tight...really fucking tight. He hadn't lied about being an ass-virgin, and he'd obviously never even played with himself. It almost made Henley feel a bit bad about going with three fingers, *but nah*.

"How could anyone like that? It fucking burns." Li squirmed — almost bucking free.

Twisting his hand, Henley drove straight for Li's sweet spot, nailing it head-on with the power of three fingers. He shuddered as Li gasped for an entirely different reason, his cock leaking on Henley's leg that was still planted between his thighs. "How about now?"

"Fuck, what are you doing?" Li trembled before going slack, rocking his ass into Henley's hand as he let out a stream of groans and curses

"Welcome to the wonderful world of gay sex, kid. Up your ass and to the left, you'll find this lovely button." He gave an extra hard thrust, and Li jerked beneath him. "And sometimes, you'll get lucky enough for this little treat. I'll give you a taste."

Shuffling down, and moving his knee from Li's slacks, Henley lowered his mouth to the spot where his fingers disappeared. It was a pretty fucking picture, and he wished he'd had the foresight to pack a little camera along with the condoms and lube.

Bracing himself for the taste of lube, he licked around Li's stretched hole, teasing his rim and sliding his tongue in next to his fingers. Li moved like magic beneath him, responding so perfectly as his groans turned to whimpers.

"Is it always so...so much?" asked Li, his voice barely above a whisper as he gulped in huge breaths, his cock leaking and forming a puddle on Henley's leg.

Henley pulled back, biting at Li's ass cheek to leave another claiming mark. "I'm a kinky fucker. Most kinksters know me for being into a type of feral puppy play, but they don't know that at heart, I'm just a primal motherfucker."

He bit down a second time before grabbing the condom. Luckily, it had stuck in a pool of sweat and hadn't slid off Li's skin. Henley wasn't sure if he had a back-up in his fanny pack or not. Like most lady's purses, it was overdue for an overhaul.

"I don't know what any of that means," said Li, whimpering as Henley slid out of his body. His hole winked a few times in the low light, beckoning him right back in.

"It means I like to chase and wrestle my subs and hold them down as I fuck into them like an animal." Henley pulled his cock from his pants, rolling the condom on and slicking himself up in record time. "It means that a caveman has nothing to how brutally I want to fuck you right now. I want to claim you and mark you and fuck you over for any other man, so you'll have no choice but to come crawling back to me, begging for my collar."

The words slipped out like they were meant to be, even though Henley had never even considered collaring anyone. Collars were for committed kinksters, not him. He couldn't imagine sceneing with the same guy more than once—or twice if they were really something special.

Li was breathing low and deep, his chest heaving as Henley started to sink inside. He was tight and so fucking hot that he must've been sweltering under his open jacket that still somehow clung to his arms.

Henley took a few deep breaths so he didn't shoot off on the first thrust.

"Seems like a lot of commitment. How many times has that worked out for you, old man?" Li's voice was strained, despite the artificial barb. His ass had to be sore, but he was pushing through it, refusing to submit so easily.

It was as if he had downloaded Henley's kinks and laid them all out in the perfect body. Henley was officially rewriting his opinion on civilians.

"I'll let you know the next time I see you," said Henley, biting his tongue. *Hold on. Brakes please! Next time?* Yeah, no. He did not do a next time—mostly because no one had ever come crawling back, but also because they never put up as much of a fight as they promised. He wanted something primal, not a wrestling match with five hundred rules.

"Now shut up, or I'll make you shut up."

Whatever Li was going to say was cut off by his strangled yelp as Henley pulled almost all the way out, before slamming home again. The force of the thrust sent Li skittering forward a few inches, probably scraping the fuck out of his cheek.

Releasing Li's wrists, Henley tugged him to his hands and knees. Li hung his head low as he let out a sound tainted with pain and pleasure as Henley gripped his hips and tugged him back to meet his next thrust.

He wasn't going to last long, and neither was Li from the feel of his dripping cock when Henley reached around to give it a tug. Hopefully Li would come hands-free, which was an underrated talent, if he said so himself.

Burying himself and unloading was what was *supposed* to happen, but between one thrust and the next, Henley landed on his ass on the roof, his cock not wrapped in heat, but instead pointing up to the stars like a stray compass. Li hovered over him a second later, smirking at him with his hair frazzled and his pupils blown wide. His cheek was reddened and there was a spot of blood at the corner of his lip that Henley had no guilt about whatsoever.

He's fast. Henley hadn't even felt him move before he was looking up at the stars and praying to baby Jesus. He blinked as his head spun and his cock throbbed, so close that he ached all the way to his toes.

"So that's it? You pin me once, and you call that an epic fuck? Maybe we should switch places so I can give you pointers," said Li, because he obviously had a fucking death wish.

Leaning in, Li crashed their lips together, plunging his tongue into Henley's mouth without hesitation and clearly attempting to strip him of every bit of control. It stole Henley's breath and his will in one fell swoop.

It almost worked. But a second later, Li shoved Henley's pants the rest of the way off and he felt a dry finger against his asshole. *Shit just got real. Real exciting, that is.*

He was done pulling his punches.

Smashing the heel of his hand into Li's solar plexus, Henley wrapped his legs around him, twisting to the side before slamming Li onto the roof. Li's head bounced at the hit, so he'd probably end up with the same budding headache that Henley had. It only made everything more exciting.

Sliding between Li's thighs, he pushed Li's knees to his chest, thrusting his cock home in one brutal thrust. His condom had managed to stay on, thank goodness, but the drag was slightly dry, making Li clench around him until he was so tight that Henley could scarcely breathe.

Tugging Li's pants from his ankles, Henley grabbed his wrists, using the slacks as an improvised rope to bind his hands together. By the time he finished the double knot, Li had started to struggle again, wrapping his legs around Henley's hips and squeezing. It only pushed him in deeper, grazing his cock over Li's spot with a well-aimed slam.

"Fuck." Li arched his back, momentarily going slack as Henley gave a few more quick thrusts.

His cock jerked against Henley's belly, a line of pre-cum staining Li's shirt. Henley spread Li's leg wider, leaning down to give his cock a little more friction with his fanny pack.

Li let out the sweetest shriek before he started to come, his seed seeping through Henley's shirt and the corner of his fanny pack. *Damn*. His pack was *not* machine washable, and hand-wash items may as well have been disposable.

Grabbing the pack, he slipped it sideways so it was resting against his hip instead of hitting Li's cock, before he let himself start to pound in earnest. Li was still making tiny noises, but Henley couldn't stop. He couldn't have stopped if there had been a gun to his head.

Two thrusts later, he was finished. He pushed his cock as deep as he could get before dragging Li up for a kiss that was mostly teeth and tongue. His cock flexed, tingling pleasure spreading from the base to his balls, then beyond. His breath caught, and every muscle went taut as he peaked, emptying himself with a long groan.

"Am I squishing you?" asked Henley, pulling back to try to catch his breath. He lowered his head to Li's chest, where the man's heart was pounding fiercely. He wished he could stay there for a minute or ten.

"You're about sixty pounds lighter than I am," said Li, his voice a low grumble.

Henley nearly startled as Li threaded his fingers through his hair, brushing the sweaty strands away from his eyes. It was a move that he hadn't expected, and one that he should have been doing. Aftercare was just as important as the scene.

Was that a scene? It hadn't been scripted like his scenes usually were, and they hadn't even touched on safewords.

"You carry it well," he said instead of moving an inch. The rumble of Li's laughter had his eyes going half-lidded. Now that sex was off his to-do list, sleep had skipped right to the top.

"Can you pull out, though?"

"Sorry," said Henley, reluctantly leaning back, gripping the base of the condom and tugging free. He murmured a second apology at Li's wince.

"Does it always hurt?" asked Li, slowly trying to sit up and cringing along the way.

Hello, guilt trip. Henley forced a grin on his face as he grabbed his pants and pulled them up, zipping and fastening the button. He tossed the condom over the side of the building in the direction of the goon below who had gone silent. Sweat cooled rapidly on his skin, leaving shivering goosebumps in its wake.

"I probably wasn't the best guy for your first time. Slow and steady were never my style. In my defense, I usually don't get any complaints," said Henley, helping to free Li's hands from his make-shift bindings. He'd actually done a pretty good job.

"I wasn't complaining," said Li, looking over the side of the building. They'd managed to get uncomfortably close to the edge during their struggles with only a few feet between them and a sudden drop. "I can see what you mean about this spot, though. It's definitely one of my two new favorite spots."

Chuckling, Henley offered his hand, helping Li to his feet. "Anytime you need another tour, I'm your man."

Chapter Three

Henley

The music was even louder, or maybe it was the hangover that Henley was still nursing, that had his brain feeling like it had gone head-to-head with a pressure washer. It wasn't like him to drink, but it also wasn't like him to offer a second chance at his dick.

He was a one-fuck wonder — and always had been. So why the hell had he offered round two to Li? The bottom of the bottle of Crown Royal hadn't given him an answer, except to the question of how comfortable his bathroom floor was.

It also reminded him that he wasn't in his twenties anymore.

Rubbing his temples, he leaned against the vibrating glass, peering out into the night. The rain from earlier in the day had mostly dried, leaving a few sporadic puddles on the desolate road. Even with the dampness, it looked so much better than the club.

Martinez Junior still wasn't listening, which wasn't surprising. Henley glanced sideways at the reflection in the glass to where Martinez was dancing in clear view of the street. Maybe his charge had gone deaf within the walls of throbbing glass and sweating bodies — or maybe it was because he was high on enough coke to bankrupt a Catholic church.

"Damien, you need to get away from the windows," yelled Henley as he reluctantly turned, shielding the kid from the glass that stretched along the entirety of the outside wall of the club. It was the same move he'd practiced four times in the last hour.

Henley was a few inches shorter, but the kid was like a twig of malnutrition and meth next to him, so he was easy enough to cover.

Damien shot him a glare, his eyes so bloodshot and his pupils so wide that it was a miracle he could even see. If someone really wanted to kill him, all they needed to do was slip something into his drug supply.

Not that I'm considering it. He ground his teeth as Damien turned away, grabbing the nearest set of hips like he owned them. The woman jerked away, slapping Damien's face when he didn't let go right away. He wobbled from the hit, stumbling back before Henley could deck him. *Not cool.*

Killing the kid would probably get him fired. No…definitely. His boss wasn't exactly the forgiving type, and she had more resources in her pinky finger than Henley had in his entire portfolio. Martinez Senior was another matter, but Henley had dealt with worse.

Gently pushing two ladies aside, Henley gripped the kid by his collar as he tried to turn back to the window and shake his ass like he actually had moves. Damien wobbled as Henley tugged him a few steps, supporting the kid's weight as he stumbled.

"You fucking listen to me, *sir*," said Henley, snarling as he held back from punching the kid who was still trying to dance. "If you want to end up dead, you can dance in front of these windows all you want. Hell, I'll put up a fucking sign for you. Otherwise, you need to do as I say." Henley released his hold to rub at his temples that throbbed with renewed persistence.

He closed his eyes as a wave of dizziness struck him, his tongue gluing itself to the roof of his mouth. *Don't puke.* Shouting and hangovers did not mix. He could hear Damien spluttering with indignation as the music cut out for the few seconds between songs.

"Get off me. My father —"

The beat rocketed back into existence, the force of it like a belt squeezing his chest. *Oh threats. Bring it on, rich boy.* Henley forced his eyes back open, despite the strobe lights flickering over his face. He blinked in confusion at the blank space where Damien had stood seconds before.

What the — ? The kid was gone, the few women close by looking at the ground with blooming horror on their faces seconds before the screams started — or maybe it was a siren in the song. Henley wasn't sure.

Oh shit. He wasn't gone at all. He was on his back with a bullet hole the size of a quarter through his forehead. His mouth was open, his eyes wide and crossed from the impact to his brain. A vermillion pool crept away from his lifeless shell, tainting the pointed stiletto of the nearest lady.

"Fuck," Henley shouted over the screams. He touched his cheek, his fingers coming away red as the strobe light swung his way again. He hadn't heard the shot, but there was only one direction it could have come from.

He turned to the glass, eyeing up the shattered round hole that was just a touch larger than the one left in Damien's skull. Cool air seeped through the tiny space, fogging the glass as Henley slipped along the edge of the window to the nearest beam before ducking for cover.

The trajectory looked like it had come from up high, a full foot higher on the window than where Damien's head had been. There was only one spot that fit the bill for that.

The shooter had been on the roof — *his* fucking roof. His roof that had more alarms than fucking apartments, and that was *supposed* to be secure. His phone hadn't buzzed, meaning that none of the alarms had been tripped.

Taking a deep breath, he peeked around the beam, looking straight up to the top of his building and the security light that did a shit job standing guard. He touched the gun in his holster but didn't draw it. There was no way he could make that shot.

There was a single blink of a silhouette across the light, moving so fast that Henley hardly had the chance to figure out what he was seeing. It was gone a second later, disappearing from the edge of the rooftop.

I'll just have to be fast.

With Damien's blood barely starting to pool on the ground and the music still blaring, he booked it through the thick cloak of bodies, slamming the club door open and dashing toward his apartment building.

His lungs burned as he sucked in a breath of cool air, the taste of fall on his tongue. He pushed past the burn, his shoes slapping against the sidewalk before he launched himself onto the road without bothering to check for traffic. A horn blared at him from his left side, so close that his ear throbbed and his skin prickled.

Real life was nothing like the movies where the bad guys could get away in ten seconds flat on their flashy motorbikes. Disassembling a gun took time, unless you were really, really good at it, or if you felt like walking down the street with a rifle, hoping that no one called the cops.

Henley still pushed himself to his limit, darting toward the single entrance to the building as fast as he could. He may or may not have fucked with the other fire escape, leaving only one exit for anyone who tried something on his turf.

He reached his apartment door at the same time someone was pushing their way outside. It took him a few seconds to recognize Li, and a few more to get over his shock and instant surge of arousal.

Li was flushed in his thick jacket, his hair in disarray as he threw the door open. He was carrying a briefcase that looked a bit too big for paper and pens, clutched in a white-knuckled grip.

Li was also the only one who had seen Henley's trick for the door to the roof. *I am so fired.*

Henley slammed into the door with his shoulder as Li tried to escape through it, biting back the groan as his body gave a twang of protest. He half-expected the glass to shatter, but it held, the scratchy address stamped into it thudding against the side of his head.

Li either hadn't seen him coming or hadn't expected him so soon, because he tripped backward at the hit, the briefcase falling from his hand and out to the street as his head smacked into the opposite side of the door frame.

"Fucker," Henley growled as he pinned Li with the door, leaning his full weight on the glass as he reached for his knife. Li's eyes went wide as he looked down at

Henley, his lips open in surprise. A gun was too good for this guy, even if he was hotter than molten lava.

He slashed at Li with his left hand, the tip of his knife almost sinking in before Li caught his wrist in a brutal hold. Henley winced as Li ground his bones together, the knife falling from his useless grip. Li bucked against the door, sending Henley stumbling back and off balance, with his wrist still captive in the enemy's claws.

Henley had been trained by a martial arts specialist, but she'd never mentioned what to do if he caught a semi in the fight. His half-hard cock was enough to put his stance off a hair, so when he tried to use Li's own momentum against him, it only half-worked. *Damn you.*

Dropping to his knees with Li behind him, he tried to recover, tugging against Li's grip in an attempt to flip him over his shoulder. Li wrapped an arm around Henley's neck instead, planting every kilo of his weight against him.

It wasn't a total failure, though. He wasn't dead — yet.

"Who hired you?" Henley snarled, struggling to get his wrist free before Li could put another part of him out of commission. Threading his fingers together, he held on for dear life so Li couldn't twist his arm behind his back. Li dug a knee into his spine in retaliation, tightening the grip across Henley's throat.

"I don't think you're in the position to ask questions, old man," said Li, yanking Henley's hands apart before cranking his arm behind his back. Henley arched and cried out as his shoulder protested, so close to popping out of joint.

For some reason, his cock was getting hard. *Not the time.* He wasn't sure if it was because the struggle was so close to what they'd done the night before and his mind was still too wrapped up in that, or if he'd just found out that he was a masochist. Maybe it was Li's voice growling "*old man*" in his ear.

"You think I'm running this solo? You'd be lucky if there aren't three guns pointed in your direction right now." Henley's cheek hit the pitted sidewalk, scraping his skin in a way so reminiscent to what he had done to Li. *Huh,* it did hurt a touch more than he'd thought it would.

He was not apologizing.

"You're fast, and my guess is that I'll be gone and you'll be dead by the time anyone else gets out here," said Li, managing to get Henley's other arm behind his back after releasing the hold on his neck. It was a good thing Li's coat was padded or Henley would have passed out from the chokehold.

His headache pounded fiercer as Li lifted him by his arms alone, his shoulders barely staying in their joints. He struggled as hard as he could, which wasn't much with his arms being practically ripped from his body as he was dragged. His heart thudded, adrenaline pumping new strength through his limbs.

Slamming his head back, he aimed for Li's nose, catching his cheek instead as he turned his head. There was an ominous crack and Henley's head went fuzzy for a moment as his brain bounced around in his skull from the impact.

"Fine… This'll make things easier anyway," hissed Li, his voice strained. Dropping down, he kneeled on Henley's spine, pushing the air from his lungs, even as his hands were released. It was a moment, but not long enough.

Something sharp jabbed into Henley's neck, the sting like his worst memories of the dentist. His skin burned, the spot that was pierced flaming hottest of all as something rushed through his veins. A foreign taste drifted over his tongue, making him gag before his head thudded to the concrete once more and darkness took him.

Chapter Four

Henley

Henley took a deep breath of tainted air, letting it out as his chest and back ached from the strain. The fact that he was breathing was a surprise in itself that he didn't take for granted. He took another breath, fighting against the ache as he forced his eyes open.

A hospital room. Fucking fantastic. His blue gown that left nothing to the imagination was the only thing on him except for a thin blanket that probably had a thread count lower than the sheets in a rent-by-the-hour motel. He quickly shut his eyes again as he spotted the nurse at the end of his bed who was jotting something down on a clipboard.

The air was filled with a mixture of blood, death and sterilizing spray that made Henley want to sneeze. He didn't mind the blood and death part—he'd seen enough of it that it didn't really matter anymore—but the cleanup still got to him, even after so many years in the field.

The cleanup happened after the adrenaline had died and there was no one left to kill or protect. That was the time when he would look down at himself to take stock of his injuries that he hadn't felt through the rush. It was when shit got real.

Usually he tried to push the faces of the lost ones from his mind, but how could he do that when he had almost died at the hands of the man who had been one of the best fucks of his life?

Correction – the best. Li was the best fuck of his life, hands down. Other subs had paled in comparison, and casual hookups might as well have been his own hand compared to the way he'd gone off, his balls emptying until he had nothing left to give.

Li had been perfect. His responses weren't rehearsed or some ploy to fit into a crowd where he didn't belong. Li probably hadn't known that they had played out one of Henley's all-time kinky fantasies.

But the kid just *had* to be a fucking assassin — one who had slipped away, leaving a needle sticking in Henley's neck like a poison dart. It was a wonder that he was alive, because he was almost certain that the needle hadn't been meant for him.

The nurse shuffled at the end of the bed, and he felt the brief sweep of her warm fingers against his wrist before she withdrew, the door clicking behind her as she left. The scent of her perfume slowly dissipated until there was nothing left.

The syringe had probably been a back-up plan for Damien. Well, the bullet had worked, thank you very much, and Henley was going to be out of the job.

He should have listened to his gut when he'd seen Li struggling with the lock on the apartment door. And he definitely shouldn't have shown him how to bypass the roof alarm with a well-placed card. He wasn't going to regret the fuck, though, not even if he was fired or suspended for eternity. No, that fuck was going down in the hall of Henley fame.

Opening his eyes, he leaned forward, groaning at the ache in his ribs that flared from the movement. He tugged the sling from his arm, stretching out the limb to try to ease the sharpness in his shoulder. The other one didn't hurt near as much.

He glanced at the clock, wincing at the time that glared back at him. It was nearly four o'clock in the morning and well past his usual shift end and check-in time. It had been about three hours since his altercation with Li, too, and who knew how long since Martinez Senior had found out about his son. There would be more than one person looking for him.

"Oh good, you're awake."

Henley flinched at the sound of the nurse returning. It must've been a slow night for them to be so *attentive.*

"Any dizziness, sir, or trouble breathing?" she asked him as she approached, retrieving a small light from her pocket before shining it across his eyes. He flinched at the overly bright beam that seemed to cut straight into his retina. He'd been hungover before, but whatever Li had given him was like a freight train had chugged along his entire body.

The nurse was cute, with short blonde hair and blue eyes that anyone could get lost in. Anyone but Henley, that was. He didn't want soft eyes or a round face or kind hands. He wanted calluses and a fight and fuck for his life.

Something is wrong with me.

"I'm not dizzy, and I always breathe like this, hon." Henley let out a sigh to prove his point. He turned away from the light, rubbing his hand over his eyes. *Be nice!* Nurses had so much shit to deal with that they didn't need his attitude on top of it, but it was hard being nice when people wanted you dead.

"Do you know where you are?" The nurse smiled softly, so patient.

He glanced at the clock again, the numbers clicking by steadily.

"It's 78845 Westbridge Street," Henley grumbled, shutting his eyes as the light came back. His head pounded, each thud reverberating throughout his body.

It's your own fault. Henley grumbled to himself, glaring at the nurse who was now watching him a bit nervously.

"Are you hearing voices, sir? You could be hallucinating. We aren't one-hundred-percent sure what drug you were given, but we are certain it was some sort of anesthetic." The nurse grabbed her stethoscope, lining it up to Henley's chest. "Take a deep breath for me."

"The only voice I hear is yours, sweetheart," said Henley, squashing his fatigue and sucking in a breath as the cold stethoscope touched the bare skin at the dip of his gown.

The nurse let out a strained chuckle, starting to back away. "I'll come check on you a bit later when you're feeling up to it." The door opened and clicked shut as the nurse withdrew.

Time to get the fuck outta here. Flicking a few buttons, Henley silenced the alarms on the monitors before unplugging the intravenous pump and slowly unwinding his IV from the inner workings of the tube. It looked like it was straight saline, and he could use that to cure the rest of his hangover, but he would have to take it quick.

Saltiness coated his tongue as he opened up the fluids to full blast, pushing out of bed and looking around for his clothes. He was dressed by the time the bag of fluids was almost empty, so he shut it off, pulling the line from his vein with a hiss.

Pain tolerance was not his forte. Fucking people or fucking them up? Now that was another story.

Peering out of the window that took up the top half of the door, he spotted the nurse as well as a cop dressed in full uniform, a gun and Taser at his hip. *Just what I need.* It wasn't that his department didn't co-operate with local police, but it was expected that he would avoid the opportunity to work with them at all.

And a cop fumbling around in his drugged and hungover brain was the last thing he needed. He would probably just end up telling them everything he knew. It was one of the reasons he rarely indulged in anything more than a few beers—another thing that Li had fucked up for him.

He strode to the window on the opposite side of the room that overlooked a small green space. Flipping the locks and prying it open, he took a breath of the freezing air. It was an older-style window, with safety stops that had been installed at some point. They were easy enough to unclip so he could drag it open a few more inches. It seized under his hands when it was three-quarters open, the rusted pane beyond help.

"Fuck." He glanced over his shoulder to make sure the coast was still clear. He was small but not small enough to fit through the tiny space he'd created. Grunting, he pulled at it again, trying to summon the strength in his jellified limbs. Two more inches and one aching shoulder later, it screeched to a permanent halt.

Sticking his head out of the window, he chuckled to himself. He had been expecting the fourth floor or something, but he'd ended up on the ground floor with the grass only a few feet away from his face. It was bleached brown from the frost that clung to it and would probably be prickly as all hell, but it beat gravel.

He sucked his gut in, wiggling his way through the window headfirst. If he'd had his cellphone, it would have been the perfect time to play the *Mission Impossible* theme song. He hummed it under his breath instead as he squeezed his chest through the glass.

Shit, my phone. He strained to look back with his entire upper body hanging out in the cool air. His fanny pack and weapons hadn't been with his clothes. *Double shit.*

He squirmed one more time, his ass catching on the lower pane before he finally slid through and collapsed onto the grass. If the cops had his stuff, it was as good as gone. On the bright side, it was an excuse to buy a new knife, but he would still have to go through a mourning phase for his favorite gun.

The first bit of dawn battled with the security lights that surrounded the hospital, his breath steaming the air as he puffed. He slunk along the edge of the building, keeping tight to the brick as he continued to hum. Ducking behind a scraggly hedge, he gave himself a few extra seconds to finish the song and catch his breath.

The drugs were obviously still in his system, making him woozy like he'd just given three rounds of blood.

Leaving the safety of the hedge, he broke into a run, weaving through the hospital outbuildings. Despite the early hour, there were a surprising number of people milling about the parking lot, moving to and from their cars. A Hyundai honked close by as the locks engaged.

Step one – get a phone. Any phone would do, as long as the call was under four-and-a-half minutes.

Step two – find Li. Although he hadn't decided if he was going to fuck Li or kill him once he located him.

"Excuse me," said Henley, as he stood tall and approached the edge of the parking lot where the shadows were still long. There was a lone man wearing blue scrubs with his face buried in his phone as he leaned against his Porsche. He looked up for a second, his gaze sliding over Henley quickly before he returned to his cellular.

"Excuse me," said Henley again, pitching his voice a bit higher, but not loud enough to catch the attention of two ladies wandering past. One of them laughed, tossing her purse over her shoulder as she pulled her hair from its tight ponytail.

"I heard you the first time," the man in the scrubs said, powering down his phone before slipping it into his back pocket. His voice was gruff and tired, with a deep shadow of scruff on his face. He gave Henley a small smile as he approached, the sparkle of his teeth not reaching his eyes.

"Would you be able to answer a question for me?" asked Henley, grinning when the doctor went on instant alert, the exhaustion sliding away.

Stalking out of the shadows, Henley moved until they were uncomfortably close, their chests inches apart. Henley blinked slowly, licking his lips and looking up at the doctor through half-lidded eyes. The doc's eyes went wide, but he didn't take a step back. *Perfect.*

"I have a bet going with my friend. Can you help me out with it?" asked Henley, trying to make his voice seductive. Usually, he'd be fucking thrilled to be in the general proximity to an attractive man, but he must've been worse off than he thought. Li had fucking broken him.

"Okay," said the doc, his voice dropping into a husky timbre as he shifted closer, licking his lips as Henley gave him a sweet smile. He was incredibly attractive, even if he did look so tired, and he was a full head taller than Henley.

Henley shifted closer, sliding his hands over the doc's hips as he brought their groins together. Most guys would have pushed him away, but thank goodness for the horny bastards who made his life easier.

"I told her that all doctors have big cocks to go with their big hands, but she insists that it's the other way around." Henley reached for the button on the doctor's jeans as he said it. The doc's breath stuttered, his pupils blowing wide in the semi-darkness.

"Yeah?" He blinked, looking over his shoulder at the others in the parking lot before he shook his head. No one had looked their way.

Sliding his hand over the doc's ass at the same time he smoothed down the front seam of his slacks, Henley lifted the phone without the doc being any the wiser. He paused along the seam of the doc's slacks, before rubbing a few more times.

"Looks like she's right." Henley cackled as the doc tensed, his sudden lust morphing into a glare. Henley could almost see the steam pouring out of his ears. It was always the guys with the biggest egos who were the easiest to trick. Henley didn't doubt that his sweet nurse probably couldn't stand the guy.

"I'll call security," said the doc, pushing Henley away.

"No, you won't." Henley turned, walking from the lot and melting into the remaining darkness. He had the phone to his ear before he hit the alley at a run, leaving the doc behind him as he sprinted away. His ribs ached with each deep breath, his legs getting weaker with every step.

The phone rang once before it connected, his boss' voice slicing through the morning air.

"Where the fuck are you?"

Always the romantic. Henley would have sighed if he'd had the extra breath. Shelia tolerated him on most days because he got the job done…eventually. Sometimes things fell off the rails. She didn't have a history of being too forgiving unless he strolled through the door to her office with a grin and a cracked case. He'd never fucked up quite so bad before, though.

"Nice to hear from you, too," he said, ducking down the street that ran behind the hospital. An ambulance whipped by, its lights flashing as the siren whirred.

There were a dozen houses spotted along the street, every one of them dark except for a single porch light. A few moths battered at the light as he ran past, their fluttering wings clicking in the air.

"Did you have to kill the kid *and* blow your cover?" Shelia asked, letting out a sigh that would make any mother proud. "I know he pissed you off, but I'm sick of you burning bridges because of your temper. Three months of deep cover down the drain, not to mention that Martinez is on a war path. I'd be impressed if you had actually accomplished anything within that time, but once again, I'm left covering up your mistakes with nothing to show for it."

"I didn't kill him," said Henley, ducking down an alley and breaking into a sprint. His head swam and his vision blurred, but he shook it off.

Three months was nothing to get to a man like Martinez, who trusted no one for good reason. He'd worked his way up from goon-for-hire to being on Martinez's payroll in that time, but he'd barely spent any time in the mansion, too busy looking after the fucking kid.

Maybe he should have filed a few reports...

"My insider has you shouting at Damien Martinez, then the next thing anyone sees, he's dead and you're taking off. When they cleared the area and caught up with you, you were already in an ambulance. We've managed to keep your location under wraps for now. I pulled a few favors with the hospital, but that won't last long."

Henley pulled the phone from his ear to glare at the timer that was steadily counting higher. "I don't have a lot of time, so save the bitching until later. The kid had a hit on him, and the guy managed to shove a needle in my neck before I could take him down. Is that my fault, too?"

"Yes."

Bitch. Henley panted, his headache pounding to the front of his mind. Slowing to a walk, he ducked behind some bushes, leaning back against the prickling shrubs that had started to lose their leaves.

"Where are you? I'll send someone to pick you up," said Shelia.

Henley shook his head, despite the fact that Shelia couldn't see him. "Just a sec." He tucked the phone into the back of his pants, moving out of the bushes before shimmying up a fence into someone's backyard. The house was still dark, but a light in the yard reflected off the still waters of an in-ground pool. Pools usually meant pool sheds, which were a great place to lay low on a cool day.

"I'm not coming in. I need to track the sonofabitch who shot Damien Martinez and take care of him," said Henley, breaking into the pool shed with a well-aimed hit. The door crumpled like a cardboard box.

So freaking cool! They have rainbow pool noodles. He could not think of an excuse to bring them along. "My weapons were seized by the cops—"

"Seriously, Henley?" asked Shelia with another long sigh. "You'd think I didn't fucking train you at all."

I am so getting my ass kicked when I get back...if I get back. "Well, I could break into the police station and get my shit back—but not until tomorrow. I'm still hungover and drugged as fuck." Even as he said it, he stumbled, sending a rack of garden tools to the ground with a loud crash. Why were there garden tools in a fucking pool shed?

"Corner of Park and Erb. Look under the bench." The line went dead as Shelia hung up on him with only seconds to spare.

He knew better than to be insulted. It actually sounded like she was a little worried about him. If she hadn't cared then she would have made him get his own weapons back. He would be surprised if she wasn't on the line with another agent already, getting them to cover his tracks.

He was more surprised that he hadn't been fired.

Two years of jumping around in the city between jobs then immersing himself in Martinez's affairs so that when the threat went out against his son, Henley was able to slip into their ranks as a mercenary-for-hire like sugar in molasses.

Which reminded him... If he had to split town for a while, he had to call up Clint first. It had almost been by chance that he'd stumbled on Clint in the grocery store, making a dick joke when Clint had grabbed for an extra-large zucchini. Instead of acting like an aghast civilian, Clint had laughed and started up a conversation before he'd invited Henley to his kink club, which had opened up Henley's eyes to the kinkiest world of awesome.

He wouldn't have made it over the last two years without the community.

But now, he had his own kinky motherfucker to track.

Grabbing the phone again, he dialed the only other number he knew by heart. It rang once before connecting with a few beeps and a burst of static.

"We secure? It's Rockwood," said Henley, cradling the pool noodle under his arm as he tried to figure out a way to sneak it along with him. Rockwood was probably one of his coolest fake names, although he only used it with a few people.

Ben, his geek-for-hire who could track any-fucking-thing, probably knew Henley's first, last and middle name, but he used the alias with him all the same.

"You know it," Ben replied.

God. He sounded like a kid over the phone. Ben was fresh out of university and had figured out quickly that he made more in the private sector than he ever would fixing people's phones at Best Buy. Henley was certainly glad to be a part of that revelation, because Ben had made his life a thousand percent easier.

"How's the new kitten? Frosty, right?" asked Henley, rubbing along his ribs where a bruise was making itself known. He didn't even want to try to touch his neck where it still ached from the needle.

"Right here," said Ben, his voice pitching even higher. "Aren't you, you little rascal? She loves the new set-up. I made her a perch that sits right over my screens so I can keep an eye on her while I watch everyone else."

Henley nodded along, grunting a few times as Ben went into a spiral of too much information about his cat. Henley loved cats, but he'd heard more stories about Frosty than he ever cared to divulge.

"Good. Good." Henley spoke up when it sounded like Ben was finally spiraling down. "I need you to find someone for me." He listed off everything he knew about Li, except for the size of his dick, then added that in as an afterthought, just to hear Ben splutter.

"Give me three hours," said Ben, the sound of his fingers flying over computer keys like music to Henley's ears.

"Three? Christ, kid, you must be bogged down for it to take that long. You used to have it to me in like five minutes." A bit of an exaggeration, but whatever.

"Fine, two, but you owe me cat treats."

"They're already on the way."

Chapter Five

Li

He had five rules. Five simple rules that kept his head on his shoulders and his ass out of prison.

Li shook his head, running his fingers through his hair before wincing as he touched the bruise on the back of his head. His cheek still throbbed with his heartbeat, already tinting purple where Henley had slammed into him.

Five easy-peasy rules, and he'd broken most of them with one simple job. His target was dead, which was great, but everything else was fucked.

Including his ass.

Killing Damien had been one of his easier jobs, and the loss of one coked-out rich boy meant nothing to him. It was everything else that had his heart pounding and his chest aching as he gasped for air.

He'd promised that he would never have sex in order to get a job done. In the past, he'd repeated it to himself when there was an attractive person in his scope, so he'd remember there was a reason they were in that position.

Some of the hitmen and women he'd come into contact with used seduction as their main tool. The problem was it only worked if your target swung the right way, and fucking someone was a great way to get attached to them.

Unless they had the whole black-widow-spider vibe going on.

It wasn't like he'd planned on having sex. Damien was a guy, so it hadn't even crossed his mind to be on guard. His blond hair and bloodshot eyes matched his red nose and droopy cheeks and hadn't struck a single chord of want in his entire body. The thought of even touching him gave Li the sudden urge to wash his hands. And Li wasn't gay, either—obviously.

It had been obvious before Henley, at least.

Henley, who had a rainbow sticker on the butt of his gun and a pink knife that Li had stashed in his truck before he'd gotten the fuck away from the scene. Henley, who was like one of those little dogs who had way too much personality for his frame so he ended up jumping on everyone in his proximity with his contagious enthusiasm. His dark hair and boyish looks hid his strength and had thrown Li so off guard.

But when Henley had made a pass at him and offered to show him to the roof, when that was exactly where Li had needed to scope out, then his rules hadn't seemed to matter. He had been shocked speechless at Henley's advances, but he hadn't been disgusted. On the contrary, his cock had tingled to awareness for the first time in months.

He wasn't sure when it had all gone wrong. One second he had been looking down into the alley to see one of Damien's bodyguards getting head, and the next, Henley had had three fingers buried deep as he touched something that Li had never thought would be touched by another person.

But his no-sex rule, which was there to protect himself, his future and his someday family, was blown to bits. And the worst part was, he couldn't stop thinking about it. Every moment was seared into his thoughts and body, parts of him still tingling in remembrance of Henley's touch.

And the *sex*. He hadn't even known that it could be like that. Sex with women was mostly fulfilling, and he'd thought that he'd want to catch himself a wife someday. Sex with a man had never been in the cards. Hell, it hadn't even been in the deck.

But instead of ritualistic preparations for his upcoming hit, a cock up his ass had distracted him completely. He'd gotten sloppy, fucked up his exit and had left the pain in his ass lying on the street with a needle in his neck.

He scratched his chin at the bit of soft scruff that had started to grow. He usually kept himself completely clean-shaven, but that was just another thing that he had fucked up. That, and the hunk of hair that Henley had managed to tug out during their struggle. Li hoped he'd gotten it all, but if he hadn't, then the cops had his DNA.

He should have just tossed Henley into the back of his truck. His basement was roomy enough to keep a hostage, and there was nobody around to hear screaming. But he refused to break another rule. He wasn't going to kill an innocent because he was in the wrong place at the wrong time.

And that was exactly what Henley was—innocent. He was just a bodyguard trying to protect a coked-out kid—and a pretty pathetic bodyguard, at that. He was the opposite of what a bodyguard should have been, too—short, lean and with an attitude a mile long.

Damien had been so easy to kill that Li should have sent Henley a tip as a thank you. But he wasn't sure if Henley would take it the wrong way or not. He had seemed a little upset when he'd smashed Li into the door frame. *It was just business.*

Luckily, he would never see Henley again, so technically, he didn't have to worry about it.

But why couldn't he get him out of his mind? The timbre of his low laugh and the unexpected way he had held Li to the ground so he was powerless on the rooftop, followed him like a ghost—not to mention, the husky tint of his voice when he had told Li to say stop or to push him away.

He had given Li a dozen outs, but Li had still managed to have sex with a man.

"Call the boss," he said, his Bluetooth activating and dialing for him as he gripped the steering wheel of his truck, turning off the main street as a siren sounded in the distance.

Is Henley still on the street? Will he even live? The needle hadn't been meant for him, and although Li had only given him a fraction of the dose, he wasn't exactly a physician. He shook his head. It didn't matter.

The speaker above his head buzzed twice before the line connected. Li waited for the telltale sign of three clicks that indicated that the line was secure. His boss was nearly as paranoid as him, and it had kept them both from discovery.

He had no idea how many others like him were out there. He had tracked a few, removing some of the competition early on in his career. They had yet to discover *who* had taken out their precious assassins. *Oops.*

His student debt had cleared quickly when he was the only one on call.

"It's done," said Li, swiping his hand down the steering wheel, just to feel the leather. He squeezed the material until it creaked before he finally released it and let out a long breath. There had been a time when those words had meant a lot to him, but now they were nothing. "But there were complications."

"Did you need a cleaning crew or a doctor?" asked his contact, her voice distorted and flat.

If he saw her on the street someday, he would never recognize her. Faces only meant more liability for both of them. She gave the orders and he followed them…to a point. They both knew that there were rules that he would never willingly cross.

"Neither." He glanced out of the window as he turned into a less desirable part of town. His Chevy pickup blended in, just like it had on the busy street with a bustling club and a few apartment buildings. No one looked twice at a regular old pickup.

What do I need? Maybe a woman for the night would clear up any budding confusion, but his cock practically wilted at the idea. But Henley? He grumbled, slamming the heel of his hand against his groin.

He needed to lie low until he was sure that nothing had been left at the scene. He worked solo, and although his contacts were occasionally fine with providing a cleaning crew or an underground doctor, his protection was his own problem. If anyone ever caught him, he would have a bullet in his head before he could say *sayonara*.

He wouldn't talk to the cops, but his contacts never could be too careful.

After nearly thirty seconds of silence, the call ended with a click. Li shook his head as he tried to erase the image of Damien's wide eyes as his head had turned into a blender.

He turned onto the highway, his blinker clicking as a cruiser whipped by him with their lights flashing. A few of his hits stuck around in his thoughts, but he hoped that Damien wouldn't be one of them. Killing him had almost felt like a mercy.

Damien's schedule had been a monotonous cry for help, to say the least. He had seen it all before. Rich parents would rather spend their time making money than comfort their kid after a rough day. The kid turned to others to fill the empty void left behind, and when that didn't work, drugs were the easy choice.

But Henley had made it almost too easy. He had to be one of the worst bodyguard's out there—or he just didn't care. Henley hadn't even checked Damien once he fell with a bullet between the eyes and hadn't made any effort whatsoever to keep him unseen in the first place.

Driving five kilometers above the speed limit, nearly half-an-hour passed before Li turned off the highway toward his little patch of paradise. The land had cost next to nothing, because it was worth exactly that, but the time he'd put into the place meant everything to him.

Of all the places in the world he had ever been, his home had always called to him when he was away for too long. It was the only place he could relax and let his guard down, forgetting about his life and his future.

Clenching his teeth, he fought back the anger that surged in his gut. He'd never done a job so close to home, and he would probably have to leave it behind if he'd blown his cover. He should have killed Henley and secured his identity, saving himself from arrest and death, or he should have turned the job down in the first place.

Which was why *that* was rule number two. One thousand kilometers and up was usually his motto. Anything he had to take a plane to get to was even better. He didn't want anything closer that could somehow lead back to his place. But the killing business had been surprisingly slow over the last few months — and bills were bills.

He turned off the road, slowing as he hit pitted gravel. Hopefully Henley was still alive on the street and hadn't had a reaction to the pentobarbital. People had started to emerge from the club as Li had thrown himself into his truck, and the sirens had already been whirring in the distance.

It was always good to have a back-up plan or three, and it had been easy enough to grab the syringe from his padded jacket before he'd slammed it into Henley's neck. He should have given him the whole thing and put him straight into a coffin. That would have wrapped everything up with a neat little bow.

He passed the last few ramshackle houses as the gravel on the road started to thin into worn dirt. Grass and weeds peeked through the center line where the stone had thinned the most. The city didn't maintain the road so far out in the country, so it hadn't seen a grader or a plow since he'd lived in the area. He was more likely to see a deer than a person in his parts.

The road quickly devolved into a barely defined path with warning signs to turn back. If any intruders missed the 'no trespassing', 'no exit' and other signs, there was a good chance they would never see the entrance to his place.

The tiny break in the trees gave a new meaning to 'hidden driveway', and he still managed to miss it on occasion. He'd paid an exorbitant amount to have the electric lines buried, so to an outsider, it looked more like a wide game trail than a place where someone would live.

The lane itself was pitted, with huge holes that threatened to consume his tires if he plowed straight through them. Trees closed in on every side, scratching at his windshield and dragging along the edges of his truck with great swipes that left colorful leaves caught in every nook. In the dark, he could barely see a few feet ahead.

Hovering his foot over the brake, he peered into the darkness, pausing for every animal that startled as he approached, their eyes shining in his high beams. A buck danced away from the light, velvet dangling from its antlers. He could hear them calling in the dark sometimes, the clacking of their antlers cutting into his bedroom as he lay awake.

Outside the forest, he could kill in a heartbeat, and it didn't matter if it was cold steel or a warm blade that needed to get the job done. In the forest, he'd found peace. The idea of leaving it behind had tension lancing across his shoulders, twining his belly tight.

I should have killed him. Was a broken rule number three worth leaving everything behind?

The trees split apart suddenly, leading him to the small clearing where his home lay. From the outside, it wasn't much, especially in the dark. There were no exterior lights—nothing to give away his position to anyone who flew a drone over the woods. Even the trees themselves loomed over the cabin, disguising the roof a bit in the summer.

Most of the leaves had already fallen during the last few frosts, leaving only the sturdiest maples still brightly- hued. His eaves were bursting with the colorful compost, his rain barrel slick with mucky water.

From the outside, the cabin was tiny, looking more like a hunting cabin for one. Even if someone did stumble upon it, they would probably be afraid of going inside because it looked like they might fall through the porch.

Li had gone through a lot of trouble to make it look that way, leaving the paint peeling and the porch at an awkward angle, simply to cover his tracks. The roof was the only place he wasn't willing to compromise, with new shingles that still picked up moss every spring in the damp closeness of the forest.

Behind the cabin was a small clearing that deer often visited, munching on the thick grass as they bathed in sunlight. Li would watch them from the window, worried that they would startle if he stepped outside.

Parking the truck beside the cabin and under one of the evergreens that left needles everywhere, he opened the door and stepped out into the oppressive silence. Taking a deep breath, he let it flow through his lungs until it hit his veins, melting his exhaustion away. The moon was high and bright, nearly full against a blanket of stars. The rain from earlier had left its mark, though, chilling him straight to the bone.

Reaching into his pocket, he retrieved one of his burner phones, pounding the power key until the screen came to life. Burners were a dime a dozen, and he'd already gone through three as he'd gathered intel on Damien.

He dialed the number by heart, putting the phone on speaker as he retrieved his key and let himself into his cabin, more by muscle memory than sight. The inside was incredibly underwhelming, too, with a single bedroom to the left and a tiny kitchen and living room combo to the right. The bathroom was tucked away at the side of the bedroom, no larger than a closet, with a dark brown door that was warped from repeated changes in humidity.

It still smelled like home, though—like moss and clean air and that bit of moisture that he could never get out of the walls. His clothing reeked of it when he left, lasting until it was covered by something metallic and brutal.

He pulled his coat off and flicked on his lights, resetting his alarm and retrieving a few things from his pockets before setting them on the side table to be disposed of later. A few syringes, some tainted cocaine and a couple of pre-rifled bullets would all be burned until there was nothing left but a touch of melted plastic and metal.

The chocolate bar was still there, his stomach grumbling as it reminded him of his two missed meals. He peeled the wrapper off with his teeth before shoving it into his mouth.

The phone line connected with a burst of static and a few successive beeps as the line secured. He had his own programming to thank for it that time.

"Hello?"

Li glanced at his watch at the sleepy greeting, cursing at the time that glared back at him. It was almost two in the morning and about four hours before his contact would even think about getting up for the day. He could always blame the time zones, though.

"It's me," said Li, zipping the pockets in his jacket closed before slowly starting to divest the weapons from his body. He cursed as he realized that he'd left his rifle in his truck in the rush. Shaking his head, he shoved the rest of the chocolate bar in his mouth, licking his fingers clean.

"Little bro, how have you been, buddy? It's not that I don't want to hear from you, but it's like two o'clock in the morning." His voice went quieter for a moment, just at the edge of Li's hearing. "No, baby, go back to sleep." A sleepy murmur followed.

Li shook his head at his brother's enthusiasm, rubbing his hand over the back of his eyes. "Sorry. I'm in Ireland right now. Time zones are shit. I need a favor, Jesse."

It was the same excuse that he'd used before. Ireland, Zurich or a Russian town that he couldn't pronounce. Jesse would answer no matter where and when he was pretending to be—even if Li was only a drive away.

"Anything for you, bro, just give me a second." His voice went quiet again followed by the sound of kissing. "Love you, too, baby, but I gotta get up. Not now—later."

Li cringed, staring at the phone as he tossed his spare gun on the side table. The chocolate coating the inside his mouth suddenly felt off, like he'd swallowed kilograms of sugar instead. As confused as he was about himself, he had no desire to hear his brother getting it on, especially when the other person sounded like a guy.

"Are you gay?" asked Li, shaking his head as soon as he asked. "Sorry. That doesn't matter, as long as you are happy." *Does that mean that it doesn't matter that I just had sex with a man, either?* It felt like it mattered. It was so monumental that he was worried that the world might stop spinning if he thought about it for too long.

"Thanks, and yeah. You met Sebastian at the last get-together, remember?" Jesse rumbled, letting out a sigh. "Wait! You canceled on that one, too."

Silence stretched as Li swallowed, biting his tongue until it ached. What was he supposed to say? He couldn't tell Jesse that he had been in Munich during the last family reunion with a German scientist in his scope. He couldn't tell Jesse *anything*.

"What's the favor?" asked Jesse, finally putting Li out of his misery.

"I need information on one of my friends. There was talk that he might have been killed tonight, and I need to know if he's alive or not," said Li, leaning back against the wall and closing his eyes. He hadn't ever told Jesse what he did for a living, but there was no way he didn't know.

"I didn't think you missed," said Jesse, his tone flat.

"Jess, I—"

"I know, little bro. It doesn't mean that I don't worry about you, though. What's this guy's name?"

"Henley," said Li, breathing out the name and biting his lip at the memories that it brought back. "I don't have a last name. He worked for Martinez." He rattled off the address of the club.

"Ireland, eh?" asked Jesse, the sound of tapping keys following his sarcastic reply.

"Yeah." Li closed his eyes, his chest aching. The rule that hurt the most was number four — keeping his life from the ones he loved.

Letting the sound of Jesse's breathing wash over him, he imagined standing beside his big brother, leaning over his shoulder as he tapped away on the computer. Jesse would probably smack him before shooing him away so he could get his work done. He'd done it all the time when they had been younger.

Fuck, I miss them. If anyone had told him that being an assassin would be so lonely… Who was he kidding? He would be in the same spot.

"Nothing," said Jesse a few minutes later. "Looks like Damien Martinez bit the dust, but there's no mention of any Henley. It's still early, though. This news was just posted ten minutes ago. Let me do some digging, and I can get back to you."

Li looked down at his phone. He couldn't give his brother the number to the burner phone that would have no SIM card as soon as the call ended. "I'll call you back tomorrow." He reached for the end call button without pushing it, his fingertip trembling as it hovered.

"Little bro?" Jesse paused, the incessant tapping coming to a halt.

"Yeah?"

"We miss you. Christmas is a few months away, and it might be Mom's last. You need to make it work if you want to see her one last time."

Li bit his lip, trying to stifle the tears that instantly brimmed. His mother hadn't known who he was when he had snuck into her care home the month before. She had screamed when she'd woken with him sitting at her bedside, her mind and body broken from Alzheimer's disease. He hadn't been able to bring himself to slip by his father's grave before he'd left town in a rush.

"I'll make it work." The lie burned on his tongue, and Jesse let out a sigh. "Talk to you tomorrow, Jesse."

"Take care, little man."

The line went dead, and Li pulled the SIM card from the phone with practiced precision, snapping it in half before tossing it with the rest of his disposable gear.

"I need a shower."

Chapter Six

Li

Two weeks was long enough to lie low, in Li's opinion. He had started to climb the walls on the first week, and he was down to tinned foods by the second. He hadn't planned on his impromptu isolation, so he'd only had a few cursory items stocked up.

Like chicken stock. He shuddered as he made a future note to never buy chicken stock again. It was great for soup, but when he'd drunk it plain out of the carton, he'd nearly puked. Because of it, he knew exactly what salty chicken fat tasted like. *Blech.*

So, when his phone had chimed to life on the fifteenth day of isolation, he'd dove on the opportunity for a new job, fleeing from his home to board a plane that had taken him two-thousand kilometers away.

Sitting in a dive bar with a plate of chicken wings and battered mushrooms in front of him was not the worst place he'd ever been. The grease alone was the best thing he'd eaten in two weeks, and his target was two tables over, feeling up a young woman who looked barely legal.

Leaning back in his chair, Li glanced up at the water-stained ceiling, wondering how many times the bar's floors had flooded with rainwater. Some of the spots were still damp, the slow country music only adding to the residual mildew of the place. The air was warm, though, and no one had interrupted him except the waitress, who was more than welcome.

His target, Bill Greene, was definitely getting killed, but Li still hadn't decided on *how* yet. A gun was his usual tool, unless he could find another way that was less messy, but a gun would also be too quick for Bill. Li had only been following him for twenty-four hours, and it was twenty-four too many.

Some men, like Bill, were just dirtbags. The last woman he had forced was destined to be his last. She happened to have a cousin who had as much money as influence, which meant that Bill had gone from a dirtbag to a dead man. It was only a matter of time.

"Can I get you anything else, hon?" the waitress asked as she paused by his table for the fourth time. Her blue eyes sparkled in the low light, and she was more attractive than any other person in the bar. She gave him a flirty wink that had him frowning.

What the hell is wrong with me? He'd fucked women before, as long as they didn't get in the way of his work, and she was pretty. She was tall, with legs for miles and a sweet smile. Her tits peeked out of her top, giving Li a little *hello*, and she looked like she was ready to party.

But when he looked down at his crotch, there was nothing—not even a twitch as he imagined the woman naked and on her knees beneath the table as he sipped his cheap beer.

Strangely enough, he got more of a reaction out of his cock when he looked up to the bar at a guy who was perched on his stool drinking a pint. His Adam's apple bobbed every time he swallowed, and his biceps bulged as he lifted his drink higher to finish it off.

I'm not gay, but bi is looking like a distinct possibility. Not that he wanted to approach the guy at the bar. He looked too close to Li's own height and was thicker than the man he dreamed of every time he closed his eyes. His isolation had been difficult for more than one reason. *Damn you, Henley.*

He'd tried to look up if Henley had survived, reading every news article and tweet about the incident, but it was as if the bodyguard had disappeared. It set his teeth on edge, but it hadn't stopped him from exploring himself late at night when he should have been sleeping.

"I'm good," said Li, giving the waitress a smile. "But can you do me a favor instead? I want to send that lady a drink. Could you manage that for me?"

He pointed at the couple seated next to his target and his escort, giving the waitress another smile when she bit her lip.

"I don't think her man will appreciate the gesture, but I can do it, if that's what you want, hon."

He nodded, slipping her a tip that was more than the cost of his meal. Her eyes went wide as she eyed the bill, her cheeks flushing. "Or maybe she might ditch her man instead and come sit over here."

Li watched as the waitress delivered the drink, the condensation on the glass tinting a circle in the cheap tablecloth. The lady blushed and her date turned with rage and indignation as the waitress pointed toward Li with a tense smile.

Pushing his empty plate to the side, Li tossed a few more bills by his napkin before he stood and strolled toward the table, weaving through the bar as if he had all the time in the world. The man had flushed red by the time he arrived, smoke practically coming out of his ears.

"Did you get my gift?" asked Li, as he looked down at the woman. She turned her gaze on him, fluttering her lashes as she lifted her lips at the corners. Taking a swallow of the gifted drink, she let out a quiet hum. She was quite pretty but still did nothing for him.

"What's your problem, prick? Can't you see she's with someone?" The guy pushed his way to his feet, a few inches taller than Li and built like a fucking tree trunk. His hair was buzzed, and he had a few tattoos peeking from the collar of his shirt. Something about them just made Li want to lick the salt from the guy's skin.

Henley had ruined him.

"I thought you were her brother," said Li, subtly sliding a small piece of paper from his pocket before he held his hands up in defense. "Pretty lady in this kind of bar? I didn't think her *man* would bring her here." He looked to the woman, who was blushing furiously, her eyes and mouth wide. "A beautiful woman like you should be treated like a queen."

Li took a step back as the guy lunged for him. His hip hit his target's table, sending a few glasses tumbling sideways. The waitress looked up from where she had leaned against the bar to watch them, a laugh behind her hand. The bar had gone silent, all eyes on them.

"I'm so sorry," said Li, shrinking back and holding up his hands in surrender. "Honest mistake. I'll be on my way before I cause any trouble."

The man puffed up like a peacock, preening under the blushing stare of his lady in his victory. Li waited for people to look away when they realized there wouldn't be a fight before he turned to his target, picking up his spilled glass and refilling it with the pitcher at the table. He slipped the piece of paper into the glass, making sure it dissolved instantly.

It was a special kind of paper that definitely didn't come from a tree.

"Sorry for the disturbance, sir. Enjoy your evening." He handed the glass to his target, who took a sip, as if he was obligated. The sip was all politeness, and exactly what Li had expected.

The girl never looked to him, keeping her eyes on the soaked table. There were bruises around her neck that made Li wish that he had gone with a route that was a touch more painful. At least she would be safe soon.

Li stepped out of the building, peeling the thin gloves from his hands as a few laughs broke out behind him and the door swung shut. The dark parking lot was clear, with only one person pulling out of the lot, their headlights glaring as they turned onto the road. Waiting until they disappeared, Li grabbed a bag from his jacket pocket, stuffing the gloves into it.

The gloves were skin-toned and tight enough that it was almost impossible to tell that he was wearing them. His wig came next, along with the prosthetic nose and chin and the eyelashes that had taken him three tries to get on right. His makeup would have to wait until he found a place to burn everything.

He would be remembered at the bar, but it wouldn't be him they recalled. In about twelve hours, his target would be dead, but he wouldn't start to show symptoms for the next four or so. Even if the police suspected something besides a heart attack, it was doubtful that they would ever connect a nearby argument with a lethal dose of digoxin.

Another easy-peasy job under his belt and enough cash to get the new Smith and Wesson he'd been eyeing. He would be back home by the time the guy's liver had cooled to room temperature. Chuckling, he tied the bag off, shoving it back in the inside pocket of his jacket as he reached for his keys.

"You seem like you're in a rush."

Li froze with one hand on the handle of his *borrowed* car, the other still in his pocket. The car was only stolen if the owners noticed it was missing—or if he didn't return it.

He knew that voice, because he'd heard it every night in his dreams as he was filled by a phantom. His cock twitched, as if it could reach for Henley itself if Li turned him down.

He hadn't expected to see Henley again, especially not on another job two-thousand kilometers away.

"Just heading out," said Li, turning in the direction Henley had spoken from. The dark spot between two neighboring vehicles was empty, but Li had no doubt that Henley was somewhere close. The shadows were thick, and the steel buildings nearby made sound echo.

"You should have waited longer, kid," said Henley, his voice coming from a different direction. Li whirled to the sound, but there was nothing there. His heart picked up as his adrenaline surged, pumping more through his veins than any recent job. "I've been trying to track you for weeks, and I almost gave up, until I got a hit on an airline ticket. I didn't think you would have given me your real name, Li, even if you shortened it a bit."

Li hadn't...had he? Oh God, he *had*. He had been so overwhelmed by Henley's tiny but fierce presence that he had given him his real name—sort of. He usually kept his aliases short and sweet—a new one for each job. Two weeks before he'd been Larry, the intern who couldn't afford a nice apartment because his boss was a tightwad.

"What do you want?" Li dropped his hand to the back of his belt, resting on the butt of his gun. It was easy enough to hide a piece in a bar but getting a gun across the border had been a challenge, as usual. He was lucky that he had stashes in a few countries.

"I heard you were the guy I should talk to if I need someone dead," said Henley, finally emerging from the shadows. Li's memory had overexaggerated his recollection of Henley, adding a few inches where there was only a bit of mussed hair in reality. The thickness of his shoulders, arms and the breadth of his thighs were a reality, though.

He still couldn't believe that this was the man who had pinned and fucked him on a rooftop. A hint of cologne struck him as the wind picked up, every hair on his body standing on end. He shifted his legs apart as he pulled the gun free, clicking the safety off.

"I don't know what you're talking about," said Li, crossing his arms and reaching for his hidden knife with his free hand. After finding Henley's hidden blade, he had finally caved and had added a few to his arsenal. Blades were never his first choice—too messy. "I'm here visiting family."

Henley chuckled, stalking forward until he was only two steps away, looking up at him with a wicked smirk on his face. A wave of heat immediately washed over Li at the proximity, and he glanced down to Henley's lips.

How a *bodyguard* had managed to track him, when no one else had ever been able to, was a mystery. Everything about Henley had seemed to be a shadow of a mirage, until Jesse had done some digging.

Pulling the blade free, he lowered his hands to his sides, struggling not to take a step back as Henley shifted closer.

"I did some digging of my own," said Li, recalling his stagnant days in his home where the walls had started to look mighty close. "Here I thought that you were an innocent guy protecting the wrong man, but you aren't so innocent after all. You spent five years on the inside before you got out and started working security. I would have killed you in the street if I would've known that—and saved myself the trouble."

Henley threw his head back, his laugh echoing through the parking lot until he had to bend at his waist through the wheezes. His eyes crinkled at the corners as he slapped his knee, the smile making his eyes glisten. There was a small tattoo on his collar that Li hadn't noticed before—a tiger with teeth and claws drawn.

"You kill me, kid. What are you? Nineteen? Twenty? You think I'm a fucking bodyguard?" Henley giggled, wiping the tears from the corner of his eyes before they could fall.

Li's breath caught as he focused on the weight of his gun. Things weren't adding up. He trusted his brother, and Jesse had yet to fail him. Henley had to be bluffing.

Forcing an image of false bravado, he huffed. "I'm twenty-six."

"Twenty-six years old and a body count of thirty-two." Henley glanced at the bar. "Or thirty-three in a few hours." He looked back to Li, his eyes blazing in the darkness. "We've been trying to bag you for years, kid. Never thought you would be so naïve, from looking at your file."

Dread sank deep into Li's core. The body count wasn't even close to the right number, but it did match one of his aliases—one that only a few people knew about.

There was no way. Henley? *No.*

Henley kept up his grin, closing the last of the distance between them until his breath steamed over Li's face as he tilted his head to meet his gaze. "Whatever you're thinking…I'm worse. Too bad you're my dream sub. You could have been my pup, but I'm about to make you my bitch."

Li saw the glint of metal a second before it would have slammed into his chest. He wasn't sure if it was a knife or a Taser, but it didn't matter. Either way, if it made contact, he would end up in prison or in a body bag. *Or tied to a bed, maybe.*

He blocked the weapon with his hand, dropping his gun to the ground as he grabbed Henley's wrist and twisted him around to slam him into the nearest truck. Henley's head hit with a thump that was hard enough to make Li's teeth ache. The hit should have taken him down, but the moment he relaxed his grip, Henley spun and managed to get a death grip on his throat.

"Fucker," Henley shouted, tightening his hand around Li's throat, despite the blood dripping from the fresh gash above his eye.

Li jumped back, pulling free before he flipped his knife into his dominant hand. Henley was on him in a moment, pushing him to the ground with his lighter body on top. Gravel dug into his spine, his face smooshing into the edge of his rental truck tire as the air rushed from his lungs.

Henley gripped Li's wrists with one hand while kneeling on his chest and digging his kneecap directly into Li's solar plexus.

Li gagged as his dinner attempted to make a reappearance. He was stranded, Henley's powerful body above him and his cock aching in the most distracting way. He should have been focusing on getting loose, but instead he had the strangest urge to reach out and bring Henley closer.

Breaking Henley's grip on his wrists, he rolled them, settling between Henley's thighs and tangling their legs together. They were both breathing hard, their hair mussed and a few small rocks clinging to Henley's short locks. The blood on Henley's face made him look absolutely mad.

Li's eyes nearly rolled back as Henley shifted and their groins aligned. Their lips were inches apart — so close that Li could taste the beer on Henley's breath. Henley was laid out beneath him like the sweetest treat on a platter — the one that gave him cavities and sores in his mouth every time he indulged.

Move! Get away! Kill him! Li took a deep breath as his heart hammered, staring at the man pinned beneath him. His eyes were like the northern lights up close, his pupils like the blank darkness of the night sky. There were a few wrinkles at the corners of his eyes that relaxed as he stared back, giving in, if only for a moment.

Even wondering who Henley could be didn't change what they had shared together. He had never given himself willingly to someone like that, and he couldn't picture ever doing it with another person. Perhaps that was why he had no desire to kill him.

How many times have I imagined this? What if things had gone differently, and he had ended up on top on the roof, pinning Henley beneath him and sliding his cock home? The thought made him shudder with desire. Even the knife digging into his thigh didn't hamper the lust that pulsed through him. If anything, it made him hotter.

"Have you been thinking about me, kid?" asked Henley, his voice a harsh whisper as his heart pounded against Li's chest.

Li didn't even know his grip had gone slack until Henley tangled his fingers in Li's hair, tugging him even closer. "I've been thinking about you every night and remembering the way you came on my cock. I thought you might even crawl to me like a good boy if I let you taste me again. Maybe you'd let me come inside you and plug you up with a nice tail that you could wag — but only after you run for me and let me chase you, catch you and fuck you like a beast."

Li's chest heaved, the images flashing through his head sending a burst of pre-cum to coat the inside of his boxers. He was throbbing and dripping, slicking the inside of his underwear like a wet woman beneath the partner of her dreams. He couldn't remember the last time that had happened.

Because, even though he was terrified, he wanted it. "Except, I would be the one fucking you," said Li, growling as he nipped at Henley's lower lip. "I wonder how sweet you would sound as you begged for my cock."

And where the heck did that come from? Did I just go from bi-curious to gay and kinky from a little dirty talk?

Henley surged up, bringing their lips together with a low growl. He tasted the same as Li remembered, with a touch of beer—the heat and slickness like nothing he'd ever felt. His jaw was scratchy beneath Li's hands as he pulled him closer, tighter, longing for more. *Undoubtedly a man.*

"I love a challenge, kid," Henley grumbled as he pulled back for air. If he hadn't been close to breaking Li's leg with the grip he had on it with his thighs, Li might have laughed at the audacity.

"I'll give you a chance, kid. If I can find you again in a week, then you'll crawl to me like a good pup. If I can't, then you can have my ass as hard as you'd like," said Henley, the words sending a shudder down Li's spine.

No. He should have been running or reaching for his knife to thrust it into Henley's chest. Henley was probably some kind of special forces agent. But there was no back-up rushing in and no red dot of a sniper rifle aimed at his chest. *Now is my chance!*

Henley released him, his body going lax against the gravel so Li could untangle himself. Li pulled back, reaching for his gun that was only a few feet away. He tested the weight in his grip, the eleven bullets all accounted for. It would only take one second and a quick squeeze.

Henley closed his eyes, a smile on his lips as he leaned his head back before taking a breath of chilly night air. He was only in a long-sleeved T, and it was tight enough that it left nothing to the imagination. When he let out a soft breath, Li's decision had already been made for him.

There was no way Henley had any chance of catching him again. Li had more aliases than anyone else in the business, and he'd been moving undetected from country to country for most of his career. And the thought of having Henley again, only coming out on top, had saliva flooding his mouth.

Pulling the door open of his borrowed Chevy, Li ducked into the vehicle. When he glanced back at Henley, he was still on the ground, his arms folded behind his head in the picture of comfort.

"See you in three days, Listowel."

Chapter Seven

Henley

The kid was good, Henley would give him that. He'd given Li a twenty-four-hour head start, just to be fair, and it had taken him almost twelve hours to retrace his steps and catch up.

That kind of timeline was pathetic for him, really. So either he was bound for retirement soon, or Li was better than Henley gave him credit for.

He had enough cash saved up for retirement, even with his impromptu off-the-books runaround. He wasn't quite sure why it was still off the books. He'd been mostly bluffing when he'd told Li that they had been looking for him for a long time. Ben had been able to find his name but not much else other than a few aliases to track him by.

He was a professional, that was for sure, but he hadn't made enough of an impression to be a blip on Henley's radar — at least, not before the rooftop.

Shelia had accepted his minimal update with a sigh and a click of the phone as she'd hung up. It wasn't the first time Henley had gone off schedule a bit, but he'd never done it to get his dick wet. He should have been good for a few months with the epic romp only a few weeks behind him, but chasing Li was building up to be some kind of twisted foreplay instead.

After three flights and two continents, he was crouched in a high branch of a massive tree in a park in Germany. The branches were nearly bare with their tinted leaves scattered all over the park, but he'd managed to find a spot that was concealed from onlookers.

He shivered as his breath misted in the air, tucking his hands into his armpits when his fingers started to go numb. A few conversations drifted to him from below, their thick accents nearly indecipherable. German was not his forte, although he could get by most days.

Bracing against the wind, he looked up to the nearest hotel where Li was staying, his window overlooking the park below. The lights were on in the room, their warm glow leaking out into the street as night slowly descended and the streetlights switched on one by one.

Despite the light, Li hadn't appeared at the window in the last forty-five minutes except for the brief peek he'd offered when he'd opened the curtains. If he had been trying to hide, he was doing a piss-poor job. *Perhaps I gave him too much credit.* Henley had picked Li's body count off the top of his head, but in hindsight, perhaps he should have gone with something in the single digits.

It *had* been difficult to uncover Li's name, though. He never would have been able to track him at all if Li hadn't slipped up. As for anything much deeper than that, Li was an enigma—a very sexy enigma.

Under the cover of darkness, Henley dropped from the tree and booked it across the street, his running shoes tapping on the pavement as he huffed. He was short on sleep after so many time zones, but he was still quick...ish. Sprinting was certainly easier than running for five blocks chasing after a madman with a gun. *Those were the days.*

The only hindrance was his cock, which felt like it had been hard for days. Nothing was better than an epic chase, except for one that was followed by a fuck. He'd given Li three days, as promised, and it was high time to cash in.

After that...maybe Henley would call in? Shelia had made it clear that it was either his ass or the shooter's who would go down for Damien's murder, and Henley wasn't too keen on starting over with a new life. Mr. Martinez was a powerful man, but Henley liked Canada and the kink community he had found there.

He slipped through the lobby without being noticed, avoiding the cameras in case Li had accessed them. The elevator camera was trickier, so Henley pulled the ballcap down on his head before tugging his hood up. He kept his gaze on the ground as he used his knuckle to push the button for the right floor.

Li had gotten smarter and had switched to another ID. What he hadn't known was that Henley had friends at the airport, and the ID Li had used had been flagged in a previous investigation. Henley had called in a favor to let Li slide through airport security, leaving his prey none-the-wiser.

But Li had still been cautious, switching to another identity as he'd landed in Zurich. That had stalled Henley and had deprived him of an epic night of sleep and jerking off. Li practically owed him a blow job at this point.

He scanned the room numbers as he arrived at the sixth floor, heading left down the hall. He could have tried to scale the outside of the building, but he was terrified of heights—a secret that he would take to his grave. Shelia would only find an excuse to throw him out of an airplane if she found out.

Withdrawing a universal key from his pocket—a gift from an unsuspecting maid earlier in the day—he tapped the key on the lock for the unoccupied room next to Li's. Li had almost made it too easy on him by choosing a room with an adjoining door that was meant for families. It only made Henley wonder why.

A desk crowded the right side of the room with a queen bed to the left that was stacked with four spotless pillows. It smelled clean, too, with just a touch of bleach as he crept past the bathroom. The rooms were nice and average, which still didn't answer his question.

Because Li is begging for it. He wants my cock, and he's only running for show. Henley adjusted his cock, triple-checking to make sure his fanny pack was secure. He'd picked one up at the first opportunity, packing it with lube, condoms, sex toys and one other item that made him drip pre-cum every time he thought about it.

He'd been half convinced that he had gone insane when he'd first added it to the bag. Maybe he was insane. He wasn't sure why, but Li was *different*.

His pack had been an interesting thing to get through airport security, but it had drawn their attention away from his concealed weapons. He'd managed to get the phone number of a sweet twink at the airport, too—not that he had any interest in anyone but Li.

Opening the door to the adjoining room, he was faced with a second door. It was locked from the other side, but it was a simple mechanism, not a vault, and lock picking was something he excelled at. Thirty seconds later, it clicked open, the knob turning silently in his palm.

He crouched down, taking a deep breath before he slowly pushed the door open, wincing as the hinges squealed. He paused when silence greeted him. Relaxing, he pushed the door the rest of the way open, squinting in the sudden bright light.

Looking up, he came face to barrel with Li's gun. *Whoa.* He hadn't heard the footsteps, or the swish of Li's clothing as he'd moved. He'd appeared like a fucking ghost.

Okay, so maybe it wasn't too easy. Henley moved his gaze from the gun to Li's face, taking in his scowl and the deep marks under his eyes that made it look like he hadn't slept since they'd last met. His grip was steady, his finger already on the trigger with the safety off.

He wasn't happy, and he definitely didn't look horny. Li's pants were tight enough that Henley would have known. *Huh.* Whatever Henley had been expecting, it wasn't that. Li had already passed up a few chances to put Henley in the ground, and he'd seemed excited about their little bet.

"Caught you?" said Henley, slowly getting back to his feet. Li followed his movement so the gun stayed level with Henley's forehead, his expression never changing.

"I already told you that I'm not gay. You must have a death wish if you followed me here," said Li, his grip going tight on his weapon. Henley flinched, taking a step back.

His cock was still hard, even with the gun pointed at his head. Henley had always known he had a bit of a thing for his own weapon, but apparently it had extended to Li's as well.

He'd never explored the kink further because there was no way Clint would have let him in his club, Unkinked, with a gun. He had made that clear enough when he'd accidentally found out about Henley's background.

"I made a few more calls after you tracked me down," said Li. "Turns out that I have more friends than you do. It wasn't so hard to flip a few people to get your story, Harris."

Henley flinched at the use of his birth name, his knees going momentarily weak as his mouth went dry. He'd buried that name a long fucking time ago—and for good reason. That wasn't who he was. "Don't call me that."

"It's your name," said Li, his scowl deepening. "But it still doesn't explain why you've been chasing me around the globe. One of my contacts said you were into puppy play—whatever that really means. You won't find that here, but I have lots of bullets, if you'd prefer."

Henley gulped, looking at Li's face and not the weapon. A bead of sweat dripped down the back of his neck, despite the coolness to the room. Two years of deep cover and building a life that was a lie and yet closer to himself than he'd ever been and Li had torn it aside to expose him while Henley chased after him like a horny beast.

"It's not exactly puppy play," said Henley, letting out a sigh. He didn't want to explain his kinks with a gun in his face, but he didn't have a better choice — anything to keep Li from talking about his background. *Damn, I did not give him nearly enough credit.*

"There are some aspects of that kind of play that appeal to me, but it's too sweet for me. There isn't really a term to describe what I'm into. I like the tail plugs and all that, but no masks, and the only time I want my sub to crawl is if they are begging for my cock. What I really want is someone feral and primal to dominate."

"That still doesn't explain why you're chasing *me*. I'm not gay, and I'm not interested in playing a role." Despite his words, Li lowered the gun. His pupils blew wide as his chest rose faster. It was progress.

"I'm pretty sure you are a little gay, Li." Henley licked his lips. *What are you thinking, Li?* A straight man would have told him to stop. A straight man wouldn't have been interested in the first place.

"You're hot, strong as fuck and you want to fight for dominance, which is everything I want in a partner," said Henley, the truth striking his core. Li was *everything* he wanted — gun and sense of humor included. No matter how ridiculous that sounded, it was true. He had shared moments with Li that he had never shared with another person.

"Maybe you should lower your standards," said Li, flicking the safety on.

Henley's heart slowed just a tad, his gaze flickering back to the weapon.

"I don't need to because I've already found you. Before I met you, I was just a guy in a dangerous job waiting for a bullet to come get me at some point. I've never felt as alive as I did on that rooftop. I need it again, except, not the part when you drugged me, because that just fucking sucked. I do not do well with barbiturates, and I was hungover for like three days."

Li quirked his lips into a small smile, the anger slowly evaporating from his gaze. "If you weren't such a creepy stalker, I would almost call you romantic." His cheeks flushed, the color edging toward the curled edge of his turtleneck.

"I'm only a stalker for you," said Henley, scratching at his chin. He needed to shave soon before he turned into a mountain man. Li looked like had had just finished shaving, his cheeks smooth, like they always were. "I'm stalker enough to cover your ass from my boss, too. She's gonna be pissed if she finds out that I was within a few feet of you and didn't try to arrest you."

Li slipped his gun back into the holster at his side, leaving the securing strap open for easy access. He probably had a few other weapons stashed around the room, but Henley couldn't tell from his spot at the door.

"I appreciate that," said Li. "I don't usually have special forces on my ass after a job."

"Is it worth a thank you blow job?" asked Henley, perking up as Li huffed and turned away before heading deeper into his room. The bed was identical to the one behind Henley, and unslept in, but the desk had been moved so it was upturned against the door with the notch of the top just under the handle.

"How about I just don't shoot you," said Li. He paused by the bed—a towering queen with the same spotless white pillows and duvet. He chewed his bottom lip, something that Henley had never seen him do before. Li's every move had always been carefully controlled.

"I really don't think I'm gay. I've never found any man attractive before you. But what will you do now if I turn you down? Will you just force me anyway?"

"No," said Henley, shaking his head. "I would never force you. I'm kinky, but I'm not a rapist. If you tell me you don't want me, then I'll leave. If you say that you never want to see me again, then you won't. I won't be able to protect you forever, but I'll do my best to give you a head start."

Henley ran a hand over his fanny pack to the things he was not going to need. He should have kept the receipts, but he wasn't sure if the store would even take returns—not for the cock ring—definitely not—but the other item that he'd ordered custom and on a rush.

He would burn his trail and end his life in Canada with his new friends who made him feel like a real person and not a freak. He could ghost Shelia or just put in for a transfer to somewhere very hot or very cold.

"What would you do if I said that I wanted to have sex, but that I want to fuck you this time?" asked Li, apparently oblivious to Henley's internal resignation.

Henley's cock perked up faster than light, but he held on to his sanity. "Your friend who told you that I was into kink, did he tell you that I'm a Dom?"

Li shook his head, his eyebrows drawing together. He bit his lip again, the pink flesh flushing red as he pressed his teeth together.

"A Dom is someone who sets the scene and decides what happens to his sub, where the sub takes directions and follows orders, so to speak. The sub has safewords so they can pause or put an end to the scene at any time, and that gives them more power than the Dom could ever have. A switch can be both a Dom or a sub, depending on their partner or their mood. I'm a Dom through and through."

"So, it's okay if I take it up the ass, but you're too good for it? Forget I said anything," said Li, crossing his arms as he looked away, his lip nearly bleeding from his bite. His hair caught the light, shimmering and neat.

Henley could imagine Li waiting on the other side of the door with a hairbrush in one hand and a gun in the other. But he'd gotten ready and that was the point. He'd shaved and shined himself up for Henley, even if he hadn't slept.

"I never said that. I'm fine with you fucking me, but I would still be in control. You would still be under my command, even if you were inside me. My control has been taken from me too many times before, and there's no one in the world that I would give it up to willingly." Henley tensed, years' worth of memories that he had tried to suppress rushing to the front of his mind.

He hadn't become one of the top agents on the continent by sitting at a desk and twirling a pen. He'd been captured, tortured and fucked up in both mind and body, and he had the scars to prove it. "If you tried to dominate me, I would probably end up snapping your neck. It has happened before, and all the therapy in the world isn't going to get rid of my reflexes and self-preservation when I go into panic mode."

It was only PTSD once the trauma had passed, but Henley still exposed himself to it all the time, treading on the thin line between sanity and an institution. When he retired, it was going to slam into him harder than a Peterbilt truck.

Li nodded, a look of understanding passing over his features. His gaze dropped to his shoes, submissive, even if he wasn't aware of it. "What if I told you that this would be the last time?"

Henley sucked in a breath. He wasn't sure when Li had morphed from a target to more than that, but his chest clenched painfully at the thought. He couldn't turn back with Li in his sights.

"Then I would do everything I could to worship you and make it worth your while for what little time we had together."

Chapter Eight

Li

Make it worth my while? Even if it pained him, he had to admit that sex with Henley had probably ruined him for any other person in the world. He had slept with women on almost every continent, but none of them had made his heart race. None of them made him burn.

And Henley was the complete opposite to his usual type of tall, slim and female. Maybe Jesse would understand and be able to explain it to him, but he didn't want to drag his brother any further into his world.

Henley couldn't get any closer to his exact opposite. He was a special forces career brat with a rainbow chip on his shoulder the size of the Eiffel Tower. Li should have put a bullet in his head ten times over. He had to if he wanted to save his own life and career.

But he couldn't. The thought had bile rising in his throat. Imagining Henley as a lifeless corpse instead of someone brimming with excessive personality was the same as killing a kid's puppy.

Instead of reaching for his gun, he took Henley's hand, closing the two adjoining doors before leading him to the queen bed. His heart pounded for a different reason altogether. It had *hurt* last time, but looking back, he couldn't think of a single thing that he would have changed.

Although it did irk him that Henley assumed that he was bottoming again. Li had the height advantage, and he was stronger, no matter what Henley had to say about it.

The bed was unslept in, because it was just another part of the trail of breadcrumbs that Li had left for Henley. It had all been a ploy to get Henley exactly where he had ended up — on his knees with a gun to his head. The plan had been to shake off his pathetic excuses and take care of business.

Instead, he was digging himself deeper.

"Tell me more," said Li, squeezing Henley's hand tighter as he eyed up the bed frame. His mouth was dry, and his palms went sweaty. He hadn't been so nervous in a long time.

"My friend was vague on the details, other than you were a member of a kink club. Tell me what that means." The Internet had been a dangerous hole to fall into, and it had sucked Li in while he was stuck during a layover. Being hard in an airport had been awkward as hell, especially since there had been a Christian youth group waiting in the same lounge.

"It's everything," said Henley, looking up at Li with wide eyes, like he couldn't believe that Li was pulling him closer. Li couldn't believe it, either, until the reality sank in as his ass hit the edge of the bed.

"I didn't have a lot of sex when I was younger," said Henley, holding Li's gaze steadily. His emerald eyes almost glowed in the soft light of the hotel room. "I tried every type of person, but I was never satisfied, no matter how far I tried to push things. People seemed to have a vision of who I was supposed to be, and eventually, I just followed along. But when I was transferred, I finally had a chance to start over and be myself. After I met Clint, he helped me put a few of the pieces together, and he matched me with a sub who set me free." He closed his eyes, a smile on his lips.

Li narrowed his eyes, biting the tip of his tongue to keep from asking the sub's name. Why was he even jealous? He squashed the uneasy feeling in his gut, but it burned brighter instead of flickering out. "Where is that sub now?"

Henley snorted, shaking his head as he looked to Li. "I said he set me free, not chained me down. He showed me that it was okay to want the things that I wanted, and after that, there was no turning back. I propositioned every sub with similar kinks and fucked them until they couldn't remember their own names." He gave a cocky smirk, which only made Li want to smack him more.

"Must not have been that special if they didn't come back for seconds," said Li, pushing his own hurt into his words. He wasn't sure why his chest ached more than his cock, but it pissed him off.

"Oh, they came back," said Henley, his eyes going dark. He pulled his hand free, pushing Li back on the bed with one well-placed shove to his chest. "They crawled back, crying and begging me to be their Dom, but I told them all the same thing. I don't do repeats."

He crawled over Li, straddling his hips and grinding down.

Henley's cologne sank into him, the spicy smell bringing his memories to life in an instant. His cock perked up, answering Henley's hardness with iron of its own.

"And with me?" asked Li, a little rush of heat going to his head as he thought about being the only man Henley had ever come back to. It shouldn't have mattered, but it spurred him on until he grabbed Henley's hips, meeting every grinding thrust. Henley's body was light, but his presence was overpowering, turning every nerve on until Li was certain he would combust if their naked skin touched.

"I couldn't get you out of my system after the first time, so maybe the second will do," said Henley, chuckling as he leaned in for a kiss.

Li stopped him with a hand on his chest. *Oh.* He turned his face away. Fucking was intimate enough, but he wasn't sure if he could hand any more of himself over again. "No kissing."

"Seriously? fuck that," said Henley, lifting off with a sigh before he strolled across the room, freeing the drapes from their ties. "I kissed you on the roof and you didn't have a problem with it, so what's changed? Afraid that if you kiss me again you won't be able to go back to burying your face between a woman's thighs? Ass is where it's at, kid."

"Don't call me 'kid'," said Li, following Henley across the room and grabbing him by the throat. He twisted them, walking Henley backward before pushing him to the bed and pinning him by his throat again. Henley's pulse was rapid under his fingers as he swallowed, his throat bobbing. His pupils had blown wide, his pants obviously tented. Li couldn't tear his gaze away.

Henley grabbed at Li's hand, his nails digging into his knuckles and the delicate tendons. The zing flared at the base of Li's groin as he squeezed tighter, so tempted to push that much farther. How far could he go before Henley took control again? *Christ, I want to find out.*

"You may be ready to sleep around and dip your dick into everyone's ass to get a taste, but I'm not. It's called standards," said Li, licking his lips as Henley wheezed a touch and his face started to tint. *I don't like the thought of you getting tired of me after another hit.*

"Okay, *Listowel*," said Henley, his voice a raspy whisper as he tugged one of Li's fingers, forcing it backward past its normal range. Another centimeter and it would break. "Can I call you my pup? Just for today?"

Henley's eyes went wide when Li didn't let up, clenching harder on the tanned column of his throat. His head had to have been pounding from the rising pressure. But Li didn't plan on letting up anytime soon.

Fuck Henley, fuck his kinks and fuck his deals. If Li was doing this, it would be on his own terms. He didn't get to where he was in his career by following orders and *submitting*.

"If you call me 'kid' or 'pup' again, I'll put a bullet between your eyes." Li tapped the butt of his gun that was practically begging for him to pick it up. He still had his eleven bullets, each one untraceable. "And if we do this, we do it *my* way on *my* terms."

"Fuck you," rasped Henley, throwing an elbow into Li's gut and knocking his breath from his lungs. His diaphragm spasmed and he choked, grabbing at his stomach and falling to the bed.

Li's arm was behind his back before he could blink, his shoulder cranked so hard that it was almost out of joint. His cock throbbed as the ache grew fierce and his heart rate picked up. *Christ,* he wanted it.

"If you wanted a fight, all you had to do was ask," said Henley, leaning over to whisper into his ear. He was deceptively light, but Li knew that he wouldn't be able to just shrug him off. He stuck like a leech and was twice as fast. "When sex is on the table, you always seem to end up like this. You want it hard and fast because you like my cock in your ass, and that fucking scares you."

Li bucked, kicking out and slamming his heel into the meat of Henley's thigh. Henley cursed, grabbing at his leg where hopefully the mother of all charley horses was wreaking havoc. "Fucker."

Switching tactics, Li pounced, grabbing at Henley's pants and tearing them and his boxers down his hips with enough brute force that it split the seam. The globes of Henley's ass jiggled as they were freed from his pants, and Li's mouth went dry.

He hadn't had time to admire him on the roof, and he hadn't really wanted to at the time, but *damn.* Henley's ass was slim and pert, with cheeks that were the perfect size for squeezing. They looked so firm, with a dimple on each one that formed as Henley tensed.

Li shook his head, pushing Henley up the bed before leaning in and sinking his teeth into one of his ass cheeks as the urge overtook him. He pulled back for a second, slicking one finger with spit before he bit down on the other cheek. Spreading Henley's cheeks wide, he caught a look at his furled hole for the first time.

It wasn't exactly what he had been expecting. It looked so small, pink and tight that it was a wonder that he would even be able to fit a finger inside. The thought made his cock twitch as he imagined sinking into a place tighter than he'd ever been. *Okay, so maybe I am a little bit gay.* He'd never taken the time to admire the intimate places of a woman, more interested in blowing off steam than enjoying the moment.

Throwing his reservations out of the hotel window, he pressed his finger to Henley's hole, pushing until the tight ring gave and he sank all the way inside. Henley yielded to him, clutching him tight and sucking him deep all at once. It was velvet and warmth but hard to move with only his saliva slicking the way.

Henley let out a muffled moan, his face half-buried in the duvet as he gave in to the touch. He bucked against Li's hand, pushing himself back until Li sank even deeper.

"That was supposed to hurt," said Li, licking his lips and staring at the bite he had left behind. He remembered how much Henley's fingers had burned when they first pushed inside him, and how close he had come to tapping out. But he remembered the aching fullness, too, and the way it had become so much more.

"It does," said Henley, rocking so Li moved in and out of him with slow, steady strokes. He let out another long moan as Li curled his finger, meeting each thrust.

And I thought I had issues.

"Who's the bitch now?" said Li, his words dripping with sarcasm. Henley cursed before he reached back and grabbed Li by the hair, forcing his face down between his ass cheeks.

"Finger-fuck my ass harder or I'll find someone better," growled Henley, releasing Li after one final harsh tug against his scalp.

Li vision bled into a red haze. He withdrew his finger, flipping Henley so he could glare down at him. Henley's cock popped up, so hard that it was nearly purple and dripping. It was perhaps a touch smaller than Li remembered, mostly because it had felt like a football when it had pushed into his ass the first time, but it was pretty — for a cock, at least. Not that he could recall any prettier vaginas at that moment.

After spitting on his fingers again, Li spread Henley's legs wide, plunging two fingers deep as he pushed Henley's shirt up and bit down on one nipple. Henley's fanny pack bumped against Li's abdomen, something hard digging into him. He grabbed the vile thing and tore it from his waist before tossing it off the bed.

"Hey," said Henley, pouting as his pack went flying and seemingly unaffected by two fingers in his ass. "Your present is in there."

Li rolled his eyes. "If it's a cock ring, you can forget it. I can last all day if I need to." He curled his fingers as he felt something inside Henley — like a small button through a layer of silky heat.

"Ah, fuck yeah. Right there, bitch," said Henley, fluttering his eyes shut.

Li grumbled at the pet name, stroking that spot harder before he slid a third finger inside. He had no idea how they were fitting, but despite how tight and hot Henley was, he seemed to be able to stretch and take it.

"I should shoot you for that," said Li, pulling his fingers from Henley's heat before lowering himself over him. He let all his weight fall, not caring if he crushed him or made it hard for him to breathe. Henley seemed to take him like a champ with no complaints through his wheezing breaths.

Their mouths hovered inches from each other, but Li hesitated, unwilling to close the distance. A kiss was one step closer to making things more than a one-time fuck for him. He couldn't have Henley like that and push him away.

"All my problems would be gone if I put a bullet in your head," said Li, licking his lips as he watched Henley do the same.

"Same here. Except one, because my cock would still be hard." Henley quirked his lips into a grin, rolling his hips to meet Li.

"Then why don't you?" asked Li, grabbing Henley's wrists in one hand and pinning them above his head. Henley's breath quickened, his heart pounding where their chests touched.

"Because I like you, Li. I've grown a soft spot for you — and a hard one." He winked, chuckling as Li rolled his eyes.

Of all the guys in the world, this is the one fate threw at me?

Li lowered his lips to Henley's, telling himself that it was just to shut Henley up. The heat from the touch took him off guard, and Henley's tongue teasing against his had him going weak. He hardly noticed as Henley flipped them, peeling his own shirt from his body until he was completely naked except for his striped pink socks.

Li choked, pulling back as he caught sight of the scars covering Henley's torso. They didn't make sense. His bubbly Henley, who shrugged off a strangling and threw himself into doors while laughing, wasn't the scarred beast before him. No, the man before him was a monster who had seen more than Li could ever imagine and had somehow come out with a smile on the other end.

There were at least three bullet wounds from what he could tell and a knife wound along his ribs. Part of his shoulder was warped and mottled, almost like he had been burned over and over before the skin had had a chance to heal again. The pain that he must have gone through would have brought Li to his breaking point and beyond.

The tiger tattoo on his collar was so dark compared to his tanned skin, the gray-toned lines like a fierce defense against every past injury.

"Sorry... I should have asked if you were okay with it first," said Henley, looking at a spot on the wall above Li's head as an uncharacteristic frown pulled at his lips. He played with his T-shirt in his hands, stretching the cloth between his fingertips.

"Don't be self-conscious. I was just surprised, that's all. You always look so breakable," said Li, skimming over the burn wound with a delicate touch. The skin was warm beneath the pads of his fingers and softer than he expected.

Henley flinched at the contact and Li quickly dropped his hand. "Does it hurt?"

"Not anymore," said Henley with a grim expression. "Sorry. I'll put my shirt back on so we can get back to things."

Li grabbed Henley's hand as he tried to move away. Skin was something that couldn't be changed, no matter hard someone wished it. Henley couldn't change his scars any more than Li could change his height. *I'm turning into a sap.* "Don't."

"Then don't look at me like I'm fucking broken," said Henley, threading his fingers through Li's. His palm was warm, the calluses thick between his fingers. "They don't hurt anymore, and they don't bother me, so get over your pity and let's fuck before you decide to kill me."

Li made a mental note to leave Henley the name of his therapist when it was all over. She was very good — and confidential — despite his ongoing activities.

"Well, I'm waiting for you to show your *dominance,* but at this rate, I'll still be hard by tomorrow." Li glowered at Henley, forcing his gaze away from the intricate scars.

His own skin was almost naked with his single surgical wound from when he'd had his appendix removed at nineteen. Maybe he would have to roll in some barbed wire to look more like someone in his profession.

Henley dropped his shoulders as his tension drained. His cock, that had started to flag, perked up again, wet and hot against Li's belly as Henley took a breath and leaned over him, pushing Li to the bed by his wrists with ease. "You okay if I go caveman on your ass?"

"Not a chance," said Li, tugging his hands free with a smirk. "I lured you here, and now it's time I get my reward. I won't let you hurt me, if that's what you're worried about, but I will definitely hurt your ass. I'm *way* bigger than you, and our cocks are both proportionate."

Henley licked his lips, his pupils blowing wide. "Give it your best, and we'll see who comes out on top."

Li tipped Henley onto the bed at the same time Henley wrapped his legs around his waist. They struggled on the duvet, almost falling off a few times as their wrestling became more and more heated. Henley would end up pinned, only to somehow flip Li ass over teakettle a moment later. They were almost equally matched with brawn against agility.

He lunged for Henley, bringing their lips together, even as his head swam from hardly being able to catch his breath. Every touch was like fire, naked skin on naked skin. He was exposed completely, pushed to his limit and beyond as he struggled with all his might—struggled with the decision to come out on top or give in.

With every movement, Li's cock throbbed harder, until his touches held more purpose than before. The next time he managed to pin Henley, with his face smashed into the bed and his ass in the air, he spat onto Henley's exposed hole, lining up his cock with new purpose.

He saw stars as Henley knocked him back with an elbow to the forehead, before he sucked Li's cock into his throat hard enough to distract him from the two fingers probing his ass. In the fifteen seconds that it took for Li to recover, Henley had slammed a third finger home, his rim burning in the most delicious way.

His body ached, every muscle on fire as his chest heaved from exertion, but he wanted nothing more than to keep fighting until he was either fucking or getting fucked. At some point, the lines had blurred, so it didn't matter which happened, as long as he got to come. His adrenaline surged as Henley managed to get him face down with his legs pinned and his upper body hanging off the bed.

"Ah-nngh." Li cried out as Henley thrust inside him, the burn of too little lube rolling over his senses. In one stroke, Henley was too deep and so fucking hard that Li knew he was going to break. But instead of pulling away, he bucked into the feeling, seeking it like a wild animal.

Sweat slicked their movements, the slap of Henley's palm against his ass loud in his pounding ears. He touched the carpet, trying to get his bearings as he was torn apart.

Henley grunted, wrapping his hands around Li's hips and tugging him back on the bed so he was no longer dangling with blood rushing to his head. The movement changed the angle, sending Henley's cock straight into Li's prostate.

Two strokes later, Li came, his vision whiting out as he emptied himself onto the duvet. Henley grunted in his ear, snapping his hips a few times before burying himself all the way inside.

Gasping for breath, they pulled apart, even as they reached for each other. Li collapsed on the bed, blindly grabbing a pillow when he couldn't find Henley, his mind buzzing from the sheer overstimulation. It was as if part of his primal mind that had been hidden for the last hundred generations had emerged to have a fucking party on the bed.

The duvet had long since fallen to the floor and the edge of the mattress peeked through the sheets that had somehow come off the corner. Their clothes were strewn everywhere, and the side lamp had been knocked over with a shattered bulb leaving a treacherous pile on the tightly woven carpet.

I want to do it again. Not soon, because his ass was aching and damp, his eyelids resisting every attempt he had at keeping them open. *Maybe in an hour or two.* Taking a deep breath, he inhaled the scent of sex and sweat, Henley's cum thick in the air, along with his own.

His heart thudded, and Henley's gasping breaths matched his own.

"I came in your ass," said Henley, biting his lip as he glanced over at Li. His hair was a disaster, and his entire body was flushed and naked, including his cock that was smeared with cum that dribbled down the shaft to the scratchy hair on his groin.

Oh fuck.

* * * *

Henley

Shit! Henley needed to smack himself or get his head checked. Protection had always been a fundamental part of sex for him, even before he had dipped his toes into kinky waters. He'd never stayed with a partner long enough to have the trust to even consider it without, despite if they had test results or not. And he certainly didn't trust Li.

But sliding into his ass after the struggle of a lifetime had given him the best orgasm of his life. Nothing had ever come close to that feeling before. It was only when he'd collapsed to the side and reached to remove the condom that he'd realized what he had forgotten. And the cum dripping from Li's winking ass was confirmation enough.

Beautiful. Another dollop seeped from Li's hole, dripping down his perineum to his nearly bare sac. His mouth watered and he blinked as Li's reddened furl tightened as another drop tried to escape. Three days of foreplay had left him a little backed up, and he had jetted every drop of it inside Li.

He wanted to lick it from Li's hole before more of it could drip on the sheets. Li looked dazed, his eyes wide and his forehead furrowed as he rested his cheek on the sole pillow that remained on the bed. He hadn't reached for his gun, which had been tossed to the ground at some point, or the knife that was still strapped to his bicep.

Henley had almost considered lifting the knife when he'd noticed that it was the same emerald color of his eyes. No matter what outfit he wore, it would always match.

"Can you get it up again?" asked Li, his voice barely above a whisper. He frowned as another glob of cum seeped from between his cheeks, his wrecked hole unable to close completely. Henley couldn't look away.

"What?" Henley reached for his cock absentmindedly, smoothing his palm over the head. Fuck yes, he could get hard again. He still kind of was, and arousal was still simmering in his gut. "I'm forty-two, not dead." *When is the best time to apologize?*

"Hmmm, I like it," said Li, reaching back to run a finger through the wetness between his cheeks. "It's weird, but kind of nice at the same time, and I feel so empty. Will you fill me again?"

Henley's mouth dropped open. Li's gaze was distant as he drifted in subspace, the drunken smile on his face like the sweetest victory. Henley hadn't even thought of the possibility that Li would go there, but Henley couldn't doubt that he was feeling the same. There was an energy under his skin that crackled to life. He could go another six times if he had to.

"You feeling okay?" asked Henley, creeping over Li's form and lining his cock up with his hole. With a groan, he slid back inside, his own cum slicking the way. He shuddered, thrusting a few times just to feel and watch it cover his cock.

"It's strange…" Li looked off to the side, his gaze caught by something that Henley couldn't see. Maybe it was the fanny pack or the shadow on the wall that they created.

Gripping Li's chin, he forced his gaze back to him as he thrust home again. "I'm sorry about the condom."

Li closed his eyes, his head tilting back as he let out a groan. Henley sank his teeth into the pale column of Li's throat, sucking until blood burst along the skin. Li smelled fantastic, like sweat and sex and fucking lollipops, but he tasted even better. Henley knew without even thinking about it that he would never tire of it.

"I like it better without," said Li, his cock starting to firm up. Henley reached for it, stroking it in time with his thrusts.

"Still, I'm supposed to look after you when you're floating, babe, and I dropped the ball big time." He sped up, grinding his cock until Li let out a gasp.

"Don't call me 'babe'."

Henley chuckled, kissing along Li's throat and chest. He craned his neck to capture one nipple, nibbling and sucking on the bud until Li was gasping beneath him.

"I can't call you 'pup', 'kid', 'fucker' or 'bitch'. I'll have to start saying 'you there'."

Li smiled, the edges of his lips curling at the same time his eyes lit up. It took Henley's breath away. Maybe it was the simplicity of it, like nothing would ever go wrong again.

"I like it when you called me by my name. No one calls me that, not even my mom," said Li, the open look on his face nearly heartbreaking. Henley felt a tug in his chest as he committed it to memory. *I'm gonna miss this.* Not many subs went under for him during primal play. It was all adrenaline and fighting, only submitting when they just *couldn't* anymore.

"Okay, Listowel," said Henley. Li shuddered beneath him, his walls trembling and bringing Henley closer to the edge. "Can I give you my gift now? I'll come back. Don't worry. I won't leave you empty for long."

Pulling out, Henley dove for his fanny pack, rushing back to Li and shoving his cock back inside before it had even started to cool. He set the pack on Li's belly before he pulled it open.

Maybe he was weak for offering something of such importance while Li was out of it, but he couldn't wait another moment.

"I hate that thing," said Li, flicking the fanny pack before he let out a groan as Henley presumably grazed his prostate. Henley slowed even further as the urge to claim and fuck started to fade. He was still hard, but he wasn't close to the edge, and Li could last a little while as well from the looks of things.

"It holds wonders beyond your imagination," said Henley, laughing at Li's lighthearted glare. Grabbing the condoms from inside, he tossed them onto the bed.

"Don't need these, but I hope to need some of this." He set a bottle of lube carefully next to them on the bed. It tipped onto its side as the bed shifted during his next shallow thrust.

He tossed the cock ring out next, grinning when Li rolled his eyes. He grabbed the plug from the bottom of the pack, twirling it between his fingers. It was small enough to fit in his pack and baby blue, with a brown pup tail that matched Li's hair color perfectly.

Not that he had obsessed over it for three hours or anything.

"This is what I like about puppy play. I like tails, plugs and knots, but that's about it." He handed the plug to Li, who took it like a loaded weapon.

"You can't be serious," said Li, his gaze sharpening as he edged out of his haze. "I don't know what a knot is, but I can tell you that this is not going up my ass."

Henley grinned, pulling out the last item and letting it dangle from his fingertips. He still couldn't fathom what had possessed him to buy it. He'd been so determined to remain unattached for so long that it still made his breath catch when he eyed it up. But Li had to be worth it. He had crossed literal continents for him, and he couldn't let himself forget that.

It was as close as he could get to a collar without it actually being a collar. The simple chain was beautiful but thick enough that it would take a lot of force to break it. A single dog tag hung from it — a paw shaped silver disc engraved with the letter *H*.

"It's beautiful," said Li, carefully touching the chain before drawing his hand back. "Literally a dog tag. How very like you."

"I bought it before I knew it was going to be a one-time thing between us," he said, swallowing the lump that had formed in his throat. "It's a collar. For a Dom and a sub, it's a symbol of commitment. I've never offered a sub my collar before."

No pressure. Fuck, he should have just kept it to himself. Li's eyes were wide, his body suddenly tense.

"Oh, Henley, I...I can't," said Li, sounding just as pained as Henley felt.

Henley tossed the chain to the side, the sound of metal hitting carpet like a nail in his coffin. Forcing a grin on his lips, he thrust deep inside Li. "I know. I wouldn't ask you to wear it now that I know. I'm not sure why I showed it to you, really. I meant to just grab the plug and shove it in your ass."

Li chuckled, the sound strangled as Henley hit his spot a few times in quick succession. The heat that had cooled between them built quickly, and Henley pushed Li's knees back against his chest as sweat dripped down his back. Li was still tight, even after being split open so many times within the last hour. His heat clung, pushing Henley closer to the edge faster than he could breathe.

"I like the picture that makes," said Henley, grabbing the plug from Li, who hadn't set it down, despite his protests. "I'll plug your ass after I come again, and keep you full so you don't lose a drop. And after a ten-minute snack break, I'm gonna pull the plug out and fuck you again. I'll keep doing that over and over until you can't fit another drop inside — until your bursting."

"Ah, Christ," Li cursed, throwing his head back as his cock spurted against his belly, completely untouched. His walls clamped down on Henley, pulling his orgasm from him with the force of a train.

Pulling out as he emptied the last of himself, Henley slowly pushed the plug inside. Li's hole stretched around the flared knob before snapping closed around the narrowed neck. He didn't spill a drop.

"Good," Henley hummed as he finally tore his gaze away. Li was floating again, his expression blissed out and his cock still dribbling as the tip of the plug glanced against his prostate. "I'll get a cloth to clean us up. Then I'll be ready for round three."

Li turned to him, his eyes blown wide and his expression teetering on bliss. "Okay."

Four rounds later, Henley passed out on the pillow, his balls aching almost as much as his cock. His last two orgasms had been dry, and he doubted he would be able to replenish his stocks for at least a week. His goals of filling Li up would have to wait.

When he roused a short time later, he reached for Li, intending to pull him close for the most epic of snuggles. The blankets were still warm, and one of Li's long hairs was caught on the pillowcase, but the bed was empty. Li's clothes and weapons were gone, along with Henley's. The only thing left in the room was the strip of condoms and the bottle of lube.

The plug...the collar...

Henley rolled over, shoving his face into the pillow to breathe the last of Li's muted scent. He was so utterly fucked.

Chapter Nine

Li

The plug shifted with every step, his sore ass unbearable with the unfamiliar pressure inside him. The tail tickled down the back of his leg like a dryer sheet caught in his clothes. The collar was somehow worse, though, slapping against his chest with every movement like a metronome. *H. H. H.*

There was no way he could have left that room and everything behind. There was enough evidence of his presence all over Henley and soaked into the sheets, dried in crusty little puddles that belonged in an orgy and not as part of his life. Seeing Henley between those sheets, sleeping as if he weren't the filthiest asshole Li had ever met, was enraging.

The feeling had started as soon as he'd looked down, fully dressed with his weapons stashed back on his body, along with the extra few that Henley had been kind enough to donate. The plug had still been in his ass at that point, nestled between his cheeks like it had found itself a new home. The collar had been on the ground, shimmering in the lamp light like it was made of mystic diamonds.

The heat had built in his gut, leaving him halfway between heartburn and nausea. It had to have been anger — at himself for giving in and at Henley for being who he was.

But it had only gotten worse since leaving the room.

He leaned against the outside of the hotel, tucking himself out of the direct sunlight that peeked over his head in full noon. He was used to never knowing what time it was, but he'd never felt so wrong-footed.

His chest went tight as he pushed off the brick, glaring down the German street. He was fluent, but his head ached from the effort of reading the signs as he hailed a taxi. The collar pounded against his chest as he moved, not letting him forget it for a moment.

I hate him. His hands shook as he opened the cab door, slipping into the seat and telling the driver to take him to the airport. The air was stifling in the small space, but it didn't help as he rolled down the window, the freezing air sinking in.

"You okay?" the driver asked him in German, a shiver in his frame and concern on his face.

"Just take me to the airport." Li turned away, rolling the window back up. He didn't want any questions. He just needed to be back home by himself in the peace of the forest and the crisp air of fall.

The driver gave him a rude look before he set his jaw, turning off the road in the direction of the airport.

It was going to be days before Li could go home, though, and even longer until he could sleep.

He made it to the airport before he caved. There were too many questions, and he couldn't face them on his own. There was also only one person in the world who had a chance of helping him.

Not that he needed it—the help. He'd been on his own since his mother had checked out to Alzheimer's disease, and he'd been the only one left at home with her. He'd moved out as soon as he could, leaving her with care workers when he couldn't stand it anymore. He'd been a stranger to her before he'd turned twenty.

He dialed the number by heart, his hands shaking as he lifted the phone to his ear.

"Jesse." His voice cracked as he breathed into the phone. He'd never realized how much he missed his family until that moment. He had no one, least of all Henley. If he was to drop dead, no one would give a shit.

"Little brother?" Jesse sounded sleepy again, his voice tainted with exhaustion.

Glancing at the clock, Li tried to think of what the time would be back home until he realized that he couldn't remember where he was. He closed his eyes, taking a deep breath that didn't fill his lungs.

There were German voices around him including the announcer that vibrated through the tinny speaker announcing that his flight was delayed. Everything had been a blur—a rush to get out of the hotel room, but he was still in a fog. His hands were numb as he clutched the phone tighter.

"You need help?" asked Jesse, sounding much more awake.

What time is it there? Li focused on the clock, trying to dig up the answer, but it refused to come to him.

"Sorry, Jesse. I shouldn't have called you." He looked down at his phone, staring at the screen. It was another burner, like all the rest.

"Never apologize for calling me," said Jesse, his voice going tight. "You're family. You can call at two in the morning, and I'd still be happy to talk to you. Even if I have to bail you out of prison, I'd still take that phone call, too."

Chuckling, Li shook his head before resting it on his hand. His eyelids dropped. Three days without sleep catching up to him. But when he closed his eyes, he saw Henley on the bed, his face relaxed in sleep and a smile on his lips.

"I just…I need to figure some shit out. I don't know why I called you."

"Okay."

The silence stretched, but he could hear Jesse breathing on the other end. He knew he was still there.

"I think I might be gay," said Li, his breath whooshing out of him. He glanced to the woman next to him, but she was still on her phone. Hopefully she didn't know English.

"Congratulations. You need tips or something?" Jesse snickered.

"The last tip I want is from my brother," said Li, the smile on his lips finally feeling real. The laugh in his ear was worth the way his chest tightened and relaxed at the same time. "I just, never thought I was, you know? There's a lot of shit going on right now that never should have happened, and I don't know if that's one of them. I don't know if it's real or if it's just in my head."

"Jesus." Jesse let out a breath. "Okay, I'm getting up and grabbing some coffee. You tell me about your man, and I promise I won't fall asleep."

"He's not—" Li bit his lips. Was Henley *his*? The collar around his neck said yes. When he'd refused it,

Henley had looked crushed, the light going out of his eyes in an instant. Putting it on had given Li that floaty feeling that only ever happened around Henley.

"I don't know if he's mine," said Li after a moment. "I can't tell you everything, you know I can't, but he's different than anyone I've ever met. But he's not safe." Staying with Henley was stamping his own career with an expiration date. All it would take was one fight or disagreement and someone would get shot.

"He treats you right? I'm not talking about flowers and shit."

How was a man supposed to treat another man? Li didn't want flowers, but Henley *had* bought him gifts.

"He gave me a necklace." He touched the cool metal, pinching it between his fingers. It was heavier than it had any right to be. "It's more of a collar, actually."

Jessie choked and spluttered, the phone clacking as he presumably dropped it. Li could hear him coughing, the sound more distant than it was a moment before.

"You still there?" It was probably too much information. Unfortunately, he didn't have a choice but to ask Jesse. He happened to be the only other gay man in the world that he knew.

"Yeah." Jesse cleared his throat. "I just never expected my brother to get into that sort of stuff. I don't know much about it, but I've had an ex or two who did. As long as you're safe and you look after him during that stuff, then you're good."

Li flushed, the hair on the top of his head prickling from the force of the heat that consumed his face. He'd luckily skipped over the birds and the bees talk when he was younger. "This is so awkward." He laughed, the sound startling the lady next to him. "We've had a couple of slip-ups, but I guess he looks after me, yeah."

If not shooting me counts. The condom slip-up was a definite mark against Henley, but if Li were honest, he didn't mind as much as he probably should have. He could imagine being furious, but instead, he was just sad—sad that it was the last time he would ever feel something so deliciously dirty.

"Tell me about this guy. I don't need a name but paint me a picture. What's he look like?"

Li leaned back, closing his eyes as he listed every single thing he knew about Henley, from his eyes that sparkled like actual jewels to his attitude that would give any brat a run for their money.

An announcement over the speakers cut him off and he realized he had been speaking for a long time, nothing but the sound of his own voice and the bustle around them.

"You still there?" he asked, wondering if he'd lost the connection with Jesse and he hadn't noticed.

"Yeah," said Jesse, letting out a soft sigh.

"I gotta catch my flight," said Li, grabbing for his carryon. His weapons had already been stashed in their usual spots, right under the noses of the security folks, but he had a few changes of clothes in his pack. What he really needed was a shower.

"You figure stuff out a bit?" asked Jesse.

Li ran his hand through his hair, tugging a few tangles free that he'd missed at the hotel. His mind was jumbled, the collar like an anchor around his neck. The plug shifted as he stood, more uncomfortable than pleasurable after hours.

"I gotta go." He ended the call, slipping the SIM card out of the phone before pressing the back of his hand to his forehead. *What am I going to do?*

Chapter Ten

Henley

"This is turning into a habit," said Clint as he passed Henley another beer. Henley took it with a grunt, knocking back a swallow that was entirely unsatisfying. The tingling burn was almost mute against his numb tongue that had seen Fireball and whiskey in the same night.

"At least you aren't scoping out the place tonight," said Clint, grabbing two empty glasses and stashing them behind the bar. He turned away, scooting down the bar to help some other more deserving asshole.

Henley pressed his forehead to the bar top, the cool surface soaking some of the heat from his skin. Getting shitfaced at Unkinked was becoming a nightly ritual that his liver was not appreciating, not that he blamed it. His gut was in agreement, rolling noisily as the alcohol refused to settle.

He'd tried to top a few other subs, but it had left a sour taste in his mouth after Li. It hadn't been their fault that he'd lost interest halfway through negotiations and had turned the others away before they'd gotten to the best part.

It seemed that everything was revolving around his life before and after Li. Although budding alcoholism was definitely an 'after Li' development, along with a simmering horniness that hadn't disappeared, no matter how many times he took care of himself.

Li had taken the collar. That was all it came down to. If he wanted nothing to do with Henley, then he wouldn't have taken it. Maybe he hadn't understood the commitment that it represented or maybe he was somewhere warm laughing his ass off.

Henley wasn't sure, and he didn't plan on finding out. He had kept his promise and had let Li get away, even with Shelia breathing down his neck and looking for answers. She had kept Martinez off his ass, but he knew it wouldn't be long before she recalled him and sent another agent.

Another agent would probably find Li if they put their mind to it, even though Li was one of the smartest fucker's he'd ever had to track. *I can't let that happen.* Whatever confusion there was between them, he was certain that it had been real.

"Why did he take it?" he asked Clint when the bartender passed by him again. His glass was empty, but Clint shook his head when Henley asked for another refill. If Clint hadn't been such an awesome guy who had welcomed him to the world of kink and had shown him the ropes, then Henley would have punched him.

"What did he take?" asked Clint, sounding genuinely concerned as he slid a glass of water toward him. His assistant—Maddy, if Henley remembered correctly—took drink orders in Clint's stead, mixing and pouring faster than Henley could track.

He wasn't sure what day or time it was, but the club was busy, bustling with noise and conversation. Normally the leather and skin would be enough, but not when the only thing he wanted was never coming back.

"My heart," said Henley, cursing as soon as he said it. Now that it was out in the open, he couldn't deny it. "He took the collar and the tail-plug with him when he left, and my fucking gun, too. That's two guns I've lost to him. I didn't even get to know the last one before she was gone." He lowered his head back to the counter, rolling it back and forth.

Clint knew a smidge of his background—the usual 'I'm a secret agent and carry a weapon to fight terrorism' crap. Henley still wasn't allowed to bring his gun into the club, even if it added an extra twenty percent to his sex appeal.

"But the worst part is that I'm wondering if he's wearing them out there," said Henley, lifting his head so Clint had a chance of understanding him. The image of Li perched on a rooftop with someone in his crosshairs with a plug concealed under his boxers and Henley's collar around his neck, never failed to make him rock hard.

Too bad that drinking and sceneing were against the rules, because he could pound somebody into next week at this point. Not that it would do any good. Nothing and nobody would satisfy him.

"Anything I can do to help?" asked Clint, leaning on the bar and swiping Henley's last empty glass. He was taller than Henley, but most people were. "I have a sturdy shoulder if you need one to cry on, and I could put some feelers out for you, if that's what you wanted."

Clint did have a sturdy shoulder, probably sturdy enough to give Li a run for his money. Henley knew that because he'd made passes at Clint for the last year-and-a-half and had been turned down every single time. But now that Clint was halfway offering, Henley didn't want anything to do with him. Clint had been hurt badly in his past, according to the few wisps of conversations he'd caught, and Henley had no desire to drag him through the dirt.

"Nah," said Henley, tugging on his hair, which had started to get a tad too long. He needed to go home to cool off, shower and do a full body degrease.

"Now I really know something's up," said Clint, a small smile tugging at his lips. "The Henley I know would never give a pass to that opportunity." He turned to his assistant, letting out a small chuckle as Maddy bustled around the bar. "Maddy convinced me to do an open house. We haven't done one in years, so there are bound to be a few new play partners who attend."

Clint looked up, a frown on his lips as he stared at a spot above Henley's shoulder. His forehead furrowed as he stood to his full height.

Tensing, every sense in Henley's body slapped into alert awareness. Clint knew every face that came in and out of his bar, so for him to look concerned, it had to have been an asshole or an ex-member trying to make trouble.

Henley had seen both and had helped take care of a few situations—away from the bar, of course. He hadn't seen the dungeon master lately, so they were probably in the open play area making sure everyone was playing safe. They would be too far to back Clint up.

A hand touched Henley's shoulder, the warm weight of it pulling the thickness of his intoxication away. The hairs prickled on the back of his neck as his body reacted against his will. Every second of denied PTSD slammed into him at once, until he was longer in control but merely a passenger along for the ride.

Grabbing the hand on his shoulder, Henley clamped down on the sensitive nerves on their wrist at the same time he dropped from the stool and kicked their legs out from under them. They hit the floor with a resounding thud, with their arm extended in Henley's grasp as he readied to snap the bone with the barest hint of pressure.

He slammed the offender's face into the ground, digging his knee into their spine as a dizzy spell overtook him. Everything wobbled for a moment as his stomach jerked from the sudden movement, and he swallowed the burp that tried to make its way out of his throat.

Smirking, he glared down at them, his hazy brain recognizing who he had pinned. He was about to laugh and cry at the same time, until they bucked beneath him, breaking his hold and tipping him back until he lost his balance and splayed out on the ground.

His ears rang as his head bounced once before they swung their huge hand into the side of his head, boxing his ear hard enough that he was sure he would have hearing loss. A moment later, an arm pressed against his neck as he was pinned, a heavy body restraining every muscle in place.

He blinked, a slow closure and lift of his eyelids as the pressure built in his head and blood rushed through his ears. Li looked down at him from above, his hair blazing around him like a dark halo and his lips pressed into a slim snarl.

"What the fuck is wrong with you?" Li growled at him, even as he pushed harder against Henley's throat. Henley choked, his lungs screaming for air as he tapped Li's arm.

"Li?" he choked out. The music of the club cut through the ringing of his ears, and he realized that something wasn't right. As much as Li and him had wrestled and fought, Li had never pinned him like that, cutting off almost all his air as he grew closer to passing out.

That, and Li's hair had suddenly gotten shorter, and blond...and he had gained fifty pounds of muscle. Henley blinked, his vision clearing. Two blue eyes stared back at him that definitely didn't belong to Li.

"Fucking Robins." The words barely made it out of Henley's mouth with all the pressure on his throat. He would've reached for his knife so he could teach Robins a lesson, but his knife was in his new pretend flat, along with the rest of his remaining weapons. Probably best when was drunk in a bar full of kinky shits like himself.

"So you *are* still alive. I thought Shelia sent me to pick up a dead body," Robins whispered into his ear before he leaned back and loosened the pressure on Henley's neck.

Coughing spasms racked Henley's body as his throat opened and constricted from the phantom pressure. He glanced around the bar to the dozen or so onlookers who had paused mid-conversation. A few regulars had stepped forward, ready to defend their fellow member.

Clint had a bouncer and a dungeon master, but he rarely needed more than that—not with enough friends to step up and take down any Dom or sub who stepped out of line. Clint appeared around the bar, a baseball bat in his hand as he stepped closer. Henley waved him off, hacking as he got to his feet.

"You okay, Henley?" asked Clint, tapping the bat in his palm as he eyed Robins up. "I'm not sure how you got in here, but I'll only ask you once to leave."

Henley looked Clint up and down, a warmth rushing into his limbs. Even if he didn't have Li, he still had people who cared. He turned a glare on Robins, pouring every bit of ice into it that he possessed.

"He was just leaving, Clint, nothing to get worried about," said Henley, wobbling where he stood. *Fuck, what a terrible time to be a lightweight.* It was a good thing that Clint had cut him off when he had, or he would have made even more of a fool of himself by ending his choking fit with a puking one.

"After you," said Robins, surprisingly not putting up any fight about leaving.

Grumbling to himself and blinking at the over-bright lights, Henley pushed his way through the privacy curtain to the exit. The spot where the bouncer usually sat was empty, except for his wooden stool. Looking over his shoulder, Henley saw him emerge from the bathroom before the curtains slid shut.

Elbowing his way through the door, Henley waited for Robins to step out and the door to close before he rounded on him, jabbing his neck and forcing him back against the rough brick.

"That was un-fucking-called for," said Henley, easing up his pressure before he could choke Robins out. He wasn't an asshole like that. When someone squeezed your neck, it fucking hurt. He rubbed his own throat, wincing at the bruising that was probably already starting to show.

"You know what's uncalled for? A fairy like you strolling around town like you don't have a target on your back and getting shitfaced in a gay bar while everyone else is out there picking up after you." Robins pushed him away and Henley stumbled back, his reflexes slower than a fucking snail's.

He looked up at the sun, the light thundering into his head. *What time is it, even? On that note, what fucking day is it?* Tuesday? *Nah.* He scratched his chin. Wednesday. Wednesdays always had a certain frustrating and disappointing feel to them.

"You aren't my boss, Robins. In fact, I outrank you. So unless you have Shelia tucked in your back pocket, I suggest you fuck off." Henley turned away, looking up and down the street for his car before he remembered that he had left the keys with Clint. *Probably for the best, but there goes the dramatic exit.*

"Shelia is the one who sent me," said Robins, crossing his arms. There was a smirk on his lips, and a twinkle in his eyes that Henley didn't trust. "I think she'd be disappointed to hear where you've been hiding for the last three weeks."

Three weeks? Oh man, he was dead. Shelia was the most terrifying woman on the planet—like a strict grandparent combined with a mom who didn't give a shit about the *rules.* If Henley had been straight, he would have married her fifteen years prior when he'd first met her.

He'd been cocky up until the point when she'd slammed him on his ass during special ops training. He'd never had a beating like it in his life.

"I'll take the bus," said Henley, waving Robins off with his middle finger.

"I'm driving you, and if you put up a fuss, I have the authorization to tranq you."

Seriously? He had to be missing something. He was a good fucking agent, who *usually* didn't get anyone unnecessarily killed and sometimes managed to protect the people he was tasked at guarding. Okay, he was a *decent* agent, who hadn't been kicked to the curb because he was their best tracker.

He was like a bloodhound. No one had ever managed to slip through his net.

Tranquilizing him seemed a bit extreme, though — unless they knew about Li. Which, considering the people he worked for, they probably did. Hopefully they didn't know *all* the details.

"Fine," said Henley, kicking the tire of a nearby Jeep. It was huge, black and atrocious, so it fit Robins perfectly. "This your ride? So fucking subtle. No wonder you haven't been promoted in the last five years."

Robins clenched his jaw, his knuckles bleeding white. "Get in the Jeep. The sooner I bring you in, the sooner I can wash up. I got one of your hairs in my mouth, and it is fucking nasty. And after going in that place, I need a shower."

"What a dick," said Henley, shaking his head and stepping up into the Jeep. Even with the built-in step, he still had to tug himself up. People in the kink community already got enough flack from shits like Robins, but he was in no shape to put him in his place. *Patience.*

As they pulled away, Henley tracked a black SUV in the side-view mirror that appeared behind them. It followed them through three turns, staying far enough back that most people never would have noticed it. But he had more years in the field than most, and a black SUV usually meant baddy central.

It was a terrible time not to have a gun. He let out a breath as it passed them and sped off, the tinted windows concealing whoever was inside.

Henley glanced at Robins. The guy hadn't even noticed.

They drove to headquarters in silence that was broken every so often by the crackle of a police scanner. Henley rolled his eyes as he turned the volume down, swallowing harshly as they took another sharp turn. Any more turns and he was gonna puke. Luckily there was a box of tissues on the dash if he lost his drinks.

Robins was a man who was begging to be some kind of top-notch secret agent like Henley, but he just didn't have what it took. He was fast and strong, but he was also dumber than a rock. In fact, he was more like the pet rock, who got dolled up and thought it was anything more than just a piece of stone.

Headquarters was smack in the middle of the city, where parking was a nightmare and parking meters were constantly expiring. Their destination was a high-rise that was nearly identical to the ones surrounding it. Even the people milling in and out of the front doors were completely average and nothing to fret about.

The comings and goings of the average joe was because the building housed a high-end design and contracting business that made more money than a dirty cop. Most of the employees were talented engineers and designers who had no idea that law enforcement was strewn throughout their ranks.

Beneath the layer of average joes was a semi-legal mercenary-for-hire company that fronted their employees as construction workers who always got the job done. Boardrooms substituted as holding cells with the click of a few buttons, and the money was easily siphoned through the legitimate business.

Between the illegal cracks of mercenaries, there was a government operation that was responsible for blowing the lid off more drug and weapons ops than any other in the country. It was so secret that among the mercenaries, only a few of them were actual agents. No one trusted anyone, and the guy sitting beside them in the next chair may or may not have been a secret agent.

Henley had been confused and dazzled when Shelia had explained it to him when she'd brought him into the fold. One day he'd been pretending to lay pipe as he'd scoped out a job, and the next, he'd been 007.

He'd worked as a mercenary because he was good at pretending and even better at killing. Thinking back, he'd probably been so good at hiding himself because he hadn't even known who he was at that time. It hadn't been until Shelia had transferred him, along with herself, to the Canadian office, and he'd stumbled upon Clint that he'd finally felt somewhat whole.

Pushing through the front doors, Henley looked back to flip Robins off one last time before he stormed to the front desk. He had checked in at the office every few weeks during his last stretch of employment-slash-sting operation, but not often enough for the receptionist to recognize him.

He gave her a winning smile as he moved to lean his elbow on her desk. Miscalculating the distance, he avoiding faceplanting by an inch before he recovered and backed away with a chuckle. She looked at him with wide eyes, her pastel pantsuit making his eyes bleed. He reached for his fanny pack, pulling out a blank business card and pretending to read it.

"I have an appointment with Ms. Wasten — sorry — Watson?" He looked up from the card, blinking slowly when the receptionist didn't move. His vision swam, and he grabbed the desk as he waited for the dizzy spell to pass.

He was never day-drinking again. He felt like a stay-at-home mom who preferred wine to orange juice at breakfast. Things only went downhill from there.

"Ms. Watson is unavailable, sir," said the receptionist — Theresa, if he was reading her name tag right. Just the fact that she had a name tag told him that she was first tier and knew nothing of the mercs and agents on her speed dial.

"I'll wait," said Henley, sliding the card back into his fanny pack before he stumbled over to the comfy leather chair. He leaned his head back into the headrest, hopefully the picture of serene patience, even when he was spinning on the inside.

The longer he had to wait, the more pissed Shelia was.

But that was nothing compared to the dread of her reaction when he came clean about *everything* that had happened. And he had to come clean. He wasn't a criminal, no matter what some had to say about it.

Forty-five gut-wrenching minutes later, the receptionist called his name and gave him directions to Shelia's office. As he turned to the elevator, a security guard *escort* sidled beside him. The escort was a solid six-foot muscle-bound giant with a scowl on his face that made Henley's stepmom look like a saint.

Well, that was *new*. He touched his fanny pack as a second guard snuck into the elevator before the doors closed. He'd never been barred from Shelia's office, and he'd certainly never been escorted. He gulped back a comment as sweat beaded on his forehead.

Shit. His fanny pack was right out of ammunition, and he had removed his knives before he'd gone to the club. He was completely unarmed, and the guard didn't seem to be carrying anything, either. Only someone who knew him would make sure of that.

He had rarely needed his own weapon, because half the time he just lifted it from his opponent. He didn't recognize the guards, and they either had amazing poker faces or they were muscle for hire.

"You guys both straight or did you want to do something kinky while we wait?" asked Henley, cocking out one hip and batting his eyelashes. He doubted that he looked innocent with a wobble in his step and the alcohol on his breath, but a guy could try. Plus, they were built. They weren't Li, but they looked mighty delicious through his wobble goggles.

They didn't react. Not even a lift of an eyebrow.

Swallowing thickly, Henley hoped his gut would stay calm. He was ready to puke by the time there was a quiet ding and the elevator doors opened onto the sixth floor. He wiped his hands on his pants before he stepped out, flanked on either side by the Brute Twins.

The office building was thirty floors, and Shelia was the most executive agent out of every single one. Anyone would expect her to be on the top floor, which was why she fronted as part of the financial team on the sixth.

Her skills of camouflage blew Henley's mind, which was why he tried not to think about them too much. It was too much like Li and way beyond what he was capable of.

The guards followed him off the elevator, hovering three feet away on either side and matching their pace with his own uneven one. Two more appeared from nowhere, sliding ahead and behind him until he was completely surrounded. None of them spoke or looked his way as they marched him along to his doom.

To an outsider, they would look like a group of businessmen on their way to a meeting with a client, even if their scowls seemed a little extreme. They were all in pressed suits with a tiny earpiece in their ears that were nearly invisible if you didn't know what to look for.

His heart pounded and his lungs begged for air as he forced himself to breathe slow and shallow. "Now we're getting really kinky," he said, slipping his hand into his fanny pack. There had to be something in there he could use to defend himself.

A roll of condoms and a bottle of lube slipped through his fingers. The cock ring was there, too, which he had found buried beneath the hotel covers after Li had made his great escape. If he had been sober, he probably could have thought of a way to kill with a condom, but he came up blank. *Over his head like a bag or in his mouth like a gag?* No condom was that good.

"Quiet," the bodyguard behind him grumbled. Henley turned to the sound, catching himself before he could stumble sideways into the gallery of empty office cubicles. There was hardly anyone on the floor and only the distant chime of a single ringing telephone.

"Well, hello," he said, making a show of eyeing the guard up and down. He was big, broad and had more tattoos than Henley could count, but his dick stayed silent. Li had fucking ruined him.

"The other three I'll charge, but you, I'll do for free," said Henley, twirling around so he was walking backward to keep up. This guy looked vaguely familiar. "Tim? Tom? It doesn't matter, because you'll be the one screaming my name."

"They warned me about you," said Tim, his voice a low grumble that should have had Henley's dick perking up. *Nothing. Fuck.* "It's a good thing that I don't have to worry about you much longer, apparently."

"Apparently," said Henley, rolling his eyes and turning to face front again. He relaxed his body, because when the hit came, it would hurt like hell. There was no way he was getting out of it.

They marched him into a boardroom, moving to single file to fit through the small door. The room looked like any other office boardroom, except it was perhaps a bit small. Henley knew better. There were more cameras and microphones in the room than any non-paranoid person would ever need. The door was solid steel, and the walls were reinforced with rebar-laced concrete. The polished table was bolted to the ground and the inconspicuous office chairs were, too.

Tim pushed Henley into the nearest chair before the guards posted themselves at the four corners of the room. Perhaps he had underestimated them by thinking they were just mercenaries. Either that or he was there to die—and not for questioning. It was easy to dispose of someone when no one knew who they really were.

With nothing better to do, Henley pulled a piece of gum from his fanny pack, honestly surprised that they hadn't taken it from him already. Then again, he had passed through no less than ten sensors during the slow-as-fuck elevator ride.

"Offer's still on the table, boys," said Henley, moving to sit crossways in the chair and resting his legs on the armrest. "My guess is that we are going to be here for a while, and when I get bored, I get horny. It's the best way to pass the time." He popped his gum and raised an eyebrow at Tim, who had a small flush over the bridge of his nose.

"Now we even have the table." He slid his palms over the surface, giving Tim a wink.

"That's enough." The door slammed open, and Shelia stormed into the room, her lips pressed into a thin line and her eyes narrowed. Her blonde curls bounced with each step, drawing the eye away from her tiny waist and narrow hips. She tapped her toe once before moving to sit in a chair across from Henley, sliding a folder along the polished top.

Henley grabbed it automatically, correcting his posture like a child who had just been scolded. He swallowed again as he took in Shelia's pressed pantsuit, complete with black and red flowers and a dazzling necklace. She always fit in with any crowd, whether she was in the line at Starbucks or at the right end of a long-range rifle.

"Care to explain yourself?" she asked, tapping her red nails on the surface of the table. They were probably dipped in poison or something with how shiny they were.

"Care to have the muscle fuck off?" asked Henley, swallowing his burp and dropping his illusion of nonchalance. He'd never done an interrogation drunk, but he was ready for the promised adventure.

"They're in," said Shelia, which was all the explanation that Henley needed. They weren't contractors or mercenaries at all. They were agents. No wonder they had been warned about him.

"Damien is dead, and his father wants your ass on a silver platter. You single-handedly put a five-year operation at risk, and I have half a mind to give you to him to teach you a lesson, although I doubt it would stick. You've been AWOL for going on six weeks, and your weapons still haven't been recovered. So, either you tell me what you've been up to, or I tell the boys to have some fun." Shelia tented her fingers, staring over them.

"My kind of fun?" Henley asked with a grin. Shelia glared in response, and he slumped in his chair with a huff. "The first three weeks were mostly legitimate. I was tracking down whoever put a bullet through Damien's head. I seem to recall I told you I was going to do that."

Shelia cracked her knuckles before slipping her watch from her wrist. Henley gulped, pinching his thigh to try to tone down his sarcasm.

"Did you find him?" she asked, touching the gold band of her watch. It was probably a bomb or something, ready to blow if she didn't disarm it every hour.

"Yes."

Henley looked to the four agents posted at each corner. As much as he flaunted his sexuality and made passes at everyone with a dick, he didn't want anyone to know he had formed an *attachment* to someone.

"And? Do you at least have a name?"

"I do."

Shelia's eyebrow twitched and a brief smile flashed over her lips before her glare reappeared. She tapped her nails again, a terrible sound that had a headache forming at Henley's temples even though his hangover should have been a long way off.

"See, the funny thing is, Harris, that we know exactly who the shooter is. We've known him for years, but not a single agent has managed to track him down. We haven't come close to getting a name." She grabbed the file, flipping the cover open to reveal a list. "He has thirty-seven kills that we know of on this continent alone."

Henley spied the name at the top of the file. *The Ghost.* His stomach dropped to the bottom of his feet.

Li, his bratty sub with a kinky streak a mile wide, was one of the most prolific assassins that the agency knew of. His signature had appeared out of the blue seven years ago and he'd been active ever since. There was never any evidence, and he never made a mistake. The guy was a fucking legend.

"Fuck."

Henley reached for the file, turning it around and flipping through the pages. There were a few photos, but mostly it was just names — so many names that it made his eyes bleed and his cock hard. *Something is definitely wrong with me.*

It wasn't the murder that was getting to him, but he'd seen Li in action, and he remembered how he moved. What he wouldn't give to see it again.

"Did you take care of him?" Shelia asked, her gaze going sharp as she watched him thumb through the names. There were more than thirty-seven names and a lot of question marks. Li had been a busy boy on almost every continent except for Antarctica.

"Yeah," said Henley, letting out a long sigh, "but not in the way you think. I fucked him, then I let him leave."

Henley wasn't sure he'd ever seen Shelia look so surprised. Even the guards shifted a little, the first reaction from three of them.

"You fucked him," Shelia deadpanned, "knowing he was your shooter."

Henley bit his lip as his face flushed. It sounded terrible when she said it like that, even if it was true.

"Well, the first time, I thought he was a civilian. But the second time I knew he'd killed Martinez. I didn't know he was The Ghost, though." If he had, he still would have done the same thing. Li was something special, no matter what his profession was.

"You should have killed him or brought him in, and I shouldn't have to tell you that," said Shelia. "You've been fucking him all these weeks, just trying to postpone the inevitable?" She huffed like she couldn't believe it. "We've been together since almost the beginning, Harris. What the fuck happened to you?"

"I wasn't postponing anything," said Henley, flicking the file shut and moving to stand. One of the guards grabbed his shoulder, slamming him back into his seat. His tailbone ached as it cracked against the unforgiving surface. "I was giving him a head start."

"You fucking idiot," snarled Shelia, standing and moving around the table before she grabbed his chin. Her nails dug into the pressure points on the sides of his jaw, and the fire went straight to his skull as his headache bloomed.

"He knows how I tracked him down, Shelia. He let me catch him. He won't let me catch him a second time." He tried to jerk his chin away, but her small hands were surprisingly strong.

"His name," she said, pressing until he was sure that he was bleeding.

"I can't," said Henley, his chest aching at the thought of giving Li up. There were other agents like himself that would eventually be able to track Li down if they had his name. Even with the head start, they would catch him.

"You don't have a choice," she said softly, loosening her grip before sitting on the stretch of table in front of him. He looked away as her skirt peeked open. That wouldn't work with him. "Harris, look at me."

She was changing tactics, her voice soft and innocent, as if she wasn't about to kill him or have him killed. She could be the good cop and the bad cop when she had to be. She had tried to teach him the act, too, but he never could pull either role off very well. Even though he knew it was a ploy, it still made his head spin.

"You know what side you're on and what you have to do, Harris." Her perfume swept over him as she leaned in. "You aren't a criminal like him, no matter what he tried to say to convince you otherwise. You're a good man, and you have to do the right thing before it's too late. Help us bring him in. I'll push for non-lethal." She tapped his chin once before dropping her hands.

"Li. His name is Li," said Henley, looking at his feet. The guilt was immediate, surging through his body like a wall of depression that threatened to drag him down. "But you won't find him. There's only one way of catching him now, and you know it."

Shelia gave him a long look before she shook her head. "He means something to you. I don't trust you to bait him."

Henley wondered if dangling himself like a worm would draw Li out. *Okay, maybe.* Li hadn't made any effort to contact him, and he'd given him many opportunities during his binge drinking. And Shelia was right, he couldn't be trusted.

But she couldn't be either—not to keep her word to bring Li in alive.

"He was following us on the way here," he said, recalling the black SUV that had trailed him for a few blocks. "And he wasn't subtle about it." He wasn't sure why, but everything Li did, he seemed to do for a reason. Maybe it had been a show of support, or a threat. "He might be coming to kill me to make sure I don't talk—or he'll take me out as revenge."

"Then we'll have to make it easier for him," said Shelia, her voice dropping back into business mode. They were employer and employee, not friends, no matter how well Shelia knew how to twist what was between them. "Consider this your last assignment."

Chapter Eleven

Henley

His palms were clammy as he was escorted out of the building and onto the street like a lamb being let to slaughter by a team of over-muscled farmers. The guards disappeared the moment he was out of the doors, leaving him shivering and woozy in the sunlight.

Swallowing dryly, he scratched at his wrist where a new tracker lay beneath the small cut that had already started to heal. It had been no larger than a microchip, but he'd still squealed when they had punched it into his skin. It ached, too, and moved under his skin when he nudged it with his finger. At least it didn't glow.

Shelia had known that he wouldn't cut off his own arm, and that he couldn't retrieve it with his left without causing some damage to his nerves or worse. One slip of a knife to the delicate tissues where it lay and he risked bleeding out or paralyzing his fingers.

I gotta get it out. He scratched at the skin, dried blood lifting away from the bruised dot.

His friends were dust, except for the few he had made when he'd joined the kink club. There was no one there who knew his real name and actually had a hint about what he *really* did for a living except a select few, including Clint. Clint had been a nurse, too, and probably had hands that were steady as fuck.

But going to the club would put them all in danger now that Henley was being followed. And he was sure that someone was following him. No one drove black SUVs unless they were doing something bad...or planning to.

He shook out his hand, wincing at the ping of nerves that crawled along his wrist. His T-shirt was too chilly for the autumn air that had grown brisk as the sun started to fade. Shadows dug their claws into the well-lit street, turning every alley and walkway into an enemy.

They hadn't even given him a gun. He was too much of a risk.

He would have done the same thing if he had been in Shelia's position. Actually, he would have put a bullet in the head of any agent who went AWOL after sleeping with a target. But he had always been on the cautious side, whereas Shelia liked to tread the line.

Scrubbing up and down his arms, he turned into the first alley past the office, sinking into the shadows and wrapping them around his skin. A stray cat hissed at him as he passed a bursting dumpster, the acrid scent bringing tears to his eyes. Dumpster cats were the worst.

He had two options stretching ahead of him. Well three, really.

The first was a definite death sentence. He could make a run for it and try to have his tracker removed before his fellow agents caught up. He was good, but he wasn't good enough to pull it off solo.

From there, only two choices remained. The short way, where he turned back to meet the footsteps that had sidled up behind him shortly after he had left the building. Or the long way, where he put up a fight and gave Li a chance to run instead.

Picking up his pace, he darted down another alley, heading back out to the street. He heard a scuffle of footsteps behind him as his follower sped up. It was honestly sloppy of Li to be so darn noticeable — unless he wanted Henley to know, or he didn't care.

But still, he was certainly being followed by agents. Li should have known that.

He spotted another black SUV as he broke out onto the lit street, his breath huffing into the air as he paused to look through the glass. *I swear that isn't the same car.* The license plate was off, if only by one digit.

The shadowed outline of driver and passenger moved, barely visible on the other side of the tinted glass. Something flashed in the passenger's hand as the steps behind him moved faster as they broke into a run. Looking back, he caught the first look at the man who he'd thought to be Li.

Shit. How many times can I fuck up in one day? Li wasn't behind him, but instead it was someone else who had even less invested in the law. Their hoodie was pulled up, concealing their identity from any onlookers, but Henley remembered their body shape. He remembered because he had watched them for so many nights at the nightclub while protecting Damien Martinez, who had been bound for an early grave.

Henley should have recognized the license plate the moment that he had noticed it following him, but he had been too fucking drunk when he'd left Unkinked. He was still a bit drunk, with the edges of his vision blurred and a persistent headache at the base of his spine that had him aching for water.

He broke into a run, pushing his body as hard as he could as he ran out into the dismal traffic of the city. A passing cab honked as he missed the fender by a few inches, and he flipped them off over his shoulder. The oncoming SUV stopped as he sped right past it, the doors opening and erupting with shouts as he slipped between the narrow buildings on the opposite side of the street.

Fuck, he was thirsty, and his bladder was heavy, bouncing along like a balloon in his gut. He could thank Shelia for that. Bathroom breaks had never been a part of interrogation, and she had used every one of his weaknesses against him. *And I broke like a water balloon on a hedgehog.*

Shaking his head, he changed his mind about day-drinking, stay-at-home moms. They were fucking champs if they could go through that every day and still pick up their kids from school.

He pushed himself faster, reaching for his fanny pack as he broke out onto another cross street. The city was made of giant square blocks with alleys connecting the centers of each one. It made it great for an escape attempt, but it also turned the whole place into a fucking maze, where everything looked the same as it blended together.

Cold air bit into his lungs as he drew breath, and he forced himself along faster until every muscle burned with exertion. The shouts faded farther away, but the squealing of tires and the hum of an engine drew near, pushing him onward.

With a three-week sabbatical under his belt, he was spent almost before he had started. He was honestly impressed with himself that he'd made it as far as a few blocks before his legs felt like they were about to fall off.

The footsteps pounded closer, hammering the pavement as he started to lose steam. One of them was a fast fucker, not built for brawn like the rest of the bodyguards who Henley had met during his stint with Martinez.

When he'd started his undercover gig there, he'd thought he'd never stop drooling with all the tattooed eye candy at his disposal. But looking back, he realized they did nothing for him — not even a twitch from the underground junkyard.

Grabbing the edge of the building, he used his own momentum to spin around, facing the fastest pursuer head-on. He shook out his hands, trying to get the feeling back into his fingers before reaching for the zipper on his fanny pack. Before they could close the distance, he pulled the cock ring from his pack, cupping it in his palm.

It was heavy and unyielding, and more for display than any practical use. But it had been a custom. *A hundred bucks down the drain.*

He threw the cock ring, aiming for his pursuer's forehead. It hit with a hard thunk that hopefully felt like a rock that had been kicked up by a speeding truck. His pursuer stumbled, grabbing at their head as they cursed and stumbled to one knee.

There was only the one goon on that side, and he was fresh out of cock rings, so he spun back to the street, taking off as fast as his legs would carry him.

"Oh shit," he whispered, his breath escalating into panicked bursts. Two more SUVs were barreling down the street, arching toward him like a battering ram. If it had been earlier in the day, traffic would have cut them off, but with afternoon turning into evening, there were only a few parked cars and one distant motorbike.

He plunged his hand into his pack, scraping the bottom and crumpling the fake business card. All he had left was lube and condoms — and not even the fun, flavored kind.

He ran straight at the trucks, breaking off at the last second as they swerved to a stop. Barreling past them long before the passengers had managed to climb from their seats, he ripped his T-shirt from his chest, grabbing the lube as he dropped the fabric to the ground. They were getting closer, their legs fresh while his were already dead-tired.

Opening the cap, he splashed the lube on his chest and arms, biting against the cold that leeched into his skin. The bottle had been nearly full, so he emptied the entire thing on his torso, saving the last squirt for his back. He tossed the empty bottle to the side, grabbing for a strip of condoms.

Really? What the fuck am I supposed to do with them? He let one strip fly over his shoulder, grinning as it smacked one of his pursuers in the eye. He hadn't thought his aim was that good.

One strip left. Maybe he should keep it, just in case they were planning on torturing him in *that* way. They were obviously trying to catch him and not kill him. He would have had bullets in his body already if he were just going to end up dead meat.

He ran onto the next street, almost slamming into another SUV.

It was official. Martinez had way too much money to spend on identical cars. Maybe Henley could convince him to donate some of it to a children's hospital or something in honor of his deceased son and all that.

That might not go over too well.

His steps stuttered as he stumbled, trying to miss the broadside of another vehicle as the door opened wide. A hand emerged, clamping down on his bicep, and immediately slipping off, coated with a thick layer of lube.

"What the fuck?" the goon called out as Henley escaped from his grasp.

"Gotta be prepared!" yelled Henley, his voice barely a croak with how dry his throat was. Could he die of dehydration while his bladder was bursting? He wasn't sure how that worked.

He rounded the back of the SUV, grabbing the rear windshield wiper to steady his step. Unless Martinez had more vehicles jammed up his ass, he had to be in the free and clear soon.

A broad chest slammed into him, and he bounced off, stumbling to the ground. The guard had popped out of nowhere, and Henley's lube tactic hadn't done anything against a brick fucking wall.

Multiple sets of hands were on him in moments, grabbing at every part. Some slipped off, hindered by lube, but others found their way into his hair or the material of his pants. He let out a screech, kicking out and sinking his heel into someone's crotch.

Score. He fought the urge to fist pump, as a length of rope wrapped around his wrist. He was tiny, and he knew it. He shouldn't have had a chance against so many guys that were double his size and had trained in martial arts or at least went to the gym.

But cats were small, too, and just like them, Henley could turn into a hissing and clawing beast when he was cornered.

He pulled out all the stops, throwing punches into throats with his free hand, and kicking dirty places with both feet. A few of the goons dropped, and he struggled harder, despite the way the rope burned into his wrist until blood burst beneath the chafing bind and his bones ground together.

A hand got too close to his face, and he chomped down on it, nearly snapping someone's finger in two. Blood filled his mouth and he gagged at the taste. It wasn't the type of hydration he had been looking for.

"Shut him up!"

The voice registered as someone vaguely familiar from his workdays with Damien. It was probably one of the bodyguard or goons that he had propositioned. He craned his neck back.

Yep. It was the hot one who had turned him down before fucking some chick's face in the alley as Henley had been going primal on Li on the rooftop. He'd pulled his hoodie down and his face was flushed red as he panted, just as out of breath as Henley was.

Those were the days.

Something slammed into his forehead, leaving a trail of fire in its wake. Henley blinked back the tears as blood seeped from the wound and down into his eyes, his head throbbing as he let out a shout.

He writhed, ready to break his own wrist if it gave him an opening to get away. If these fuckers got him, Shelia was the least of his problems.

Had she known?

Fuck. He blinked, hoping that he was wrong. She couldn't have known that Martinez was that close to bagging him. Setting him up like that wasn't really her style. But she *had* been ready to let Li take care of him for her, so she could keep her fucking nails blood-free.

His moment of distraction was his doom. The butt of a gun crashed down on his forehead a second time, obliterating all thoughts except one.

If Li found out I went down so easily, he is going to kill me, just to teach me a lesson.

* * * *

Li

Li shook his head, crouching on the rooftop as chaos erupted beneath him. Gravel crunched under his boots as he shifted, trying to remain impassive, even as his heart started to pound. He shrugged, pulling his jacket closer as the wind started to pick up.

Pulling a hair tie from his pocket, he bound his hair out of his face. He needed the picture to be clear, so he could memorize every moment and every face.

Martinez's crew had grown in the last month, nearly doubling since Li had taken out his son. It looked like he had become paranoid of late, or he had hired more guys just to take Henley down.

He still couldn't figure out why they had placed all the blame on Henley in the first place, though. Yeah, Henley made a shitty bodyguard, and he had been the leader of their little sideshow, but he hadn't actually shot the kid.

Letting out a sigh, he let his eyes fall shut at the sound of tires squealing as they left an empty street behind. His gun was beside him, completely assembled and ready to go, the dark barrel glistening in the security light of the building.

Not a single one of them had looked up as he'd moved from rooftop to rooftop, scaling the buildings with his gun case strapped to his back. There had been one moment when he'd almost thought that Henley would get away. He'd stifled a chuckle as he'd watched Henley douse himself with lube, and the disgust and shock from Martinez's men had been a classic.

It had given him a minute to catch his breath and sight in his target.

Henley had writhed in the crosshairs as Li had let out a breath, steading his hand and his heart. He'd blinked, waiting for the right moment to take him out.

But if he had taken that shot, he would have changed everything.

Shortly after Jesse had uncovered who Henley really was, Li had hacked into their headquarters, gaining access to every security feed and microphone. He'd been watching for weeks and waiting for Henley to show his face and tell his superiors everything.

Li had passed off every chance to take him out, but watching Henley getting interrogated by his own people had nearly broken him. He had *tried* to protect Li, and Li wasn't even sure why he was furious about it.

He lay back against the rooftop, his collar shifting under his jacket until the cool metal lay in the center of his chest. He couldn't fathom why he still wore it. Ever since he'd snuck it from the hotel room and put it around his neck, it had hung there, thunking against his chest with every step. *Because I can't stand the thought of taking it off.*

He slammed his fist into the ground, grunting as a few loose rocks cut into his skin. He was leaving evidence behind with every drop that escaped from his hand and every hair that clung to the dirty roof. If anyone was to look hard enough, they would have no trouble tracking him down.

He'd been a ghost for the last seven years of his life, but before that, he'd had a somewhat normal upbringing. Somewhere, there were probably dental records of him that he hadn't managed to erase, and his parents had filled out the DNA kit when he was younger, in case he went missing. Even if he had managed to erase most of that part of himself, his family was still alive.

Not that his mother would recognize him with her mind riddled with disease. And not that his brother would give him the welcome home that he always promised. It was one thing to talk to someone on the phone, but it was another to have them in your living room and offer them tea.

He wasn't sure when he had stopped trying. A few days after the hotel, he had turned down a job, and since then, he'd been idle. He'd gone back to the place where it had all started, leaving himself wide open to be found if anyone had cared to look, while keeping an eye on Henley as he drank himself to oblivion night after night.

Henley had kept his promise, drowning himself in a bar instead of looking for Li like he should have been.

Every time Li had watched him from afar, the collar burned on his skin like a brand.

Hacking the security feed in the club and seeing Henley with another sub, however brief it had been, had made his chest go impossibly tight. He'd wrapped his hand around the collar, trying to tug it free, but the links resisted long enough for him to see Henley turn away from the sub with a shake of his head and a sigh.

I can't take it off.

The tail-plug, he was less attached to. He had tried it once on its own after the airport, but it had no appeal compared to the way it had felt when Henley had pushed it inside him. Maybe he wasn't doing it right.

Rubbing his hand over his face, he blinked his eyes open, staring up into the stars that had managed to peek through the layer of light pollution that the city offered. There was nothing there for him anymore.

Time to go home.

But that was what he had been trying to do for three weeks, and instead, he had followed Henley around the city like a lost pup. He wondered if his home would even feel the same anymore, even if he did return.

"He's gone," he whispered to himself, his voice sweeping away on the wind. Henley wasn't his problem anymore. Martinez would kill him—maybe not right away but eventually. Li was going to let that happen.

And Li would disappear again and turn back into The Ghost. He would have his life back, and the collar? That would just be a memento to remind himself of the things that weren't worth the risk.

He pushed himself to his feet, scraping his heel over the ground to cover the few drops of blood that had dripped from his injured hand. The wound had already closed, the cool air seeping into the tiny cuts and soothing the edges. No one would find the evidence of him being there.

No one would ever find him again.

Chapter Twelve

Henley

A pounding headache was the first thing that assaulted him as he blinked his way back into consciousness. His mouth was so dry that his throat ached like he had a cold, and his tongue was numb. It was probably a good thing that he couldn't taste very much, because from the little he could smell, he had been sick more than once.

He vaguely recalled the memory of retching repeatedly as he'd rolled around in the back of an SUV, the head injury and booze too much for him to take. He'd been knocked around more than once, until he had apparently stopped waking up and flailing at his attackers.

At least he didn't have to pee anymore. And he didn't feel wet, which was a bonus. He dropped his gaze to his lap, his vision filling with naked skin and his arrangement of scars. *Oh.* His clothes were gone, and his skin was sticky in the I-need-a-shower-immediately kind of way.

His shoulders ached as he tried to tug his numb hands, the rough rope binding them barely hurting as it scraped against his skin. They were wrapped tightly and separately restrained just behind his back and attached to the chair. He couldn't reach to break his thumb, and even if he could, the ropes were tight enough to stop his circulation.

His ankles were wrapped in the same sturdy binds around the chair's legs, his toes tingling in and out of his awareness. His left foot was pale, while his right pounded red and looked a tad swollen, the scar along his leg from a previous broken bone aching fiercely.

Flitting his gaze around the room, he tracked every detail, trying to record it with his foggy mind. The walls were concrete, with only one window high above his head behind him, and one door. There were a few chairs and a tray that didn't bode well for him, but otherwise, it was empty.

The floor was damp beneath his toes, hopefully just from condensation, and there was the distant scent of mildew that lingered. It was the type of place where rats had family reunions.

A shiver racked his frame, and he shuddered against the metal chair. His teeth clacked and he squinted against the overhead light, which was bright enough to put an eclipse to shame. He was so fucking cold that he was sure hypothermia was only a few hours away. He loved the cold, but the room was too much, like it hadn't seen heat, even in the midst of summer.

He craned his neck back, trying to spot something through the single window. It was cracked, though, and although it looked bright on the other side, it was impossible to tell the time. His shriveled stomach didn't give him any clue either, with the nausea pounding at his temples.

Twelve hours or two could have passed, for all he knew.

The only part of him that didn't seem to hurt was the circular bruise where the tracker lay beneath his skin. Rubbing it against his bindings deliberately, he let out a breath of relief. Wherever the hell he was, Shelia would know. Her team would come for him…hopefully.

He rolled his shoulders, trying to relieve the strain, and only sending a biting wave of fire down his arms and back. The next time he moved was going to be a bitch. He shifted his ass on the metal chair, trying to get more comfortable instead. At least that part of him didn't hurt any worse than usual. His tailbone still throbbed, but it didn't feel like they had tortured him below the belt while he had been in dream land.

The lube on his skin had long since dried, but he was still a touch tacky as he leaned away from the chair, seeking any position that would relieve the ache in his arms. The fire flared to life and a groan slipped through his lips.

His first priority was the impossible task of getting out of the ropes.

The single door slammed open, bouncing off the concrete wall hard enough that a touch of dust puffed into the air. A man in a suit appeared, his face in shadow against the even brighter light at his back.

Henley could have recognized the balding head and paunchy belly anywhere, though. Martinez Senior hadn't aged well, and at fifty-three, he looked closer to a limp-dicked seventy-six.

Three bulky guards filed in after him, marching in sync like they had something to prove. Henley spotted two he recognized, dismissing the hot goon and turning his glare on Robins.

"Fucker," snarled Henley, before he could help himself. The lift at the corner of Robins' lips was all he needed to know. He had sold himself to the highest bidder.

"I see you two know each other," said Martinez, grabbing another metal chair that wasn't bolted to the floor and moving it so he could sit in front of Henley. He crossed his suited legs, his knees straight like the prim and proper rich asshole he tried to portray. It was too bad that his dye-job was atrocious and he reeked of enough Gucci cologne to make Henley's eyes water.

Henley sneezed, his body spasming against the chair as every joint and bruise flared to life. Blinking away the gathering spots in his vision, he let out a breath, trying to focus on Martinez through his pounding brain.

"We've worked together before," said Robins, "but I have a feeling we don't work for the same people anymore." He let out a low laugh.

Henley swallowed. Robins wasn't in the loop about who he really worked for, but it sort of sounded like he had picked up an inkling that something was going on. Shelia directed the mercenary side of things, too, but Robins may have just tried to dig too deep. The thought had a shiver working its way up his spine, and Henley couldn't stop it with so much cold in the room. *Don't look weak.*

He'd never been much of an actor — not like Li — but he was strong. *Oh, Li, what I would give to see you one last time.* Setting his jaw, he pushed his thoughts away.

"They fired me, yeah," said Henley, wishing he could spit the foul taste in his mouth on Robin's shoe, but he had no saliva to spare. "They didn't seem to care about throwing me to the wolves after I fucked up." He turned a light glare on Martinez. "I'm sorry about your son."

Martinez paused, a brief look of confusion passing over his face that settled the rage that had been there since he'd walked into the room.

"There's no excuse," said Henley, trying to muster up guilt that he didn't feel. "I should have taken the bullet for him, or at least seen the shot coming. I wasn't able to track down the shooter, either." He hunched in the chair, trying to look smaller than he really was. It didn't take much. If only he hadn't been naked, so they wouldn't have been able to see his muscles beneath his skin.

"I can't bring him back, but I can make the people that let him die pay," said Martinez, crossing his arms and cutting off Henley's attempted plea. "Two of my men already have, but Dino has proven to be invaluable." He glanced over at the bodyguard that had turned Henley down.

Henley snorted, shaking his head.

"Something amusing?" asked Martinez.

"Nah, I just thought Dino's name was Thor or something because of the size of his hammer." He looked up to Dino. "You look like a Thor, don't you think? All those muscles bulging out of your shirt just makes me want to lick you from head to toe." The thought actually made him want to gag.

Martinez turned a remarkable shade of prune while Dino reached for the gun attached to his belt. It looked like he had gotten an upgrade in that department, along with his promotion.

"I told you that we should have gagged him, sir," said Robins, stepping past Martinez and landing a kick on Henley's shin.

Henley hissed, trying to draw his leg up, but failing when his bindings tugged him back down. "Kinky. You know I like that shit, Robins." He bit his tongue to keep from crying out as the sting from the hit ramped up to full-blown pain.

"I want to hear him scream," said Martinez as he stood, "just like I made the others scream. I want to hear him beg before I put a bullet in his brain."

If I only had a wire. He had been sneaking around Martinez's company and his family looking for evidence to tie him to a string of murders, trafficking and drugs charges for way too long. Martinez had just admitted to two murders and had threatened a third. He would have gone away for a long time, and Henley would have had the excuse to eat an extra cupcake instead of a protein bar for dinner.

Life was so not fair sometimes.

"So, what will it be?" asked Henley, leaning back into the cold metal in an attempt to make himself look relaxed. He suppressed a shiver before it could start, tapping his toes against the ground. The rope ground into him, making the movement almost impossible. "A knife? A hot poker? Or my personal favorite — a pair of pliers?"

Martinez stared, his gaze as bleak and emotionless as a sinkhole. "I'm going to cut your eyelids off so you can't look away as I feed pieces of you to the dogs. They're hungry. Can you hear them?"

Henley could. He could hear the low simmering growl and a few barks that did not sound like they were coming from chihuahuas. There was something else at the edge of his hearing, too — the low hum too distant to really be sure.

"I'm not really good with pain," said Henley, tilting his head, "and seeing as your son's death wasn't anyone's fault but his own, could we just do some light flogging and I'll be on my way? I swear you'll never see me again."

Henley flexed his hands, folding his thumbs in as far as he could without being able to break or dislocate them. The rope slipped down just a touch, cutting off the circulation in his fingers as he managed to get it down to his knuckles.

It was funny how something that he'd thought was impossible suddenly became completely doable when his eyelids were threatened. He had tried eyelash extensions once, and he never wanted to have to go through that fiasco again.

Martinez didn't react to his words, other than to snap his fingers. Dino strolled to the metal tray, lifting the towel from overtop to reveal what lay on it. There were tools that looked like they belonged in a surgical suite, including a scalpel that would have gleamed if it hadn't been encrusted with dark blood that looked like it had long since dried.

"Could you at least clean them first?" asked Henley, keeping his voice calm, even as his heart pounded. The rope glided over the bumps of his knuckles, his left hand slipping free. He moved to focus on the right, his movements slow and muted so he wouldn't be detected. "That one even has a fly on it. What if I get an infection?"

The distant thrumming noise grew louder, the blades of a chopper whirring hidden beneath the howl and bark of dogs. Henley looked to each of the men, fighting his smirk when they didn't seem to notice.

"Can I ask one question before you start slicing and dicing?" asked Henley, rocking back in his chair as Martinez grabbed the scalpel. "Why did you turn me down, Robins? I could have rocked your world, you know."

That desperate night had been one of the lowest of Henley's history. He'd promised himself never to bring it up again, but he was about to die, so whatever.

Robins huffed, pursing his lips. "Henley, you're like a Great Dane in a chihuahua's body. You think you're bigger, better and smarter than you really are, but you always forget that you're still just a dog."

"Famous last words," said Henley as a red dot appeared on Robins' forehead.

Robins blinked, his lips curling into a smile a moment before his brains exited his body. Dino wasn't far behind, along with the third bodyguard that Henley never even had the chance to get to know.

With a jerk, he slipped his right hand free, grabbing Martinez as he gaped at his fallen comrades and plucking the scalpel from his hand. The door slammed open as he touched the scalpel to Martinez's neck, grabbing him by the hair and jerking his head backward to expose more of his throat. Martinez stumbled, landing on Henley's lap and pushing the air from his lungs.

His arms burned from the movement and his grip almost slipped on the blade. It was only years of training and adrenaline that stopped it from falling.

A dozen agents filed into the room with their guns drawn and aimed toward him. They were in full tactical gear and covered from head-to-toe in black with only their lips and chins exposed. Their gear was unmarked, because every one of them was just as much of a ghost as Henley was.

A few Henley recognized from their bodies through the bulky getup, but the rest blended together, indistinguishable from one to the next. It was honestly a fashion nightmare.

At least when he had his tactical gear on, he was recognizable because he was so fucking short. And of course, he always strapped his fanny pack over his gear, just in case he needed something a little extra.

"Three down. Martinez is still alive," shouted one of the agents over the sound of the dogs that had grown louder with the door open. "Shut those fucking dogs up." He looped the strap of his weapon over his shoulders so he could bend to clear the three downed men of their weapons. "Harris is alive—and naked, as usual."

Henley grinned against the strain in his shoulders as he held Martinez tight with the last of his strength. "That was only one time—okay, two now."

The agent chuckled as he strolled forward, covering the other agents as they dragged the bodies away before stacking them by the door for the cleanup crew. He trained his weapon on Martinez, glaring down the scope.

"That you, Tensall?" asked Henley, going with his once-upon-a-time-partner's code-name. His grip loosened on the scalpel as pins and needles raced through his fingers. His shoulders still screamed at him from his sudden movements after being still for so long, and he was about to die of thirst.

"I'm not even going to ask, man," said Tensall as he grabbed Martinez, pinning him to the ground with a knee to the spine before cuffing his hands behind his back. "Four-to-one with you naked, and you still manage to come out on top."

"Give yourselves a little credit," said Henley, rolling his shoulders and stretching to try to relieve some of the ache. He reached for the ropes at his ankles, loosening the knots with his trembling fingers before tugging them free. Shibari had luckily given him a few tips on getting tricky knots loose. "You guys did a bit of the work, I guess. And Robins is gone, so that's one less asshole left in the world who turned me down."

Henley looked over his shoulder to the sole window in the place. There were three holes in the glass only inches apart.

"Everyone turns you down, man," said Tensall as he lifted his goggles so Henley could get a flash of his face. He was smiling, but there was a strain around his eyes that didn't bode well. "But thanks for that one, too. He was a prick."

Henley's confusion was lost as he pushed his way to his feet and the room spun wickedly around him. He tried to swallow, his throat aching. "You have any water?"

"In the truck—clothes, too. We weren't sure what shape you would be in when we got here. We had the warehouse wired after your tracker led us here, and we've got more troops coming in the copter to take care of the rest of this shit." Tensall grabbed Henley's shoulder, half-carrying and half-dragging him out of the room.

"Shelia could have sent you in a few hours ago and saved the both of us a lot of trouble."

Tensall's silence was answer enough. Shelia had been sitting on him and hoping to flush out Li. *Bitch.*

"I'm not going in the copter," said Henley. He was not tackling his fear of heights on the same day he'd gotten kidnapped. His ears rang, Tensall's voice going in and out as the ground warped before his eyes.

Touching his forehead, his hand came away flaked with dried blood, the cut probably enough to merit a few stitches. *Just another scar to add to my collection.* Why couldn't he collect practical things?

"There will be a crew of three waiting at the truck to take you back to headquarters. It will take the rest of us a bit to sort this shit out." He motioned to the abandoned warehouse where Henley had been held. It was part of a massive complex with endless places to stash contraband.

Right across from the location of the sole window, there was a second warehouse that was just a touch taller. It was the only place that would have offered a clear shot, but Henley couldn't spot anyone through the confusion.

A shot rang out and suddenly the last dog went silent. Henley turned to the sound, biting his lip when he saw the pool of blood. "I could have taken them."

Tensall shook his head before scratching his forehead at the edge of his helmet. "I'll be taking the copter back before we rendezvous with the rest of the crew. Shelia will want your full report before we have a doctor check you out."

"Am I still fired?" asked Henley, stumbling as the sun peeked out from behind a cloud. It was earlier than he'd thought, with frosty dew still clinging in a few places and making his naked feet feel like he dipped them in ice. He looked down at the gravel, only a few aching steps behind him and so many more to go. The last thing he needed was for his feet to be fucked along with the rest of his body.

Will I ever hear the end of it if I ask someone to carry me? No, probably not. As much as the crew of agents were an accepting bunch, they were still masculine as fuck — except Coquina, who was definitely a woman and yet somehow still taller than Henley. She also had the pain tolerance of a woman in labor compared to him.

"Here," said a low voice that sent a tingle up Henley's spine as an agent suddenly appeared behind him. He looked identical to the rest, if maybe a touch taller than some. He may have sounded familiar, but Henley couldn't place his voice with his tired mind.

Dozens of agents had filtered through headquarters, even just in the last two years that he had been posted there. There was no way to remember them all.

Henley reached for him, only to lose his balance and fall into the agent's chest. His head throbbed as he bounced from the impact, nausea burning in his throat as his world tilted.

"Sorry...fuck." He gagged, wiping his mouth as he panted through the ache in his sides. No matter how many times he did it, getting kidnapped was never a fun way to spend any time.

Before he could say another word, he was lifted as if he weighed nothing, the agent taking off at a running jog and carrying him bridal style across the stones.

"Thanks. It's not always that small, by the way. I'm just cold," said Henley, unable to stop himself from pressing his face into the agent's neck as the world tilted again and his stomach threatened to revolt. His smell was comforting and tickled something in his memory that refused to surface. "Don't tell anyone about this, though, or I'll have to kill you."

The agent snorted, picking up his pace as they neared the truck. Tensall waved them off as he turned to join the rest of the agents. Henley looked back, spotting Martinez, who was being dragged across the gravel faster than his dress shoes could keep him standing. Prison would be a paradise compared to where that guy was going for the next few weeks for 'interrogation'.

Henley was lifted into the back of a white van, the agent carrying him crouching down before taking a seat on a bench with Henley still in his lap. The whole back of the van had bars to create a make-shift mini prison. Martinez was thrown in a second later, his head knocking hard against the cage.

Henley let himself go lax in the agent's hold, sliding his hand up to one of the many breast pockets at the front of the tactical vest and clutching it tight. He wasn't going to push the agent away if he was okay with Henley on his lap. There was something about the hold that washed away all the terror that he had just avoided.

Maybe it was because he was finally starting to feel warm as his limbs thumped and circulation returned to them. His nausea was getting worse, though, his head pounding like there was an entire drumkit in his brain.

The back of the van slammed shut, the barred door locking with a thunk as the driver took off, the sound of flying gravel piercing through the space.

"Water?" questioned Henley, only leaning away from the agent for a moment when one of the men from the front seat passed him a bottle through the bars. He tucked his head under the agent's chin, taking slow gulps from the bottle after twisting the cap off.

Oh sweet, sweet water. He was never letting himself go thirsty again.

Tossing the empty bottle at the unconscious Martinez, Henley laid his head back on the agent's chest, taking another deep breath. His sense of smell had improved with the dryness in his mouth quenched, and the agent's cologne was tickling the back of his mind. Maybe it wasn't cologne as much as body spray? It was something that he was familiar with, though.

"Clothes?"

They passed him a loose shirt and track pants that he managed to put on without moving away much from the agent. *God,* it felt good to be touched and held, especially by someone who made him feel small. It just made him crave the challenge of taking them down.

He blinked heavily as his migraine started to recede, the stress from his kidnapping starting to fade. He snuggled closer, unabashedly sliding his hand over the agent's chest and up to his throat where a tiny bit of skin peeked through the protective covering.

Something silver caught his gaze, and Henley tilted his head to get a better look. He was drawn to it, seeking out the silver with his fingers as if it were the one ring to rule them all.

Tugging it free, Henley choked on a gasp, biting his tongue to keep the sounds inside. The chain was familiar because he had spent more time picking it out than he had choosing his gun. The sturdy links flowed through his fingers, strong enough to choke but light enough not to hinder movement. Dangling from the end of the necklace was a silver talisman in the shape of a dog paw—a carved *H* in the middle of it.

The agent—no, Li—looked at him, his gaze unreadable through the goggles covering his face and concealing his identity.

Henley's heart felt like it was going to burst, and he slowly moved closer, keeping one eye on the disinterested agents in the front seat. Leaning close to Li's ear, he took a deep breath, a shudder racking his body.

Li... *Oh God. I must be dead.* Tears prickled at his eyes as he started to shake. He hugged Li closer, wrapping his arms around his neck and holding on for dear life. Li lifted his hands to Henley's back, smoothing over the little dip before the swell of his ass.

"You ready, old man?" asked Li, his voice barely a whisper.

Henley nodded, dragging his nose over the side of Li's covered face. He couldn't get close enough. He wanted to breathe Li in forever and never let go.

"There's a tracker in my wrist," he whispered back, his lips barely moving.

"I know," said Li, tugging Henley even closer and putting his lips to Henley's ear. "When I pinch your thigh, hit the ground. I have to make it look like you didn't come willingly."

Henley nodded, his adrenaline surging and hands shaking for an entirely new reason. He thought back to what Tensall had said—praising him for killing Robins. Tensall's team hadn't been the one to take Robins out. It had been Li all along, like his guardian fucking angel on the rooftop.

"Do you guys have any blankets?" called Li, pushing Henley back by his hips so they weren't so tangled. "I think he's going into shock."

Henley wanted to snort. *Him? Shock? Pah!* He'd been shot through the lung and hadn't gone into shock. A little light bondage wouldn't put him there.

One of the agents up front swiveled in his seat, before turning the lock in the cage's door. Unlike the bottle of water and the clothes, the blanket was thick and bulky, just too thick to pass through the small slit in the bars.

Li stayed put, not reaching for the blanket as it was held out to him. "I've kind of got my hands full here." He looked down at Henley as another tremble passed through his body.

The agent grumbled briefly before snapping off his seat belt and squeezing between the seats to enter through the cage door. He was crouched over without enough room to stand upright as he slowly brought the blanket to them. "Not sure if the guy is even worth saving, anyway. Word on the street is that he went rogue."

Henley lunged at the floor when Li pinched his thigh, hitting the rigid plastic face-first. Blood burst in his mouth as he accidentally bit down on his tongue, his elbows aching as they jammed on the floor a second after his face.

Two shots rang out, and the hair stood up on the back of his neck. Even with a silencer, it was loud in the space, the high-pitched whistle almost on the edge of his hearing.

Looking back over his shoulder, he went to shout, but Li was a blur of movement. His shots hadn't hit the other agents, at least, not in the foreheads as Henley had thought. He sent a little thank you skyward. They were still agents, and ones he had worked with for years. They didn't deserve to die.

Li had aimed for the passenger's foot as he had stepped through the cage, dropping the agent's defenses and putting him out of commission, for the most part. The driver swerved from the bullet that had gone through his hand and into the dash, the speedometer nothing more than shattered plastic and a burst of blood.

"Pull over or the next bullets go through your heads. I think you know who I am, and you know I don't miss," said Li, keeping his gun trained on the closest agent, who was gasping and clutching at his foot. With his free hand, Li retrieved a syringe from his pocket, slamming it into the agent's neck. The agent went still, his arms going limp a moment later.

Henley scurried back, pressing against the cage as Li lunged through the door, sinking a second needle into the driver's neck as they came to a stop. The driver flopped sideways, his arm and shoulder tilting toward the narrow alley between the seats.

Li turned to him, lowering the goggles that were part of his tactical gear. His eyes blazed, his pupils blown as he stared at Henley. "Do you know who I am?"

Henley nodded, his heart pounding and his mind racing as Li's booming voice filled the small area.

"I saved one for you," said Li, pulling out another syringe and tapping it against his palm. "You see, it doesn't actually knock you out, not like the one I gave you that first time. This one just paralyzes you so you can see everything and feel everything I do to pay you back for betraying me."

Fucking hell. Henley swallowed, kicking his feet out as Li got closer.

"I'll start with your hands and cut them off while you can still scream. Once I get bored of that, I'll give you the shot so you can't fight back anymore. We're going to have a lot of fun, you and I."

"Li, I didn't mean to. I had to tell them!" Henley yelled as Li crouched closer, grabbing Henley's arm with the tracker buried within.

Henley's scream halted in his throat as Li winked. A fucking wink! Like the whole thing was a joke. Li pressed a finger to his lips before he reached for the knife that was in his upper pocket.

Henley gulped as he caught sight of the scalpel with a point that was sharp enough to draw doodles on bone.

"You aren't even fighting back — useless, but not any less fun."

Henley couldn't stop the scream as Li cut through his skin directly over where the tracker lay. His vision wavered as Li plucked tweezers from his vest, removing the tracker with surgical precision.

"There. Now no one can interrupt us."

The needle slammed into Henley's neck and darkness washed over him like a midsummer's rain. Li ran his hand through Henley's hair, his touch bringing every nerve to life a moment before everything went dark.

Chapter Thirteen

Li

If the assassin business didn't pan out, he could probably go straight into acting. Henley had slumped against him as his mild sedative took effect, the other two agents listening to every word in their ketamine-induced paralysis. Someone would be along shortly to rouse them when they didn't make their check point. That gave Li the perfect amount of time to get away.

He lugged Henley out of the cage, setting him in the passenger seat before he tossed the driver in the back and locked the cage. If Martinez roused first, Li doubted he would do anything but quiver.

He paused, taking in every inch of Henley's sleeping form. He was hurt, even if he had been putting on a brave face to keep anyone from knowing it. And the sedative was safe, allowing him to sleep, instead of trying to move him while he was in pain.

Henley had changed in their weeks apart, a few grays streaked through his hair and tiny wrinkles at the corners of his eyes, even as he slept. The battered scrape on his forehead mingled with the other bruises and cuts that Li had spotted when he'd lifted him from the ground.

His plan had been to scope out the spot, take out the Martinez crew and move in. The high window had given him the perfect view — if a touch distorted, but Henley's agent buddies had stormed in and crashed his little parade. It would have been easy enough to slip away.

He shook his head before dragging his thumb over Henley's lower lip. *Now is not the time.*

Turning away, he scoped out the surrounding area, spotting the street sign on the closest corner. *Perfect.* They were only about a block from his stashed vehicle, and there was enough cover and it was early enough in the day that he wouldn't be noticed. Just in case, he peeled his tactical gear from his body, stashing it all in a collapsible bag and throwing it over his shoulder. He grabbed Henley next, carrying him bridal style from the vehicle and leaning back so Henley's head rested against his chest.

Li was barely breathing hard when he reached the truck, easing Henley into the passenger seat and buckling him in before slamming the door shut. He was still bleeding from his head, a tiny trail of droplets following them from the panel van to his truck. Luckily, he had picked a spot with zero surveillance. He could merge seamlessly into the few cars on the road, and no one would be the wiser.

After a quick drive down the highway and a few extra loops around the city, he took one of the exits that led to his home. He was precariously close again, with enough agents behind him to storm through his stronghold.

He turned off the road after a long stretch of silence, slowing as he hit pitted gravel. Henley's head thumped against the window as the truck bounced over a few potholes. With winter approaching, the road was only bound to get worse. Every spring, more of it washed away into the overgrown ditches, and the city rarely graded it. If he had his way, his would be the only vehicle to pass down it, anyway.

His career as a ghost was getting shorter with Henley as a part of his life.

Is that what he is? He was certainly special — special enough to change Li's plans and save him rather than leave him to rot.

Certain that he could leave Henley behind, he had fled the city, only to turn around before he hit the first highway. Maybe it had been the collar with Henley's initial or maybe he wasn't as heartless as he'd hoped, but Li hadn't been able to abandon him. Even though he knew exactly what Henley had told his superiors, he hadn't had the strength to turn away.

They had time before anyone would be able to track him down — hopefully a few weeks of recovery before they had to move.

He passed the last few houses as the gravel on the road started to thin. The grass had grown through the middle until the tallest strands touched the bottom of his truck, loosing their seeds in hopes of finding more fertile soil. Some of them had started to blacken at their tips, the cold nights taking their toll.

The road quickly devolved into a path, before he turned down the tiny break in the trees that marked the lane to his home. He opened his window a crack, taking a breath of fresh air and calling on the usual relaxation that had managed to escape him over the last weeks.

Henley snorted in his sleep before he groaned, his body slumping deeper into his seat as the truck bucked its way over a partially buried culvert that Li hadn't had the time to fix.

The trees, the sounds of the birds and the wisps of a breeze that made its way down to the grass all made his paradise perfect. He hoped that the man beside him didn't tear it all to pieces before the week was through.

* * * *

Henley

Okay, wake it up. Is it today that I'm getting my wisdom teeth out? He stretched his jaw, his body responding sluggishly. His mouth didn't hurt much, so why did it feel like he was coming out of surgery?

A shiver racked his body, and something made a clacking noise like wood on metal. His eyelids felt like they weighed about thirty pounds, but he pried them open, using sheer will instead of his hands. His hands didn't seem to want to move at the moment.

Is there another surgery I'm forgetting about? His wrist throbbed, along with most of his body, his skin tight like he had grown a size in his sleep and it hadn't managed to catch up yet. *Did I break my arm?*

Blinking at the ceiling, his confusion deepened. There were solid beams above him that looked as if they'd been carved from the thickest trees around. The one directly above him was stained yellow-tan and ran about twenty feet from wall to wall. A few other beams connected with it, a cobweb clinging in the farthest corner. The walls were built of the same smooth and stained material, stacked so closely that there were hardly any gaps.

It was like something he'd seen in a magazine while he'd waited for his test results at the doctor. The yellow decorative chair in the corner, and the high dresser matched the aesthetic perfectly. It was a seamless mixture of modern and rugged, with a few hints of fabulous thrown in.

His teeth chattered, and he pulled the blankets around his shoulders. They were soft and silky but not overly warm and seemed to suck what little heat he had from his body. He was cold enough that he wondered if he'd been dipped in ice water while he'd been under.

"Well, fuck," said Henley as he shifted and tried to sit up. His vision swam as the cabin turned on its axis for a moment, his stomach flopping like he'd gone along for the ride. His wrist ached as he shuffled around in the bed, leaning back against the headboard as he slowly blinked. With his head pounding, he couldn't look left, so he kept his gaze straight ahead.

Whatever was wrong with his wrist was hidden beneath a layer of gauze that looked like a professional had wrapped it. Henley's bandaging usually looked closer to a children's portrait when they hadn't learned to color in the lines yet, so he knew he wasn't the culprit.

I remember… He wasn't completely sure. Martinez had been taken down, and Robins—he wasn't forgetting that image anytime soon. After that, there was a mysterious blur and a flash of a necklace. He had touched the necklace… *Li!*

"It's good to see you awake."

Henley started at the voice that came from his left, his heart picking up as he twisted painfully to look in the chair that had been beside him all along. His vision faded for a moment as something in his neck cracked from the movement before it seemed to settle.

"Li," said Henley as he reached for him. Li's tactical suit was gone, along with the goggles and headgear, leaving him with a black tank and slacks. The silver collar dangled from his neck as he shifted in his seat, the paw nesting below the dip of his throat.

Henley wanted to cry and rage at the same time, but his tongue had tied itself to the roof of his mouth. He never thought he would see his sub again, looking unruffled as if he hadn't just put a few more men into the ground. But the rage was there, too. Li had left him in the hotel room, slipping away with the collar while Henley questioned every moment of his life as he tried to figure out when he'd become a monster.

His heart won out and he reached for Li, nearly tipping off the edge of the bed as the blankets pulled tight around his legs. His limbs were like Jell-o, Li's shirt falling through his fingers as he tried to grasp the fabric.

"Hey," said Li, catching Henley as he surged forward. Burying his face into Li's chest, he took a deep breath, memorizing Li's scent so he would never forget it.

He would have to figure out what products Li used and add them to his shopping list, just in case he got left in the dust again. He couldn't believe that he hadn't recognized Li immediately. *You were hungover, in pain and you'd just puked your guts out from a concussion. Give yourself a break.*

"I'm sorry," said Henley, kissing Li's throat as trembling racked his body. He blinked back tears, shaking his head. What was wrong with him? He did not cry. *Ever*. He was un-fucking-breakable. "I told them your name, Li. They didn't give me a choice. I'm so sorry."

"Shhh, old man," said Li, dragging his fingers through Henley's hair. "I've had that headquarters completely wired since the day I found out who you were. I already know. Giving up my name is better than a bullet to the head."

"Is it?" Henley pulled back, blinking quickly to suppress the little wet demons that were trying to escape his eyes. At the rate he was going, he was going to end up with crow's feet.

"Shit, ow." He winced as his migraine resurfaced, the room wobbling like he was still drunk off his ass. His wrist throbbed as he rubbed the spot on his forehead that was the tenderest. The flakes of dried blood were gone, and the edge of a butterfly bandage held the jagged pieces of skin together.

"What did you give me? I already said I was up for another round, so you didn't have to drug me." Henley chuckled at Li's glare.

Li looked a bit scruffier than Henley remembered, and his eyes were definitely bloodshot, but damn, he looked good. The collar around his neck seemed to sum up the entire picture, screaming at Henley that Li was *his*.

Maybe that was why his heart was trying to beat its way out of his chest? He'd never had anything for himself before—not a name, a hometown or a sub. Li was his first.

"You look good," said Henley, smoothing a finger over Li's dry lips and the scruff of his unshaven jaw. "Good enough to eat."

Li scoffed, gently pushing at Henley's chest, but Henley held on, digging his fingers into Li's shoulders.

"Don't push me away," said Henley, dropping his gaze to the medallion at Li's throat. Reaching for it, he smoothed over the engraving, licking his lips. "You belong to me, so you don't get to push me away." *Real subtle, Henley.*

Li scowled, his glower going from casual to fierce in a moment.

"Do I own you too, then?" asked Li, his voice bitter with sarcasm.

"Absolutely," said Henley, running his hand through Li's hair. It was just a smidge longer, brushing just past his shoulders and perfect for pulling. "You own every part of me — my wonderful sense of humor, my breathtaking good looks and, apparently, my guns. You can't have my fanny pack, though. That one is all mine." He looked around the room, remembering that it had already been taken from him. "Once I get it back, that is."

"Who do you *really* work for?" Li asked, his voice dark and flat. "Your headquarters was a wormhole of misinformation, but some of the agents working beside you seemed to be on a different team. No matter how hard I've tried, I've never got the actual answer to who you are."

Oh shit, this is bad. Play dumb. "I don't know what you're talking about." *Not that dumb!* Henley wanted to face palm. He'd been covering his tracks for so long that it was hard to know how not to.

Li raised one brow. "The first time I met you, I took your guns and knives and that fanny pack that had enough bullets to take out a hundred guys. The tracker that was in your wrist isn't standard issue or even military grade. I've never seen something like it before. I own you, Henley, and I just saved your ass. Tell me."

"Technically, I'm an agent with CSIS special forces. At least, that's what we go by in this country. But I'm also an undercover mercenary who was hired to keep Damien Martinez out of the morgue and land his father in prison at the same time. On my taxes, I'm a construction worker with a bad knee who's stuck with a supervisory position until I finish my rounds of physiotherapy. But who I *really* am is a forty-ish kinky fucker who likes to shoot baddies for a living."

Henley flinched as Li reached for his chin, immediately flushing at his response. Li probably wasn't going to cut his eyelids off, but he couldn't just shake off what had happened to him.

"I'm not going to hurt you," said Li, waiting for Henley to close the distance between them. Henley touched his cheek to Li's upraised palm, shuddering as the heat sank into his body. How was it possible to miss someone so much?

"You going to kill me?" asked Henley, letting his eyes fall shut. He turned, placing a kiss to the center of Li's palm. "I betrayed you. If I'm going to die, I'd rather it be by you."

"Well, I'm not going to kill you *right now*," said Li, letting out an awkward chuckle as he pulled his hand back. Henley grabbed Li's retreating hand, dragging his lips over each fingertip.

"I can hear your heart racing," said Henley, dropping a kiss to the inside of Li's wrist. "Do you want me to stop?" His next kiss was on the sensitive skin on the inside of Li's elbow. He licked the crinkled seam, drawing his tongue back and forth. His headache receded as his cock throbbed to life, giving him all-the-more reason to keep going.

"I never wanted you to stop," said Li, his gaze dropping to the bed. "Even that first time, and even though I wasn't gay, I never wanted you to stop."

Henley lifted Li's chin, forcing him to meet his gaze. "What do you want right now?" He crossed his fingers. *Please say sex. I'm sore as fuck, but I'm still ready to go.*

"If you're *good*, I'd like to make you breakfast," said Li, freezing the moment that he said it. "I didn't mean it like that."

He couldn't help being a tad disappointed. He'd been without Li for weeks, and sex had been at the top of the to-do list, but he knew sex couldn't fill the gaps in his dismal coping abilities. That, and he was starving.

"Of course you didn't. You know that you want to be good for me, not the other way around," said Henley, following the direction of his spiraling thoughts. He wasn't sure how he'd come to crave Li's touch so much. Even sitting in his arms while fully clothed, he ached to get closer and feel skin. He wanted to push Li to the edge of his comfort zone and beyond, blowing his mind every time.

"I don't know what gave you that idea," said Li, moving away before sliding off the chair. His gaze was locked on the floor, a flush across his cheeks.

Henley had always wondered how much acting had been behind Li's persona during their first night together and had figured it had been one-hundred-percent false. But he wasn't so sure anymore. *Only one way to find out.*

"Maybe the way you took my cock? Or the way you love to give in to me? I could be wrong, but that's my collar around your neck, and you've been wearing it since you left the hotel room." Henley grinned as Li blanched. "There's nothing wrong with that."

Li's flush deepened, the red stain spreading all the way to the top of his chest and peeking through his tank top. Li touched the collar, fiddling with the medallion in a way that looked almost habitual. "I missed you."

"I missed you, too," said Henley, getting to his knees on the bed and reaching for Li before he could slip away. "Please, don't walk away like this. You brought me here for a reason, and I need to know what it is. You feel something for me."

"You seem so sure," said Li, pinching the paw tag between his fingers before running it up and down the chain. He bit his lip, his forehead furrowing. "I know I'm not attracted to any man besides you, but I don't know what's really between us. I can't sleep without dreaming about you, and during the day, I can't stop thinking about what you're doing and if you're safe. You drive me insane."

Henley grinned. "I drive a lot of people insane." He was fucking proud of it, too. "But I only want to be with one of them. I've only offered one person my collar — the same person who I never thought would take it. Why did you take it? You could have left it there. Hell, you could have shot me, too, but you didn't."

"I don't know," growled Li, his voice dropping as he took a step back and crossed his arms, the collar swaying against his chest.

Fuck that.

Henley grabbed the loops of Li's pants, tugging him back to the bed. His wrist ached from the movement, and he gritted his teeth against the pain. "Yes, you do. It's the same reason that you wore the plug. Don't try to deny it."

"I..." Li trailed off. "I'm not gay."

Not this again. Henley rolled his eyes. "You say it like it's a bad thing." He tugged Li closer, until his groin was inches from his face. "Being gay is one of the best things about my life. I can't get anyone pregnant, and I've never met a guy who expected me to marry him after sleeping together once."

"It's not bad, exactly. It's just not me," said Li, pointedly looking away. "Men are...just men. I don't think about sleeping with them the way I do about you."

Henley sighed, shuffling and popping the first button on Li's pants. Slowly he unzipped him completely, tugging his pants down to rest on his hips. Li didn't react verbally, but his face flamed brighter.

"I have a proposition for you," said Henley, pulling Li's boxers down and exposing him to the air.

"Of course you do," said Li, a tiny smile on his lips.

"If I can make you hard without touching you, then you have to consider the possibility that you might be gay. I'm a guy with a fabulous dick, and if you get hard for me, then there is a chance," said Henley, shuffling back on the bed and arranging the pillow. The bed was only a double, so he wouldn't have much space to get really into it, but it was better than a cot.

In truth, every one of Li's words had him brimming with pride. His sub got hard for him and only him, which was like a dream come true. He'd always wondered why some Doms coveted their subs, but for the first time, he understood. He would kill anyone who tried to touch Li. *I'm not telling Clint that, though.*

"It won't happen," said Li, fisting his hands as he glared at Henley, his pants sagging that much lower on his hips. "You'd have to touch me to get me hard."

"Humor me."

Li let out a long sigh as he pinched the bridge of his nose. "Fine, just get it over with so I can get out of this room and make breakfast."

"Okay, *Listowel*," said Henley, dropping his voice as he laid back on the pillow before shuffling it around until it kept him partially propped up. "You can grab a chair if you want. It might help you relax." He lifted the hem of his shirt, clenching his abs to show off his kinda-sorta six-pack. Dipping into his belly button, he tossed the bit of lint on the other side of the bed before Li could notice. Nothing killed a hard-on faster than navel lint.

At some point, Li must have washed him, because the stickiness was gone from his skin and he smelled daisy-fresh compared to how he should have. Picturing Li on his knees, sponging him clean as he slept, had Henley aching. He'd never been a service Dom, but sometimes he could see the appeal.

"I prefer to stand." Li followed the movement of Henley's hand as he drew a line between his abs, smoothing the hair on his belly as he traveled south. Li licked his lips as Henley paused at his waist band before moving back up.

"Suit yourself," said Henley, ducking his hand under his shirt to roll his own nipple. He licked his lips as the sensation shot straight to his groin, letting his eyes fall shut. It dulled the pain in the rest of his body, almost as well as valium.

"Did you like the plug? I bet it was a tight fit in that little hole of yours. I can imagine you gripping it just right, your body begging for something bigger and deeper at the same time you felt so full."

Henley opened his eyes, the image too much for himself. Li's cock was visible just below the hem of his shirt, the spot looking a tad fuller than it had before. Li had flushed bright again, too, his rosy cheeks like a beacon in the room.

"Yeah," said Li quietly, looking a little lost as he shifted. He had relaxed his fists, but his shoulders were still tight and sitting much too close to his ears. A massage would have suited him perfectly.

Pulling his shirt over his head and tossing it behind him, Henley ran his hands over his torso, skimming along his sides and plucking at his nipples with each pass. "Did you imagine me filling you up with my cum, then plugging you after? You would be so happy that you'd wag your ass back and forth, the tail tickling your thighs as it swung. Maybe I'd slide your boxers on after and trap it inside you, the itch of the tail and the press on your prostate a constant reminder of who you belong to."

There was a definite twitch of Li's cock as he rose from the firmer side of half-mast. *Too fucking easy.*

If only he had figured himself out in college, then Henley would have been an actual master instead of a two-year newbie when it came to kink. He still fucked up, and everything was still so new to him that he longed to go back and rewrite his past.

He slipped his borrowed track pants over his hips, tossing them in the same direction as his shirt. His cock was hard and leaking, pre-cum dripping down the shaft to dribble around his groin. He gave himself one easy stroke with his good hand, letting out a hiss as his toes curled. *Fuck, that felt good.*

"You like seeing me dripping for you?" asked Henley, flexing his hips so his cock bobbed up and down. "Or maybe you want to see something else instead?" Spreading his thighs and lifting his sac out of the way, he gave Li a peek of his hole. He knew he probably looked tight. It had been a long time since he'd let someone take him, because it was harder for him to stay in control when his prostate was being pounded into submission.

"Do you want to touch me? Here or here?" He cupped his sac with one hand and pinched his nipple with the other. "Or maybe here, where I'm tighter than anything you've ever felt before." He dropped his hand to his hole, stroking himself with one finger. "You'd need to lick me open or lube me up, Listowel. I'm nothing like a woman. The only thing that would drip for you would be my cock."

Li's chest heaved, his pupils blown wide as he panted, open-mouthed. He had gone fully hard at the first peek of Henley's cock and had started dripping pre-cum when Henley had circled his own hole.

"Tell me. What do you want to touch?" asked Henley, dipping the tip of his finger just inside. He was too dry and too tight for much more.

"Your ass," said Li, so quietly that it was almost a whisper. He reached for his own cock, but Henley stopped him with a shake of his head. Surprisingly, Li dropped his hands back to his side and Henley didn't hold back his *'good boy'*.

"Don't touch yourself. I want to see you come just from looking at me." Henley sucked one finger into his mouth, moving it back down to his ass and sinking it inside to the first knuckle. Fuck, he *was* tight, but luckily his tailbone didn't hurt as bad anymore. "You should get the plug so you can put it in my ass. My hole will look so good stretched around it, but not nearly as good as it would wrapped around your cock."

Li's cock jerked, another dribble of pre-cum dripping from the head. It was an angry red, almost purple, with how turned on he was. Coming untouched was a nearly impossible feat, but Henley had faith. *Not gay, my ass.*

"It won't fit," said Li, licking his lips as he leaned closer to the bed.

Henley tilted his head, eyeing up Li's cock. Maybe Li was right. He was big—or at least proportionate to the rest of his body. He was a touch on the thin side, but long enough to more than make up for it, and he had that perfect curve that gay men loved.

"We should try. I don't know if it will. I'm so tight, and fuck, one finger hurts already. I'd be good for you, though. Even if it hurt, I'd let you fuck me." Maybe he shouldn't have put too many ideas into Li's head. Henley wanted repeat performances, and he wouldn't get that with an aching ass.

Li let out a deep groan, reaching for his own cock again. Henley lunged off the pillow, his muscles aching as he slapped Li's hand away. His lips were inches away from the dripping head, and he could almost feel the warmth of it. He blew on the head, watching as Li's hips stuttered and his chest heaved.

"Do you want my mouth?" asked Henley, sticking his tongue out, but keeping far enough away as to not accidentally touch Li. "I could take you all the way down my throat and suck. You could fuck my mouth and make me choke."

Li nodded, reaching for Henley, who dodged to the side.

"Then tell me that it doesn't matter if you're gay or not. Tell me that you want my mouth, my ass and my cock. Fucking say it."

Li shook his head, biting his lip so hard that it looked like he might start to bleed. His body was tense, his hands fisted at his sides again. He wasn't going down without a fight. *And I wouldn't want it any other way.*

Henley grinned. He loved a challenge. Falling back against the bed, he spat on his hand, slicking up his cock and spreading his legs wide. He bucked his hips into his hand, fucking himself with abandon as Li watched, his gaze begging.

"Do you like what you see?" asked Henley, waiting until he was seconds from coming before he dropped his hand, reveling in the throb of his lost orgasm. His balls grew even heavier as his load was denied release. "*Nnnn,* fuck."

One moment, he was staving off an orgasm alone, and the next, Li was on him, kissing him like the world was about to end. Their cocks slipped together as Li humped him like a madman, Henley's release thundering closer. He couldn't breathe as Li possessed his mouth, apparent longing and wonder in every touch.

Hooking his leg around Li's hip, Henley rolled them, grabbing Li by the throat as Li's back hit the bed. He ground his ass against Li's cock as he straddled him, using his cheeks as a fuck tunnel and groaning every time Li pressed against his hole.

"Do you want to fuck me? Do you want to fuck a forty-year-old *man?*" Henley slammed his hips down harder, his cock slapping against his belly from the force.

"Yes!" Li grabbed Henley's hips, urging him on faster.

"You ain't straight, baby," said Henley, bringing their lips together and fucking his cock down onto Li's. His orgasm slammed into him like a train, stealing his breath and pushing a groan through his lips that could have made the walls shake. Whether from the stimulation, or the slickness of Henley's release, Li followed a second later, digging dark bruises into Henley's hips.

Grabbing Li's collar, Henley twisted it, cutting off Li's air with an easy pressure that barely made his wrist zing. Li choked, bucking under him as his orgasm stretched on. "Don't fucking deny yourself, pup. Take what you want, and let me show you things that will blow you mind."

He released his hold on the collar, letting Li take a few gasping breaths before he brought their lips together again. His cock was still hard, ready for round two as their touches got fiercer.

"Show me," said Li, his voice dropping into a growl as he rolled Henley onto his back. "If you can, old man."

Fuck yes.

Chapter Fourteen

Li

Li choked, wiping his hand over the back of his mouth and grimacing at the taste. Having Henley in his bed was like nothing he'd ever dreamed of, but his cum tasted like salty pudding that had been left out in the sun too long. That, and he was a bit pissed about the way his throat ached from when he had opened his mouth and Henley had just kept shoving until he was certain he would never breathe right again.

"I'll give you a tour before breakfast," said Li, grabbing his clothes and throwing them on while Henley lay face-first on the bed, looking comatose. His ass was a pretty picture, even if Li hadn't even managed to touch it during their brawl. Even though Henley had obviously been sore, he'd put up enough fight that Li had backed down in fear of hurting him.

He still wasn't sure why he cared. By all rights, he shouldn't have gone back for him in the first place.

"I'll be there in a minute," said Henley, waving him off without looking up. His sides were still heaving like he'd run a marathon.

"You're out of shape, old man." Li snickered as Henley groaned before giving him a side-eye.

"Fine, fine, I'm coming."

"Thanks for the heads up. It might've been nice ten minutes ago," said Li, shooting a glare right back. Maybe he could get used to the taste and texture of cum...but not without some warning.

Henley snickered as he snagged his clothes, hissing as he twisted his wrist.

"You okay?" Li kept his hands at his side, biting his lip so he didn't reach out. If he touched Henley again, who knew what he was going to do. "I have some pain killers if you want."

"Nah, I've seen worse." Henley shrugged, rubbing his shoulder before following Li out of the bedroom door.

Li knew he'd seen worse. He had seen the evidence on Henley's body, etched as scars that would last for an eternity. He'd found more than he remembered from the hotel room as he'd scrubbed Henley's body after he'd brought him home. At first, he had planned on leaving him as he was, tucking him in bed to sleep the meds off. But one sniff of his overripe and lube-covered body, and Li hadn't had a choice.

"Kitchen and living room combo," said Li as he waved to the right side of the cabin where a cozy but neat kitchen with not nearly enough cupboards was squashed next to an uncomfortable silver couch. There was no fridge or microwave, just a sink and a tiny stove that only worked on one side.

"Smaller than I expected," said Henley, glancing back at the bedroom that was spacious compared to the rest. "Where the hell is the fridge?"

Li smothered his grin. "Bathroom is through that door. I suggest you wash up."

"Don't push me, pup. We both know I can take you down." Henley raised one eyebrow before he disappeared through the door.

Li hid his laugh behind his palm as he caught Henley's surprised sound at what he had discovered. The toilet, if you wanted to call it that, was one of the automatic composting types. It didn't smell the freshest, but Li hardly used it anyway.

"You good?" he asked as Henley dragged himself out of the bathroom looking a touch mortified.

"Decorative pillows and an outhouse *in* the house?" Henley squawked, shaking his head. "It's like my worst nightmare in there."

"Let me show you dreamland, then." Li strolled back to the bedroom before opening up the closet and shuffling his clothes aside. Hidden on the back wall was a small gray oval that was barely larger than the pad of his thumb. He touched the sensor, stepping back as the false wall started to move.

He shot Henley a grin as he started down the tight stairs, the lights clicking on one by one as he moved to the lower level. The basement was more than three stories down and surrounded by enough protection that no cell signal could ever escape. The only vulnerability was the air vent, which Li had taken great pains to hide and maintain.

He heard Henley gasp as he dropped from the last step, looking around the area with open awe.

This was where his heart was, and the only place Li ever felt like he was truly free. He was so protected that no one had a chance of getting him, even if they did have reinforcements and wicked technology.

The walls were white, with one dark blue one where he'd set up most of his living space. There were no windows, but he'd installed enough pot lights that it looked anything but claustrophobic. The real hail-Mary was the kitchen that took up nearly a third of the space with stainless steel appliances and a massive range.

"So why is everything but your bedroom underground?" asked Henley, blinking at the kitchen before he grabbed the door to the fridge and swung it open. "Ah, there's the beer."

"For an undercover agent, you aren't very good at concealing things," said Li, shaking his head.

"I'm good at everything," said Henley, grinning as he put the beer back and reached for orange juice instead. "Especially fucking."

Li chuckled, shaking his head. "No argument here." He grabbed two cups, placing them on the counter for Henley to fill. "From above, this place looks like a shitty little cabin that belongs to a hunter, and the deed on the land agrees with that. The rest is deep enough to keep it hidden from satellite imagery and heat-sensing technology."

Henley chewed his lip as he poured the juice. "And the bedroom? Aren't you most vulnerable there? You'd think that would be buried deepest."

"Until someone starts a fire and you have no escape." Li lifted one eyebrow, giving Henley a look. That, and he was a touch claustrophobic. "Even with the security on the property, I wasn't willing to take that chance. Plus, I have to explain the electric bills somehow. I couldn't do solar panels with all the trees, and I don't want to bring attention to myself if someone asks questions."

Li grabbed a frying pan, cracking an egg and firing up the flame. The propane roared to life, fed by the tanks that he hauled back from the store in his truck himself. There was no way he'd risk having a truck come back and stock a larger tank.

"Do you bathe in the woods, or is there a hidden shower down here somewhere?" asked Henley, looking around the space.

Li flipped his egg onto a piece of unbuttered and untoasted bread—because that was how he rolled—before strolling out of the kitchen. He circled around the living room couch, tapping at a black oval on the wall. Two taps with his thumb and a silver keypad flipped open from the blank wall. "Code 4242 will open the bathroom."

"And I thought *I* was paranoid. No wonder they call you The Ghost. You even guard yourself when you shit." Henley ran his hand over the wall next to the keypad, probably looking for the hidden seams.

Li had done the work himself after the foundation had gone in. He knew where every nail was and every seam beneath the perfectly taped and mudded drywall. There were *no* cracks.

Li tapped the sequence in and a hidden door clicked open on the other side of the room. The door squealed on the hinge as it slowly fell open and he mentally added WD-40 to his next grocery list.

"Are there other codes?" asked Henley as he strolled to the bathroom, humming in appreciation as he looked at the normal toilet and shower.

"Yes," said Li, closing the panel with a click. He moved to the kitchen, grabbing a second glass of juice for himself.

"You've shown me your gun, and I held it *real* good for you. Now you have to show me the rest of your gun room. It gets me hard just thinking about it." Henley called from the bathroom as the shower started.

"Not happening," shouted Li.

Henley pouted through breakfast and Li's tour of the panic room that was tucked away next to the bathroom. Li didn't blame him. In the private sector, he could afford the fancy gadgets, where Henley had been stuck with government-issue.

"Where are we?" asked Henley, gazing around as his breathing started to pick up. Li had noticed as he'd continued the tour, the tension settling over them both as Henley tapped his fingers and looked back to the door.

Without a word, Henley stood from the chair where they'd settled in silence, marching back up the steep incline to the land above. Li followed, watching as Henley's breathing evened out as he reached the top step. Henley darted to the window before throwing it wide.

"I have an issue with enclosed places," said Henley, tracing the screen. There was a tiny hole, just big enough for a bug to squeeze through, but no more. Li added it to his long to-do list. He'd been away more than usual lately, and things had started to pile up.

"You have a problem with a lot of things," said Li, placing a palm on the back of Henley's neck. "I saw you in the scope when you were in that warehouse. You had the same reaction when we got close to the edge on the roof on that first night and when you wouldn't get close to the window in the hotel."

Henley shrugged, wincing as something pained him. "Shit happens. I deal with it, but sometimes it tags along with me."

Li dropped his hand down Henley's spine and Henley let out a breath as his shoulders relaxed. "I'm sure you know what I mean, Li. You've had to have had some close encounters with shit you'd rather forget."

Li grunted, moving his hands to Henley's hips. Henley tipped his head back to rest against Li's chest. Li rarely initiated contact between them, and it was strange touching Henley without the other baiting him. It soothed the ache in his soul. To be wanted was the best sensation in the world.

"I've seen a lot of faces at the wrong end of my scope, but I stopped remembering them a while ago. Sometimes I see them…in my dreams. I don't get close enough to *really* see them, though. Is that why you can't give up control?" Li nuzzled his neck and Henley tilted to give him better access before nodding once.

"Aren't there therapists out there for that?" Li asked, his lips leaving a damp impression on Henley's skin.

"The best therapist in the world can't erase the memory of someone trying to bury you alive or toss you off the roof of a skyscraper," said Henley, letting out a shudder as his pulse started to pound against Li's lips. "Can we talk about something else?"

"Avoiding it won't help. It'll probably make it worse."

"I know," said Henley, digging his finger hard into the screen and breaking the space wider. "Can we go outside?"

"Let me show you my paradise," said Li, taking Henley's hand and tugging him from the hole in the screen. Maybe he wouldn't fix it after all but take the screen down altogether to help Henley feel safer.

Taking a deep breath as they stepped out of the cabin, Li let his defenses down. The trees were tall, with a few branches leaning over the cabin and concealing it from above. Beneath the trees were layers of green and brown in hundreds of shades, but the clearing had bits of domestic grass along with wild weeds and a few vines sneaking up the side of the cabin. It was cool within the trees, cooler than the city always felt against his skin, and it was so quiet that he could hear his ears ring.

"Do you garden or hunt or do anything like that out here?" asked Henley, his fingers still threaded with Li's.

"I don't hunt," said Li, "and I usually try to avoid meat, actually. I'm fine with eggs and milk and stuff, but I'm not a fan of slaughterhouses."

Henley snorted, rolling his eyes. "You have got to be kidding me. You'll kill a random guy, but you won't eat a burger?"

"It's different," said Li, tugging his hand free and crossing his arms. "The cow didn't do anything wrong, but my target certainly did. I always do my background checks, so I know who I'm killing before I put a bullet in their brain."

"An assassin with a code," said Henley, sarcasm biting at his words.

"An agent without a code is nothing worse than a mercenary," said Li.

He saw the moment when every bit of joking fell away from Henley's face and anger swept into his eyes.

He didn't even have time to raise his hand before Henley's fist slammed into his nose. His vision blurred as he fell back, the air pushing from his lungs as he dropped.

Henley followed him to the ground, straddling his waist and grabbing his collar. There was no play as Henley twisted his hand and cut Li's air off with a brutal tug. Li's eyes flew wide, real fear setting in for the first time. It had been a long time since he'd been afraid, and it settled in the air like a palpable demon.

* * * *

Henley

Henley drew back as if he'd been burned, stumbling to his feet and toward the tree line as Li drew in gasping breaths, choking as he rolled onto his side. He couldn't look at the pink lines that had been carved into Li's neck, knowing that he had put them there.

His anger ruled him, along with his fears, and Li had struck every button on the head with a golden mallet. Maybe he was nothing more than a mercenary. He was certainly willing to sell out the one he loved for a paycheck.

Wait… Love?

He whirled around, staring back at Li who was just lifting himself off the ground. Li dusted his pants off as he stood, sighing at the grass stain along his thigh before he let out another small cough. His hair fluttered in the breeze that swept through the trees, his eyes sparkling in the natural light.

Henley had never seen him in the sunlight before. He was stunning. But he couldn't have loved someone for their looks or he would have fallen dozens of times before.

Perhaps it was the way Li had writhed beneath him, holding back, even though he had the strength and the agility to overpower him. Maybe it was the way Li always gave in to him, putting up a fight to shield himself from reality.

But that wasn't it, either. Sex had never made him fall in love before. If anything, sex made it impossible to love someone. The moment they came, their walls fell down and Henley saw the type of person he was fucking for the first time. Only Li had drawn him back for more.

"I'm sorry," said Li, scrubbing his hand over his neck before touching the blooming bruise on his cheek. It would probably be black before the end of the day.

Henley looked skyward, like he could solve everything if he tracked the clouds long enough. There were a few white wisps and the unnatural trail of a low-flying jet headed to the city. They were closer than Henley had thought. To think, Li had been hiding under his nose all that time.

"Nah, I'm the one who's a dick." Henley reached down, burying his fingers in the grass and tugging at the strands until they broke away, earth still clinging to the pale roots. "You've done everything right and I…haven't. You should shoot me now. One and done. You can't trust me."

Henley couldn't meet Li's gaze to find out if he was contemplating it or not. If he had been in Li's situation, he would have considered it. Henley was already fucked and barely hanging on, between his built-in training and his issues.

"If you want one more fuck, I'm sure we can arrange that," said Henley, forcing a grin on his face as he turned back to Li.

"I'm not going to shoot you. I still can't figure out which one of you is *real*...the depressed old man who has seen too much for one lifetime and lived through worse? Or the happy-go-lucky one with rainbows shooting out of his ass?" Li spoke slowly, eyeing Henley like he might lose it at any moment.

"I'm not depressed," said Henley, looking back to the sky. The way the sun filtered through the leaves, casting everything in a green glow, had a certain peace about it. Not that he felt that peace. He wouldn't have peace until he was six feet under, that was for sure.

Okay, so maybe he was a *little* depressed.

"Don't say I didn't warn you," said Henley, heading back to the cabin, and leaving Li's slice of paradise behind. It wouldn't last long while he was alive.

Chapter Fifteen

Li

Li stretched his hands out to the other side of the bed as he blinked into awareness. It was cold, without a hint of Henley's heat touching the surface. It wasn't wholly unexpected. Henley had spent the rest of the previous day in silence until they had curled up at opposite sides of the bed to sleep.

Henley had faced away from him, presumably staring at the blank wall as he'd pretended to sleep. Li had faced Henley's back, counting each breath as Henley's sides rose and fell. He watched the lines of Henley's strength that managed to shine through his loose T-shirt, mesmerized. Li could only hope to look that good when he was in his forties.

But the question really was, why the hell was he looking in the first place? It wasn't that he was still in denial about the attraction between them but the fact that Henley should be dead.

Henley had called him out in the midst of the trees, throwing his arms wide as he practically begged to be shot. And Li had…panicked.

Henley was hiding something, but Li couldn't think what it could be, other than his past. Did Henley really think that he was too damaged for Li to be interested? Because the reality was that Li had tried hard not to be interested, but nothing had worked. Henley could probably transform into a pine tree at this point and still turn Li on.

He tangled his hand in the sheets, searching for any bit of warmth. The upper floor of the cabin was always brisk in the morning hours, even in the height of summer. With fall solidifying, he would have to pull out his fleece blankets soon.

At least that part of his home was simple — and the perfect disguise. There were no pipes to freeze and little heat to speak of to draw attention.

It could be bleak in the winter when he curled into bed, heaped with blankets with his toes still freezing and his breath misting the air. Around zero degrees was usually when he caved and opened up the heating system, so the warmer air would circulate from below and keep him from dying of hypothermia.

"Henley?" He sat up, tossing the blankets back and shuddering in the sudden cold. His arms and legs tingled with energy from his slacking over the last few days. The rescue had interrupted his workout time in the hidden gym below, and his body was starting to feel it.

There was no answer, and not even a sound other than his own voice. The basement door was shut — locked with his fingerprint after Henley declined Li's offer to program his. That in itself had worried Li.

Henley couldn't have made it clearer that he wasn't planning on staying. But Li had thought he would have had more than one day before he took off. He'd been gone for a while for the bed to be that cold.

Tossing on a thin jacket and jeans and pulling on a pair of running shoes, Li stepped out into the forest, letting the door fall shut behind him. The crisp mint of evergreens hit him first, mixing with the earthiness of grass and the slight sweetness of a few maples that were close by.

A rabbit skimmed along the edge of the clearing, darting into the trees as it spotted him, a dandelion still dangling from its mouth. There were no deer or foxes scampering about in the protected place, and the birds were quieter than usual. If Li didn't know any better, he would have thought there were trespassers on his land.

There was a brief call of a jay off in the distance, probably warning of a coyote's presence, but nothing closer than that.

Kneeling, he spotted a few scuffed marks along the forest floor a few steps from the cabin entrance. A turned-over leaf, and a patch of dark needles didn't mean much to most, but it was a clear sign for him. The forest left clues everywhere, and it had taken him years to figure out how to find them.

Another jay — this one closer — let out a few braying caws. He turned to the sound, looping around to the back of the cabin. The clearing stretched out for about thirty feet all around the cabin, with a few trees closer that helped conceal some of the roof. The whole place had looked like a construction zone when he'd been in the process of building it, but it was back to being one with nature, with some of the younger trees playing catch up to reach the stature of their older neighbors.

Li paused as he rounded the cabin, a breathtaking sight greeting him just around the bend. Sunlight slitted through the leaves, painting the grass and person below. Every time the wind blew, the light danced, spiraling and twirling as it kept the shadows at bay.

Henley was in the middle of the soft grass that had grown too long for most conventional lawns. He had one hand on the ground, his body inverted into a handstand with his legs stretched wide into near-perfect splits. His body was still and utter perfection in the pose, with sweat beading on his skin and his arm trembling from the effort.

He was also completely naked.

Li licked his lips, pressing his wrist to the front of his jeans. The air was freezing, but Henley's cock looked no worse for wear. It was hanging down toward his belly, half-hard with a rosy blush at the head.

"I've heard of goat yoga, and hot yoga, but never naked yoga," said Li, taking a step toward Henley and testing the proverbial waters. Henley's mood seemed to switch faster than the weather in the ocean.

Henley grinned, his smile inverted from his position as he slowly straightened his legs, pointing them to the sky. Switching arms, Henley lowered his legs again until they were parallel to the grass below him. His movements were so controlled and harmonious that Li never would have guessed that he was the same man who had had a borderline panic attack in the basement the day before.

It also explained how Henley looked so good for his age. Because now that Li had given himself permission to look, he hoped Henley would never put clothes back on. He wasn't just strong, but lean, too, his boyish body looking more like a man than Li had ever seen it.

"I thought I would take your advice and think about things," said Henley, his voice quivering with strain. His chest flushed red, a bead of sweat rolling down to his neck.

"And this was the best way to get blood to your brain?" asked Li, shuffling closer before he sat cross-legged on the ground. Even though he was a few feet away, he had a great view of Henley's cock, which looked like it was getting harder.

Li could sympathize. Sometimes just running on the treadmill gave him a semi that would not quit.

Henley nodded, gritting his teeth before he touched the ground with both hands, straightening his legs to the sky again. His face was flushed red, the tendons on either side of his neck defined as he grunted with the effort. Damp needles and partially composted leaves clung to his palms as he shifted from one to the next.

Li let out a breath that he hadn't realized he was holding. His breath caught again a second later when Henley started tilting both of his legs to one side, his abdomen clenching from the effort. It was...*wow*. Licking his lips, he forced himself to blink.

Shuddering as he hardened further, Li ran his hand through his hair, tugging a loose strand free and dropping it to the forest floor. He longed for a hair elastic to pull his hair back so it could never obscure the view from him again. He wished he didn't have to blink either, so he could commit every moment to memory.

"I might see a therapist," said Henley, startling Li from his less-than-appropriate thoughts. "What's the risk? Right? I mean, unless they decide I should be committed, which is a possibility." He slowly swung his legs to the other side, groaning at the effort, which appeared seamless.

"Just be yourself," said Li distantly, not even sure if it was him talking. What was Henley even talking about?

Henley's cock dragged his thoughts right back down as it shifted from one side of his belly to the other like a pendulum as he moved. It was filling out, getting harder with every breath.

"Yeah, 'cause that always works out. Let's try that out and see what h-happens," said Henley, his voice stuttering with exhaustion. "Ask me how I feel."

"How do you feel?" Li parroted back, shaking his head as his cock throbbed.

"I feel like naked is best right now, because it might tempt you into chasing me through these woods and having your way," said Henley, grinning as he finally lowered his feet back to the ground. He stayed in a low crouch, his chest heaving as he wiped the sweat from his face. "What's your therapeutic advice on that?"

"You want me to..." Li trailed off as his mind blanked. "You said that you had to be the one in control." He pressed his palm to his covered cock, fighting the urge to pull it free.

"And maybe I need to let go." Henley traced a pattern on the forest floor of nonsense scribbles. "Maybe that's my problem. I'm just a control freak."

"Or you're just afraid of what would happen if you trusted someone," said Li, biting his tongue when his words came out harsher than he'd intended. He shook his head, trying to overcome his arousal. Shifting closer, he inhaled, the smell of sweat and man greeting him. His mouth watered.

"I *don't* trust anyone," said Henley, rolling his eyes. "It's basically the first rule of my job. Trust is a great way to exploit someone — even better than sex."

"That's fucked up, old man." And bleak. So very bleak. Not that Li was one to judge.

"What?" Henley snorted. "You're going to fall in love one day, marry a woman and have your two point five kids? Give me a break."

Well, that wasn't the plan *exactly*. Li had always hoped to have one child whom he could teach all the good and bad things about the world. Two always seemed like too much work, and what if he liked one more than the other?

But there was the woman factor. Would he want to be with a woman after being with Henley? He thought of breasts and slick, tight holes that weren't furled rings. He could see himself touching a woman again but doubted they would give him the same feeling as Henley did.

"Oh my God, that *is* your plan," said Henley, throwing back his head and laughing as he fell back on his ass. Leaves and dirt clung to his sweaty skin, instantly turning him into a filthy mess.

Was it bad that Li just wanted to get him dirtier? It was like something feral had awoken when he'd met Henley. The sex was...second to none, even if he was the one to end up with the sore ass.

"Are you telling me that you want me to force you?" asked Li, finally realizing what Henley had told him. A chase through the woods, and Li *having his way*, sounded a lot like something that tipped over the line of consent.

"Don't change the subject, but no. I want to give up control to you to see what would happen. We would both have safewords, and we both have to consent to it before we started. You need to be ready if I fight back, and don't stop unless I safeword. What I want is kinky sex, which is a completely different." Henley stared at Li as he spoke, his words like fire over Li's skin.

"Oh." What else was he supposed to even say to that. "When you always said to tell you to stop if I needed to…"

"That was me giving you a safeword," said Henley, letting out a sigh. "If I would have met you at a munch, or at the club, things would have been different. We would have negotiated and gone over limits and all the important stuff. But when I saw you and realized that you were on board, I skipped those steps and went straight for the good stuff."

Li imagined what he would have done if Henley would have started by discussing safewords on the roof that first night. Things would have gone very differently. He probably wouldn't be where he was.

"But I don't want one of us to get hurt," said Henley. "If my training kicks in and I break your neck, I'll never forgive myself." He let out a shudder.

Li raised one eyebrow, leaning back on his hands and trying to portray the picture of relaxation. "You seem to think that you'll be able to overpower me."

Henley might have been strong, but Li had more than a foot of height, fifty pounds of muscle and similar training as an advantage. He couldn't do naked yoga, but he could fight.

"I have. Twice, if I recall. More than that if we're counting every time." Henley gripped his hands into the soft earth, his fingertips disappearing under the top layer of soil.

"I let you." *Oops.* Li hadn't exactly meant to say that out loud. There were about a hundred other things he could have said without using those exact words. "If you don't believe me, come at me."

"I'm filthy...and sweaty," said Henley, wiping his hands down his legs and only smearing the dirt further. "You can't expect me to think that you let me win every time."

"You want it dirty and primal," said Li, a touch of a snarl creeping into his voice. Henley's cock twitched before his eyes, spurring him on. "I can make it even between us. You won't come out on top this time, and when you run, I'll catch you. I wouldn't want to be your ass when I do."

Li blinked. Where had that come from? Henley was rubbing off on him in more ways than one. Pushing his curiosity aside, he tugged at his jacket and shirt, lifting them over his head instead of bothering with the buttons. He hesitated on his pants as goosebumps crept over his skin. It was fucking cold.

"I'm terrified," said Henley, rolling his eyes, even as he moved into a crouch before perching on the balls of his feet. "But I can't deny that I'm enjoying the view. Please continue."

"You think I can't beat you?" asked Li, tugging his pants and boxers down in one go and cupping his cock briefly as the cold air made it throb.

"That's exactly what I think. It doesn't matter how strong you are if you are the one who wants to submit. You don't have the balls to fuck me," said Henley, his voice deadpan, but his words cutting.

"Asshole."

"Fucker." Henley's lips pulled into a grin. "Is it cold out or did you get circumcised while I wasn't looking?"

Rationally, Li knew what Henley was trying to do. If Henley excelled in one thing in life, it was goading people on. It didn't stop Li from closing the distance between them and striking out with an open hand, laying a slap across Henley's cheek that rang out like a gunshot.

A jay called in the woods, and a twig snapped nearby as some kind of animal took off at the noise. Henley tipped back on his ass, thudding onto the damp earth where dew still clung in tiny drops. He clutched his cheek where a red stain was already blooming.

"Enough. If you're not going to fight me, then I'll just take what I want," said Li, his mind gone and his cock throbbing in the cold air. Henley's eyes went wide, his pupils growing as his cock twitched.

When had negotiating ever worked for the two of them, anyway?

"What's your safeword?" asked Li, letting a second slap fly as Henley turned a glare on him.

"Red," said Henley, his eyes starting to mist as he clutched both cheeks. "What's yours, Listowel?" His voice quieted until it was barely a whisper.

Li mulled it over, trying to think of something that he wouldn't say while running around naked in the bush. There wasn't much that came to mind. "Red for me, too, I think. Now run, before I tear your ass up right here."

Henley dropped his hands, turning a fresh glare on Li. This time, when Li raised a hand to strike him, Henley caught his wrist, twisting Li's arm behind his back before he could blink.

Henley's cool, naked flesh slid against his as he scrambled faster than a spider monkey. Li's hole throbbed as Henley's cock dragged over his hip, so much hotter than the rest of Henley's skin. Even if he did lose, he would still win.

No, I'm not giving up. I can't let Henley keep thinking he's some kind of damaged goods that isn't worth anything to anybody.

Li rolled into Henley's momentum, using the momentary confusion to get his arm back under control. Wrapping his legs around one of Henley's thighs, he squeezed while tangling a hand in Henley's hair, pushing him to the ground so his back hit the forest floor with a thud.

"Anything off limits?" asked Li, already panting and throbbing so hard that he had to come in the next few minutes or he was going to die. Moving his knee up the inside Henley's thigh, he touched the bottom of his sac, pushing up until it squished softly. Henley let out a gasp, his cock dripping a line of pre-cum.

"Don't crush my balls." Henley struggled to try to get free, but Li was so much stronger.

"Same here. And tap out if you're going to pass out." Li tightened his grip, grabbing both of Henley's wrists and trapping them down by his sides. Leaning back, he dodged the headbutt that Henley sent his way as he growled and struggled for freedom.

"I'll give you a head start," said Li, waiting until Henley finally stilled, his chest heaving for air. "Three minutes before I find you. Better than your three days, and it should give you time to slick yourself up."

"I won't need to," said Henley, his struggles renewing until he almost bucked Li off completely.

Li gritted his teeth before forcing a grin onto his face. *This is going to be so much fun. Heterosexual life, sayonara.* "We'll see."

* * * *

Henley

There were so many reasons that it was a bad idea, but every one of them washed down the drain with each throb of his hard dick. It hurt more than expected to run flat out. All the bouncing and smacking sent pleasant and unpleasant zings through his groin with each bound.

But it slowed him down if he tried to cup his balls and cock to keep them from bouncing. At least Li would be faced with the same situation — maybe worse because he had that little something extra. An extra two inches long, an extra quarter inch wide and that bit of foreskin that made it look like there was a treasure hiding just out of sight. All that made for a very special something extra.

Why am I running? Henley slowed his pace, breathing hard as his lungs begged for air. His aches from his brief captivity had started to fade, but he had pushed his injured wrist a touch hard during inverted yoga. Ten years before he wouldn't have needed recovery time, but the speckles of gray in his hair begged to differ.

He gave his cock a soothing tug, wincing at the tender throb it gave from the contact. He shouldn't have been running at all. It wasn't like Li would ever win in a fight against him.

Henley fought dirty, and he was willing to use every trick he knew to come out on top in every way. Li's style was more clean-cut and straightforward, which was ironic for a bad guy. Henley would have to do a thorough search of the fucker's basement to see if he had an actual rule-list posted somewhere. He was definitely the type.

He was willing to admit that, for a split second when Li had pinned him to the forest floor in all his naked glory, he had felt helpless. He'd experienced every stage of grief within that second, and it had left his head spinning and his heart pounding.

Denial, then anger, because there was no way Li could have overpowered him. A bargain on his tongue had been trapped between his teeth. At last, he had gone lax with a sudden wave of powerless depression and finally acceptance.

The rage had come rushing back when Li had suggested that he slick himself up. That was *not* happening, because there was no way that Li's giant fucking cock was coming anywhere near his ass — not then, and not in the foreseeable future. Not unless Henley was the one that was lowering himself onto Li's cock, with Li's hands bound above his head and his eyes covered with a thick blindfold. Then...maybe.

Li was a confident little bastard when he wanted to be, though. He *had* rescued Henley and outsmarted him and a team of agents — but he was still a fucking kid with a gun.

Henley growled at himself as he picked up his pace again. If he'd been smart enough to grab some pants, then he could have climbed a tree. Instead, he was stuck watching each of his steps leave huge tracks in the thickly padded ground.

He stooped over, picking pine needles out from between his toes as they dug into him. He didn't exactly have calluses on his feet, mostly because he wore shoes like any sane person.

Li was not sane. He had proved that with his epic amount of paranoia that made Henley look like a Canadian farmer who'd never locked their front door.

Pausing, he leaned back against a tree, letting his head fall against the rough bark. His footsteps had left a clear trail through the forest, giving Li a path brighter than the yellow brick road.

He was naked, hot and a tad nervous. Not afraid — just nervous…and pissed off. He had to do something to get things back under his control before he let something happen that he wasn't sure he was ready for.

* * * *

Li

Henley couldn't have been that much of an idiot. Surprisingly, he had taken off into the forest, the pert globes of his ass taking Li's brain temporarily offline. How he had never noticed that he might have been gay before was a mystery. Maybe because he had never met someone quite like Henley.

And thinking about the other men he had met and imagining their naked asses did nothing for him. It really shouldn't have mattered, but it did. When you believed something about yourself for your entire life then realized that you were wrong, it made you wonder.

He followed at a more sedate pace, giving Henley exactly three minutes to get ahead. Stepping into the forest was like stepping into an entirely different frame of mind. Some of his confidence vanished as the light thinned to speckled shade. The air was closer between the trees, making it harder to breathe, despite the crispness.

And it was cold — ball-shriveling and erection-killing cold. Without the heat of Henley's body sliding along him, he was soft in minutes. No, not sliding — struggling. It had been the struggle that had turned him on, and the way that Henley had given in, even if it had just been for a second.

His cock gave a hesitant twitch before he cupped it in his cool palm. If he didn't get warmer, it wouldn't matter if he caught Henley or not.

But Henley was taking the challenge completely off the table. His footsteps were dark smears among light tan. It was like a beacon through the woods.

Li placed his feet over each mark, jogging in a few places where Henley's stride had lengthened. It was the only way he could properly hide his footsteps in the forest, and Henley had conveniently gifted that to him. *Worst secret agent* ever.

A fox startled in a nearby patch of undergrowth, darting across his path and turning up another layer of soil. Its red fur was bristled and thick as it let out a high yelp and took off. Pausing, he watched until it disappeared, and the silence settled over him again.

He had been walking for about ten minutes when the footsteps he'd been following came to an abrupt halt. Li paused, glancing around through the thick trees and even denser underbrush. There were few trails through the forest created by deer and other game cutting the same way over and over. If he had been fully clothed, he would have still hesitated before jumping into the brambles that lay just beyond where the steps had disappeared.

There had been no evidence that Henley had covered his tracks, and the trail was surrounded by mostly thorny bushes and raspberry plants that had already been picked clean by wildlife. *Henley wasn't insane enough to jump into that, was he?* The short and only answer was yes.

Li took a step back, looking up into the canopy of trees. The hairs on the back of his neck prickled as he spun in a circle, trying to spot his prey. The canopy was thick, but the bark on the trees was jagged and hard, not like the smooth paper of birch trees. He could imagine how much it would hurt to try to climb.

He shook his head. Henley was *not* his prey. What they were doing was sexy therapy...nothing more. His cock throbbed to life, disagreeing with him completely.

A branch snapped at the edge of his hearing, and he whirled toward the sound. Whatever it was sounded too small to be Henley. *Probably a red squirrel.* He had been caught off guard by them in the past because they didn't know the meaning of quiet.

But the feeling of being watched was still there, boring into the back of his neck and putting him on edge. Gritting his teeth, he did another slow revolution, looking for any signs of hidden tracks. There was nothing but a spiraling leaf that had already turned orange, fluttering to the ground before coming to its final resting place. His heart throbbed as his breathing picked up, every muscle going tense. His hand twitched for a weapon.

It was starting to feel like he was becoming the prey. He grabbed for his collar, twining it between his fingers and tracing over the paw print like he had a hundred times over the last few weeks. Something inside him immediately settled, the terror slipping away to fear.

Taking another step back, he shrieked as something brushed against his ankle. He sidestepped frantically, reaching for his ankle and swiping at it. A spider hit the ground, skittering away from his stomping feet and into the undergrowth.

He couldn't stop his second scream when something warm and hard grabbed his ankle a moment later, pulling and sending him to the ground in a burst of air.

Henley emerged from beneath the brambles like some kind of camouflaged God, dirt and leaves clinging to his hair and his cheeks smudged with blood from a few tiny cuts. His eyes were narrowed as he lunged at Li, landing on him and going straight for his neck.

There was no playfulness this time — only intent. Li's ass throbbed in protest as he thought of taking Henley dry if he were overpowered.

It wouldn't matter. Henley wasn't going to win.

Li grabbed the arm at his throat, digging his fingers into the sensitive nerves before sliding a leg between their bodies and kicking Henley off him. Henley landed at the edge of a bush a few feet away, a snarl on his lips and his eyes practically glowing with rage.

"I won't be fucked by a guy who is afraid of *spiders*," said Henley, his words the first sign that he hadn't turned into some feral beast.

Li would have laughed if it weren't his ass on the line. Instead, he shot his fist out with a hit that would have been enough to knock the wind out of Henley's body if he hadn't rolled away. Li dropped to one knee as the miss put him off balance, his back exposed.

Henley leaped, tackling him to the ground and pushing his face into the dirt until pine and earth were the only things he could smell. Henley's warm cock dragged over his ass, dipping between his cheeks like a threat.

Bucking with all his strength, Li reversed their positions, ignoring the elbow that slammed into his solar plexus, stealing his breath. He didn't need to breathe to win. Pushing Henley's legs wide and sliding between them, he lined his cock up to the puckered hole that he had dreamed about, nudging his weeping cock against the resistance.

Henley let out an inhuman howl at the touch, kicking and flailing in panic. Li caught a fist to his chin that sent his head snapping back and the follow-up to his ribs that had his bones creaking.

Licking the blood from his lips, Li put everything he had into the fight, his limbs growing heavy as his breath refused to fully fill his lungs. Henley looked like a wild, deranged beast, gnashing his teeth and carving into Li's skin with his blunt nails.

Li had never been so alive. Every nerve was on fire, his focus so precise that he could see each move before Henley made it. The air misted between them, sweat dripping from his body and soaking their skin. The cold couldn't touch him anymore.

Finally, he pinned Henley to the ground face-first, his wrists captured in one hand and his legs pinned under Li's own. Henley arched his back, trying to headbutt him, but Li was too quick. He grabbed the back of Henley's head, pressing his cheek into the earth until Henley let out a low groan.

Is Henley as hard as I am right now? He didn't have a free hand to reach down and check. He didn't have a free anything in that moment to help guide his cock into Henley's hole.

Sweat slicked between them, their bodies steaming in the cool air and mingling with their frantic breaths. And Henley still struggled in denial that Li had won. Every writhe was perfection and only made the heat blaze between them, until it was an inferno.

Li did the only thing he could think of to stop his struggling Dom. He lowered his mouth to Henley's shoulder and sank his teeth into the pale, scarred flesh.

Li's jaw ached as he ground his teeth hard into Henley's skin—so hard that he wondered if he would leave a scar that would mingle with the rest on Henley's body. Each scar was a hard-won lesson, and the one from Li's teeth would be as well.

You lose.

Henley let out a sound that sent a shiver down Li's spine. But it wasn't a 'stop' or 'red'. His cock slipped between Henley's cheeks, lubricated with sweat and pre-cum alone.

"This will hurt," Li snarled, bucking his hips and driving the head of his cock through the tight ring of Henley's ass.

It was so fucking tight that Li didn't think he would be able to push deeper. He tugged himself free as Henley gave another wail. He needed more to slick the way. "Be good." He released Henley's head, spitting on his hand and slicking his cock. He did it again, his spit already drying and cooling on his heated flesh. "Good boy."

He lined his cock up, grabbing the back of Henley's head because he didn't trust Henley not to try to fight him. With a hard push, he breached the ring for a second time, sliding all the way to the base with one slow thrust.

He could guess how much it would have hurt. Being fucked, even after being opened up properly, still stung something fierce, so it had to have been so much worse. Henley had to feel like he was splitting apart as Li drove in deep, his body forced to accept something that terrified him.

"Tell me to stop and I'll stop," said Li, biting at Henley's ear as he rocked his hips and gave Henley a few seconds to adjust.

"Don't stop." Henley pushed against him, his ass sucking in Li's cock like it was made for him. Henley arched his back, his body taut as he whimpered. "Please don't stop. Fuck me harder, Listowel."

Li growled, biting down until Henley let out a whimper and stilled his hips. "The only thing you have control over is if I stop or not. You can't tell me how fast or how deep. I'll fuck you how I like, and you'll enjoy every minute of it because you know it will make me happy."

Li was starting to get a bit concerned about himself. This person—this beast—wasn't him. It was coming from somewhere deep inside that had been buried for his entire life. It surged through him, taking control of his limbs and his cock.

Henley writhed, his chest heaving as he tried to kick out. There was nowhere for him to go.

Letting go of Henley's wrists, Li grabbed his hips instead, lifting him to his knees and thrusting into his ass hard and fast. Henley didn't struggle, despite the moans that made it clear that it wasn't all pleasure he was feeling. Li couldn't stop. The only thing that would have stopped him was Henley's safeword. Nothing else was going to keep him from coming in Henley's ass.

"Fucking take it," Li growled, biting his lip as he looked down and pulled Henley's ass cheeks wide with his thumbs. Henley's hole clutched his cock like a lifeline, each slide more of a drag than anything slick. His rim was already reddened and a bit puffy, getting worse with every thrust.

Li spit, aiming for the spot that his cock disappeared over and over. The beast in him roared, ready to come, his balls drawing up tight. But he couldn't be the first one. In fact, he wasn't even sure if Henley was hard.

"Come right now, Henley," said Li, leaning forward to change the angle so his cock would drag over Henley's prostate. He reached around Henley's hip, ready to grasp his cock and bring him to his peak.

He didn't need to. With a cry that startled a few birds, Henley came, his cock painting Li's hand and his hole clamping down so tight that Li could scarcely move. With all his strength, he pushed his way through the resistance, burying himself deep one last time before coming like a freight train.

He caught himself on his hands, panting so hard that he was nearly choking on his own breath. Henley was in a similar state beneath him, his cheek pressed to the forest floor and his legs trembling to the same rhythm as his fluttering hole.

Li eased his way out, wincing as he caught a glimpse of Henley's reddened hole. Gripping his shoulder, he rolled Henley over onto his back, cupping his cheek gently and running a finger over his lower lip. "You did so good for me."

Henley let out a sob, his eyes brimming with tears as he crumpled in on himself. Li caught him as the first tears tipped onto his cheeks, dragging Henley to his chest as he rested his back against a tree.

Combing through Henley's hair, he pulled him even closer until there was no room left between them. "You did so good." He whispered the same words over and over as Henley went limp, his sobs cutting through the silence of the forest.

The truth was, Henley wasn't the only one who was trembling. Li had come face-to-face with a beast that apparently lived inside his body. It must've been lurking there for his entire life, ready to pop out at the right time. It wasn't the same thing that appeared every time he killed. This was different, and at the other side of a huge spectrum.

Henley gripped Li's collar, tugging it repeatedly as his crying started to wind down. He sniffed, wiping his eyes with the back of his hand before he slowly started to pull away. Li cradled him close, not even close to being ready to let him go. He wasn't sure if he would ever be ready.

"My ass is killing me," said Henley, a small chuckle following his words.

"I'm sorry," Li whispered, lowering his face into Henley's hair and taking a breath. "I didn't mean to hurt you." Rubbing his hand down Henley's spine, he trailed to his soft and gaping hole. It was wet and tacky with dried cum, still so open and warm. He couldn't help but push one finger back inside, shuddering at Henley's gasp.

Tilting Henley's chin, Li brought their lips together, his trembles growing fierce as Henley stayed soft and pliant beneath him, giving him everything he wanted.

Only...he didn't want it anymore. He wanted Henley's arms around him, telling him that everything was going to be okay and that he wasn't a monster. He needed Henley mumbling about something dirty in the next moment to break the tension that gripped his chest like a vise. He wanted Henley to pull on his collar until he choked, before shoving him down and fucking into him in the same way that Li had done to him.

"I'm so sorry," said Li as he pulled back, the first hint of tears gathering in his eyes.

"Pup, don't," said Henley, sliding his hands along Li's chin. "You gave me everything that I ever imagined. You blew my fucking mind, broke me and put the pieces back together again. You made me feel something that I never thought I could."

"Was I okay?" asked Li. Henley's praise meant nothing if he wasn't good. His stomach twisted, until Henley's lips turned up into a smile.

"You were perfect, pup. Now let's go get cleaned up. No promises that I don't fuck you in the shower." Henley tapped Li's cheek, drumming with his fingertips before he pulled back.

"Please do."

Chapter Sixteen

Henley

Henley scrubbed every inch of Li and himself, avoiding his own hole because it hurt like a motherfucker. He should have known and at least prepped himself. Past Henley was a dick. He'd never thought of future Henley's comfort.

Li stared at the tiled shower wall as Henley scrubbed down his chest, taking extra time on the long diagonal scratch across Li's pec. Henley was pretty sure that it was from his nails, or one of the freaking raspberry bushes that had fucked up his own back.

Li had withdrawn when they'd entered the cabin, and he hadn't said a word since they'd stepped into the basement. His eyes were half-shut, his chin tucked as he stared at the floor as if he were completely lost.

It seemed that the cost of Henley's revelation was Li's spiral. And he couldn't have that. Li was still his sub, even if he had just Dommed the fuck out of him, showing a side that had shocked Henley and his ass.

He was Henley's sub and his pup, even if Li was still a bit in denial about that.

"Tell me your favorite part about what just happened," said Henley, smoothing his soapy hands up Li's thighs before cupping his cock. He filled out quickly under the stimulation, his shaft plumping and going rigid under Henley's fingers.

"I... I don't know," said Li after a long pause. He braced himself against the tile, pressing his forehead to it before letting out a long breath.

"You want to know my favorite part?" asked Henley, grinning despite Li's lack of a reaction. He leaned in close, lowering his voice. "When you told me that it was going to hurt a second before you rammed inside me." Even thinking about it made his very tired cock twitch. The slamming part wasn't what made him shudder, but the brutal warning and the growl that had been in Li's voice was.

"What?" Li blinked, finally focusing and turning his head toward Henley. "Didn't it hurt?"

"Well, yeah, obviously." His ass was literally on fire, especially with the warm water trickling down his crack. "But that was, by far, the hottest sex I have ever had. You were amazing. No—amazing isn't a strong enough word. You were catastrophically orgasmic."

"But—"

Henley cut Li off by bringing their lips together. Where was Li's infamous confidence? He had to be dropping pretty fucking hard.

"Kiss me back," said Henley as he pulled away for just a moment before diving back up for a second kiss. It only took a few seconds before Li started to respond, sluggishly moving their tongues together to share their taste. Henley threaded his hand through Li's hair, rocking up on his toes.

Li was too damn tall to do it right in the shower. Shutting off the water and bypassing the towels, he led Li through the cabin and up the stairs to the bedroom. The blankets were still rumpled from earlier, Li apparently having followed him right out of the door in search of him instead of making the bed.

Henley wasn't sure what his plan had been when he'd woken up in bed early with Li slumbering beside him. The blissful innocence on Li's face as he'd dreamed had torn Henley in two. It was too bad that he hadn't gotten away fast enough to outrun his feelings.

Li followed him like a dazed zombie, his gaze never leaving the ground while he gnawed at his lower lip the entire time. He looked so fucking broken that it pulled at Henley's heartstrings like no one ever had.

As a Dom, he'd always wanted to push people far past what they thought they could do, but he'd never wanted to break someone and watch them crash and burn. It grated on everything that made him a person and not a monster.

Pushing Li down to the bed, Henley straddled his hips, suppressing his flinch when Li's cock brushed against his sore ass. *This is gonna hurt.*

He pulled open the side drawer — the place where everyone in the world kept their most secret sex toys — unless they had a dungeon. *Fuck, I have to convince Li to turn one of his secret rooms into a dungeon.*

He'd expected lube, which he found, but there was something else nestled in the drawer that he hadn't expected. It showed how far under Li was when he didn't react as Henley pulled the tail-plug out of the drawer. If he wasn't mistaken, Li had actually taken the time to brush out the hair, keeping it neat and pristine. It had looked a bit roughed up by the time they had been done playing in the hotel room, but now it looked brand new again.

Some subs needed cuddles and reassurance if they crashed, but others despised them. Henley knew he was taking a gamble, but he didn't have a choice.

Setting both items on the bed, Henley grabbed Li's collar, twisting until the chain cut off his breath. Li blinked, his eyes going wide as they focused on Henley. Red creeped up Li's neck and face as he choked, but he never lifted his hands and never resisted.

Henley relaxed his grip with a sigh, his cock throbbing at Li's gasps. "So fucking perfect." Mid-breath, he cut Li's airway off again, pushing him a tad longer, until a hint of purple started to swirl with the red. Only then did he release the collar a second time, waiting as Li dragged in huge breaths tinged with wracking coughs.

"Do you like that?" asked Henley as he dragged his ass over Li's cock, letting the pain mingle with the pleasure. Li nodded, his eyes cloudy with something other than denial and fear.

Henley had never seen someone slip so easily from a drop to subspace, but the transition was nearly seamless.

"Answer me." Henley tugged at the collar, bringing Li's focus back. He could slip away soon, but not yet.

"What?" Li asked, blinking slowly. Li brought his hand up to touch the red line across his neck where the collar had dug into him.

"Do you like it when I choke you? When I control everything about you, including whether or not you get to breathe?" Henley fisted his cock, spreading the bead of pre-cum down his shaft.

"Are you going to take your revenge now?" asked Li slowly, avoiding the question completely. *Now that just won't do.*

Henley backhanded Li across the face, the slap ringing out in the bedroom as Li's head was flung to the side. Li's cock flexed, wetness painting Henley's ass. It hadn't been a hard hit, but it would still sting.

"I like it," said Li, cupping his cheek.

"Hands down," Henley growled, twisting the collar again and holding it until Li started bucking beneath him. Li dropped his hands to his sides, even as he choked and Henley released the pressure as a reward. "Now breathe for me, pup, and tell me what you want. Tell me what you liked."

Li fluttered his eyes shut, shaking his head as tears gathered on his eyelashes. He was at Henley's mercy in every sense, and Henley had never been more turned on.

"Spread your legs for me," said Henley as he lowered himself between them, sucking bruises into the soft skin of Li's thighs. Li had hardly any hair there, just like his chest that was smoother than most men's. It made Li insanely kissable when he didn't have to pause to pluck a hair off his tongue.

Dragging his finger down Li's cock, he teased at the seam of his sac before dropping even lower. Li tensed as Henley brushed against his rim with a dry finger. *Finally, a real reaction.*

"Are you afraid I'll hurt you?" asked Henley, rubbing his knuckle over Li's hole over and over. It fluttered against him, so tight and longing to be split open.

Li shook his head, blinking as a few tears trickled down his cheeks. "I deserve it for what I did."

Oh, so that's what this is about. He was going about this the wrong way. Guilt twisted his gut, but he shook it off. He couldn't let himself get dragged down while Li needed him.

"Last time I checked, you belong to me, Listowel. I'll decide what you deserve." Henley tugged at Li's collar for good measure before grabbing for the lube bottle and slicking up a finger.

Li let out a tiny shudder as Henley traced his rim with a slippery finger before slowly pressing inside. He moved leisurely, teasing and stroking Li's molten walls until his furl finally relaxed, letting him inside another inch. "That's right, baby. Let me in. So fucking good for me." He let the endearment slip, keeping his gaze on Li's face and smiling as Li's eye twitched with the first sign of annoyance.

Tracing over Li's prostate, Henley slowly took him apart, only moving to two fingers when Li was dripping so much that there was a pool of pre-cum on his belly. Li was jerking and moaning, his hands fisted in the sheets as if he were trying to hold on and keep from coming.

Withdrawing, Henley grabbed the plug before lining it up with Li's hole and slowly easing it in. He teased Li's hole with the widest part before letting him suck it inside, his hole clinging to it, despite the prep. Henley tugged the tail, groaning aloud as Li clamped down to keep it inside.

"There's a good pup. You hold on to your tail for me." He tugged it again, teasing Li's entrance from the inside before releasing it and watching it settle itself deep again. From Li's twitch, it must've settled with the tip against his prostate.

Too bad it didn't vibrate. *I'll have to look into that.*

Henley crawled up Li's body, bringing their lips together as he traced Li's shoulders and chest with his hands. Li surged against him, a passion that was barely restrained by Henley's own strength.

There was his boy, his pup—the one he had fallen in love with. *Fuck.*

He reached for the lube again, slicking up his own hole with a wince before smoothing a generous layer down Li's cock. Finally pulling away from the kiss, he reached back and tugged Li's tail again, his cock throbbing as Li managed to hold on to it.

"Roll me over, Listowel. Put me on my front with my ass in the air for you." Henley landed in the middle of the bed with an *oompf* a moment later, his face in the sheets and his ass waving back and forth like a flag.

"Get up here, buddy," said Henley, slapping his own ass before dragging a finger over his slick hole. Hopefully it was slick enough. Or maybe he should have been more hopeful that Li was as worked up as he was and wouldn't last long. All the lube in the world wasn't going to make it hurt any less.

The sound of Li's snort had Henley grinning and looking over his shoulder.

"I'm not a dog."

"I have a collar and a tail that says otherwise. Now get up here, pup. I won't ask you again." Henley tapped his ass again, spreading his legs to make a more inviting target. Li moved close on his knees, grabbing Henley's hips.

"Pups don't have hands," said Henley, wiggling his ass again. When Li hesitated, Henley reached back and tugged at his collar, dragging him down onto his back. He was a heavy motherfucker when he wasn't supporting his own weight.

Li's cock brushed against his hole and Henley let out a gasp that tapered off to a groan. Li was able to touch the bed with his hands because his frame was that much larger, and he had curled his hands into fists. *Good, pup.*

Squirming his ass, Henley tried to find the tip of Li's cock by feel alone, longing to get stretched wide. The softness of Li's tail brushed against the inside of his leg as he moved, and he let out a shudder.

"Come on, pup. Fuck me good."

Li reached for his own cock, probably to guide himself into Henley's hole. Henley shot his hand back, landing an open-palmed slap to the side of Li's ass. "Pups don't have hands. Now fuck me."

Li dropped his hand back to the bed, letting out a whine as he tried to hump his way into Henley's hole. The rough friction and the primal seeking of a tight hole to fuck had Henley shooting higher and higher. The chase in the woods had introduced him to Li's beast, but this was his domesticated pup, who was ready to please and do as Henley commanded.

"Fuck, yeah, good boy," said Henley as Li's cock caught, only to slip down the seam of his ass. Did Li even realize that he had let out another pitiful whine, his tail tickling Henley's thigh as his movements became more frantic? Li was probably desperate with his need to both please Henley and ease the ache of his cock.

"Come on, buddy. Fuck your Master."

Li's cock caught, and with one frantically brutal thrust, he buried himself inside. Li seemed to be lost, unable to even give Henley time to adjust while fucking into him immediately like a rabid animal. The ache was fierce, dragging up Henley's spine and pinpointing at his hole, but the pleasure was so much better.

If I could do this every day for the rest of my life…

Henley blinked back the tears that threatened, throwing himself back into the moment. He would have to find a way to make that a reality.

Li let out a growl as his pace increased, fisting his hands in the blankets beneath them and throwing Henley off balance with the power of his thrusts. His cock slammed into Henley's prostate over and over until he had no choice but to come.

His body clamped down on Li's cock, milking him like a good bitch as he painted the sheets with his cum. Li let out a loud groan, fixing his teeth on Henley's shoulder as he fucked himself deeper and deeper. Li came moments later, finally stilling as his cock twitched and flexed.

Henley grabbed his hip when he felt Li start to pull back. "Good pups keep their cock inside until they know their Master is bred." *Holy fuck.* If anyone could see him now — the badass Dom who never had a repeat performance, getting fucked without a condom and asking to be *bred*.

"Henley," said Li, whispering against his ear. He sounded so calm, but so overwhelmed.

"Yeah?" Henley asked, flexing around Li's cock just because he could.

"That was my favorite part."

Chapter Seventeen

Li

Sex would never be the same again. Coming like that, with a plug in his ass that tickled his prostate and humping like some kind of animal was the definition of insanity. He couldn't even feel guilty if he tried. All that was…gone, as if it had never been there. With each *good boy*, it had drained out of him, filling him with something else instead.

Cradling Henley against him, Li let out a long breath. Henley had collapsed on his front and Li had dragged them together on their sides so he didn't crush him.

His cock had gone from oversensitive and back to hard again, still encased in Henley's tight hole. He humped just the tiniest bit as he swelled, Henley's whimpers making him more turned on. How far could he even go before Henley finally told him to stop? He had to be sore. His hole was so red and swollen that Li wasn't sure how he could stand it.

Could he endure the same thing for Henley? *In a heartbeat.*

"You okay?" asked Li quietly, unsure if it was okay to leave his role behind and don his human hat once more.

"So good," said Henley, his voice slurred with satisfaction. He was probably lying in a wet spot, but he didn't seem to care.

"Not sore?" asked Li, unable to stop himself from pulling out an inch and driving back in. Henley gasped, tightening his grip on Li's arm.

"So fucking sore. I think you need a dick reduction, because holy fuck that hurt." Henley grabbed his ass when Li started to pull away. "I didn't say to pull out. You're going to stay inside me until you come again…maybe twice."

Li buried his face in Henley's hair, letting out a long groan at the image. Henley wanted him to fuck his ass full. Cum was already dribbling down his cock, slicking the way as the lube started to dry. It wasn't as gross as he had expected.

"I don't know if I can come again so soon," said Li. He was twenty-six, with a healthy sex drive that had never left any partner wanting before. But three was pushing it…and four? Was he supposed to be some kind of God?

"I have a hard cock in my ass that says otherwise." Henley chuckled, his whole-body trembling. "Here's the deal. If you can't come again in three minutes, then I get my guns back—both of them. And my fanny pack. I know you stole it."

Li rolled his eyes, sinking into the bed and dragging Henley closer. He trailed his fingers down Henley's sides, reveling at the goosebumps that followed in his wake.

"Time has already started, fucker," said Henley, shooting him a grin over his shoulder.

Of all of Henley's pet names for him, that was probably his favorite. Maybe he was just a masochist.

Rolling on top of Henley, he slammed his hips down, going as fast as his tired muscles would go. Every part of him burned and ached, but the throb of his cock pushed him on faster, deeper and harder. Henley's little gasps spurred him on that much more until he was worried he would float away.

"Thirty seconds left," said Henley, choking out the words as Li picked up his pace. His chest heaved, his heart pounding in time with his cock. He was so close, but his earlier orgasms were pushing his stamina further. He wasn't going to make it.

"Time, fucker," snarled Henley, looping an arm over Li's neck and dragging him down to the bed. Li's cock slid out with a pop and a gasp, cool air coating the cum-slicked shaft. Henley kept pushing him, until his back met the mattress and his cock waved in the air.

Taking a deep breath, Henley lowered his mouth onto Li's cock, taking him all the way to the back of his throat and a little bit beyond. His tight throat convulsed, and his hand dropped to Li's sac, cupping his balls. At the same time, his tongue swept out, licking the cum from the surface of Li's cock.

It was so fucking dirty, deranged and too fucking much. Li came, his balls aching from the force of his orgasm that drained down Henley's throat. Gripping Henley's hair, Li pulled him closer, until his nose touched his trimmed curls.

Henley pulled back with a gasp that turned into a laugh and a grin so wide that it was addictive. "I get my guns back, and I got to taste you, too. I didn't know it was buy-one-get-one-free day."

"You are unbelievable," said Li, shoving Henley back as he came in for a kiss. "As hot as it was to see you like that, I'd rather you brushed your teeth before our next kiss."

Henley licked his lips with a satisfied hum. "Delicious. Ten out of ten, would go down on you again."

Li laughed, running a hand down Henley's body and cupping his ass. Sex had never been so fun before. Nothing ever had.

"So gross. My dick was in your ass like three seconds ago." Li shoved Henley away again as he tried to swoop in for another kiss.

"You love me anyway," said Henley, rolling off the bed with a giggle.

Li snorted. "Yep." *Where are my pants?* Hell, where were any of the clothes he had been wearing? Probably still outside getting picked over by the crows. Henley must've left his stuff in the cabin somewhere, because he had already been naked when Li had found him outside.

Li looked up, tilting his head to the side when he saw Henley frozen in the doorway at the top of the stairs. He had the strangest look on his face, and his mouth was hanging open.

Looking down at his chest, Li swiped at a bit of dirt, only to realize it was a bruise with a bit of dried blood. Was there something on his face? The tail-plug was still in his ass, reminding him of it with every movement, but he couldn't see anything else out of place. He reached for his collar, letting out a breath when it was still there.

"I'm glad the feeling's mutual," said Henley, turning and stepping down the stairs and out of sight.

The feeling? Oh crap. Butterflies erupted in his belly, dancing and whirling to the point that he thought he was going to puke. He had let it slip. Just like that. *Idiot.*

Falling back on the bed, he let out a sigh. That had to have been the least romantic declaration in the history of mankind.

"Hurry up. I want my gun!"

Li scrambled from the bed at Henley's shout. Removing the plug carefully, he grabbed a fresh pair of pants and T-shirt from the dresser, and a second clean pair for Henley. Tossing them Henley's way at the bottom of the stairs, Li strolled over to the keypad in the basement, typing in a ten-digit code. On the other side of the bathroom, a panel opened to reveal his collection of weaponry.

There were a few that he had never even used, but for the most part, they were well-loved. More than one had saved his life, and most of them had taken a few. He wondered how many lives Henley's original piece had taken.

"All the sunshine and rainbows were messing with my collection anyway," said Li, grabbing the handgun with the rainbow sticker on the butt first and checking automatically to make sure it was empty. Henley crept in beside him, skimming his fingers over his rifle that had taken Damien out.

"You need more color in here," said Henley. He had pulled the clothing on at some point, but there were a few places where the fabric was sticking to his skin. So much for clean clothes. "Just because it's for killing doesn't mean it can't look fabulous."

Li gave Henley a look up and down. Something was wrong. The words were exactly like something that Henley would say, but his attitude was *off*. His lips were pressed into a line and his stare was so much more intense than it should have been.

Probably because Li had just accidentally told him that he was in *love*.

"I prefer safe and shiny," said Li, grabbing Henley's second gun and passing it over. Hesitating briefly over the fanny pack, he pulled it off the bottom shelf. "Your clips are in there."

Li's heart rate picked up as Henley opened the zip, peering into the pack with a smile that didn't reach his eyes. When he touched one of the clips, his grip changed on his gun as he brought it before him.

Li took a step back, a surge of fear barreling into him.

"Two mistakes, Listowel," said Henley as he snapped a clip into his gun before raising the barrel to point it at Li's forehead. "You let your guard down, and you missed this." He tugged a condom from the fanny pack, squeezing it between his fingers.

"A condom?" asked Li, taking another step back. "I'm sorry. I should have asked, but we were in the middle of the forest, Henley. How was I supposed to have a condom?"

Henley hadn't called his safeword, had he? Li thought back to every moment in the forest, then the following moments in the bedroom. The only thing amiss had been his accidental declaration.

A frown tugged at Henley's lips as his eyes went dark. His smile was gone, his face blank like a sheet of drywall before it was touched by paint. "It's not a condom. It's a tracker, and it's strong enough that they can detect it from the center of the fucking planet." He squished the package again and Li heard a small click snap through the air. "They'll be here in five minutes."

* * * *

Henley

Betrayal.

Pure fucking betrayal and shock were the only things on Li's face.

Henley had seen Li's fear as soon as he had reached for the clip with his pink fucking bullets, and he'd swallowed the lump in his throat. Everything in him begged him to lower the gun and let Li go, but he couldn't. He was an agent, and it was his job.

It wasn't his job to fall in love or fuck anybody before he arrested them. He was probably supposed to do the opposite, actually. But Li had broken down every fucking wall he had around his heart and soul.

"I don't have a choice," said Henley, biting his lip when Li's eyes went glassy. He longed to pull his sub close and comfort him, but he couldn't. "Get up the stairs now, unless you want them to find this place, too."

Li turned his back, slowly marching up the stairs, his feet scraping on every single one. His slumped his shoulders as he walked, his head low as he continued until he was standing outside of the cabin, the doors shut behind them.

If Henley hadn't broken him before, he had now. Li's breath was staggered, everything stiff as he looked around the trees. His hidden surveillance cameras wouldn't help him with a gun three feet from the back of his head. Henley had found every single camera as Li had slept on in bed, disabling them all in case his team jumped the gun.

Li had been so distracted that he hadn't even noticed. That had been Henley's fault, too.

The distant sound of a chopper was getting steadily closer, ripping through the trees and decimating the peace that had remained for the last precious hours of their time together.

For Henley, it had been like watching sand creep out of a broken hourglass, knowing that it was never going to turn. He wished he could have had the naïve innocence of Li as their time together came to a close. He'd given everything to his sub and had taken everything he could get, because he knew their time was done.

The love part, he hadn't expected.

Every beat of the copter cut straight through Henley's chest, until he felt like the one who was breaking inside. People always looked up when they heard a helicopter in the sky, but he just wanted to bury his head in the leaves and hope that it never arrived.

His mouth went dry, his hand shaking as he tried to keep the gun steady.

"This was a mistake," said Henley, looking down at the tracker still clutched in his palm. He pulled the foil back. It was small for all its power, the small red light the only indication that it had been activated.

There was more in the packet than just a tracker, though, mostly because he was a paranoid son of a bitch. He pulled the second chip free, making sure he hadn't accidentally damaged it. Even Shelia didn't know about the second one.

"Was it all a ruse?" asked Li as he looked off into the forest. He didn't even notice that Henley had faltered, his grip on his weapon going soft. "Was the mistake meeting me, or pushing me into your trap with your cock in my ass?"

That was *ouch*. Too true — and it fucking hurt.

"Most of it was real," said Henley, slipping his gun into his pants' pocket. The cuffs dragged on the ground, and the waist barely clung to his hips with the drawstring pulled all the way tight. "You should have killed me when you had the chance."

Crossing his arms, Li turned and leaned against the cabin, the picture of relaxation except for the set of his jaw. His eyes were wide and wet, his chest still heaving with every breath. "There's still time."

Pulling the gun from his pocket, Henley tossed it so it landed at Li's feet, the barrel facing off into the trees. The rainbow sticker smudged through the dirt, the ever-present sparkles dulling for the first time. "I wasn't built for retirement, anyway. This is my last job, so it might as well be my last day."

Li toed at the gun, turning it until the barrel faced toward Henley. "You need therapy…desperately."

The helicopter whirled closer, leaves falling from the trees en masse as the wind picked up. Every color streamed down around them, but neither of them moved.

Henley snorted, tilting his head back to catch sight of the bird overhead. "Somebody I love keeps telling me that. If you aren't going to kill me, can I at least get one last kiss?"

To feel Li again was a risk he was willing to take. He couldn't leave without one last touch, even if it meant a bullet in his brain. The choice was Li's, as it had always been. Slipping the concealed chip into his mouth, he threw his life away for love.

Crossing the distance, Henley leaned into Li's body, dragging him down until their lips crashed together. Li should have resisted, but he melted like he always did, submitting to him and whimpering for more.

He thrust his tongue into Li's mouth, holding him by the collar when he tried to pull away in confusion. *Here's a little more than my tongue.*

They kissed until the propellers hovered above them, the wind sucking the groan from Li's lips as Henley pulled back. His pup was flushed, tears streaming down his face and his eyes bleak and red. He was the most beautiful thing in the world, and he belonged to Henley, even in the moment when he was ready to give him up forever.

An agent dropped behind them with a thump, a rope snaking across the ground as it was released. Two more followed, red dots appearing on Li's forehead as they trained their weapons on him.

Henley had to hold himself back from reaching for the gun between them and taking the agents out as Li gave him one last desperate look. His chest tightened and he struggled not to look away.

"Catch you on the flip side, pup," he said, leaning close one last time to speak into Li's ear over the sound of the chopper. "I've always wanted to go to Mexico. There's an adult's only resort on the Riviera that's just calling my name." Henley backed away as the agents surrounded them, sending Li a wink as he raised his arms over his head.

Li's takedown was the most anticlimactic in history. He was bound, blindfolded, searched and hefted onto the copter without any resistance on his part, although

Henley had to stop himself from reaching out over a dozen times.

He let out a breath as the helicopter sped off, leaving two agents behind with their guns still cocked. They looked to each other as if they were assessing if Henley was a threat or not. He still wasn't sure himself.

Tensall peeled off his mask, strolling up to Henley and laying a hand on his shoulder. The dark paint under his eyes made him look older than he actually was. He was too young for the job, with a wife and kids on another continent who he rarely got to see. Henley knew how much it hurt him to be away from his family, but there was nothing he could do.

"I knew you'd come through, Harris," he said. "And what's the expression? Two birds, one stone? How did you know he would come for you, though?" His hand was impossibly heavy on Henley's shoulder.

Did I do the right thing by dragging Li through all this? He closed his eyes, letting out a shuddering breath. He shrugged Tensall's hand off his shoulder before looking around.

"There isn't much to this place, so I think it was just a safe house. He brought back our meals, but he didn't let me leave the cabin." He toed his way around the cabin ahead of Tensall, sliding Li's clothes out of view before they could see them. He didn't need any more unanswered questions than there already were. As far as they knew, he had been a prisoner.

"Yeah, our aerial shots say the same thing. You'd think a hot shot like him would have a bit more than a hunting cabin." Tensall peered up at the retreating helicopter, cupping his hand to shield his face from the sun which shone through the stripped trees with a new vengeance. "Oh, before I forget. The boss wants a word." He tossed a phone to Henley, who caught it one-handed.

His ass twinged as he leaned against the cabin, resting on the lip of a slightly larger log. Dialing the saved number on the unfamiliar phone, he brought it to his ear, waiting for the sound of the line connecting.

"I quit," he said into the silence.

Tensall jerked beside him, his eyes going wide. *Oh, to be young again.* He snapped the phone shut, tossing it back to Tensall. "Take care of Shelia for me, and hugs to Kira and Jess. They all need a strapping man like you to watch out for them."

Finally, he was free. If only it hadn't cost him everything.

Chapter Eighteen

Henley

Henley reclined the lounger, spreading his toes as the sun slowly turned them a deep pink. The sandal tan lines from his first day at the resort had to go as soon as possible, even if he roasted his toes a bit too much. After a hefty sunburn and a round of peeling skin, he had donned enough sunscreen to make any mother proud.

A waft of salty air brushed against his face, combined with the light scent of chlorine from the pools and coconut that always seemed to linger in the best places. He wasn't exactly sure why there were seven pools when the ocean was twenty steps away, but he certainly wasn't going to complain. He'd dipped his toes in every single one since he'd arrived. It had been a tossup, but in the end, the lazy river had lost.

Instead, he found a pool that was lost in a maze of manicured bushes. The first reason he loved it was that it was quiet and away from the steady beat of the music at the main pool. He didn't mind the music, but the occasional siren mixed into a trendy pop song never failed to put him on edge.

The second reason was the view. Nestled beneath the palm fronds and tiny huts where lizards scampered and caught ants beneath the shade, there was a group of vacationers who had caught his eye and then some. At least two of them were straight, if their girlfriends were to be believed, but that didn't mean that Henley couldn't enjoy the view. All those tanned and glistening muscles were worth a bit of sunburn.

"Is this seat taken?"

Henley glanced up to see an older gentleman motioning at the lounger beside him. He was in decent shape, with chest hair that was sprinkled with gray, and a faded tattoo that was more green than black. Too bad he was just an inch or two more than Henley's height, and about twenty pounds short on muscle.

"I'm not looking for a fuck today, buddy. Maybe tomorrow after a few tequila sunrises," said Henley. Who knew what *those* would do to his brain?

His retirement goal of working his way through the entire drink menu was not appreciated by his liver...or his bladder.

The guy lifted one gray-speckled brow, glancing at Henley's exposed abs.

Okay so maybe...just maybe, Henley had convinced himself to get a henna tattoo that said '*I like big cocks and I cannot lie*' across his abdomen. His choices had been that or getting his short hair somehow braided.

"What happens when you get to the purple rain?"

Henley's breathing came to an abrupt halt, and he whirled toward the new voice. It was coming from the lounger on his other side, which had been unoccupied three seconds prior.

He was moving before he knew it, throwing himself into the lounger and burying his face into the person's chest. It was sticky with freshly applied suntan lotion and smelled of the city and coconut. *My favorite.*

"Li, you fucker, what took you so long?" Henley crawled his way up to Li's lips, crashing their mouths together as his hands gained a mind of their own and went exploring. He caught the sound of a huff behind him and the steady pad of retreating sandals.

"Easy, old man. One of your buddies got a shot in and bruised my ribs." Li flinched, moving Henley's hand from where it dug into his side. "And do you *know* how many resorts are on the Riviera? It took me three days to track you down."

Henley snickered, hugging Li close, despite his second flinch. Li was just going to have to deal with the pain because Henley was not letting go anytime soon. He glanced over his shoulder at the tourists he'd been watching to pass the time. They paled in comparison to the beast in his arms.

"That, and I had to lose their tail. Should be a good two weeks before they get close," said Li, reaching for Henley's drink and taking a swig. "Ugh, is that straight tequila?"

Grinning, Henley grabbed the glass, downing the rest in three chugs. His stomach churned, but that could be cured with a few nachos. "Two weeks? That's it?"

"Well, you didn't give me a lot of instructions when you kissed me and shoved a chip halfway down my throat." Li kissed the top of Henley's head as he let out a chuckle. "Thanks for that, by the way. It would have taken a miracle to get out of that holding cell without it."

Henley let out a sigh, glad he even had the forethought to keep an override chip in the same condom packet as the tracker. He tried to be fully prepared, and that chip was the same as a universal door key. It would open any electronic lock with a delay of ten seconds or less. It had gotten him out of more than one tight spot in the past.

Henley drifted, curling his toes into the shade and letting his eyes fall shut as he listened to Li's heartbeat beneath his ear. He struggled to keep his eyes open to maintain a steady gaze of every inch of *man* before him, but his exhaustion was too much. Every bit of guilt washed away in a steady throb and the slow rise of Li's breath.

"Did you lose their trail on the way here?" asked Li, tugging Henley's tangled hair that he hadn't combed since coming out of the pool. He leaned into the touch, letting out a hum as Li scratched his scalp.

He had only imagined something like this in his dreams before, but the real thing was so much better.

"As far as they know, I'm in Serbia right now seeing a distant cousin, and you're on your way to get me. In" — he looked up to the sun, trying to remember the date — "two days, our bodies will be discovered in a train car, disfigured beyond recognition, but luckily my dental records will match, and your body will just so happen to be carrying a rifle that will match the one that put the bullet in Damien's head."

Li let out a laugh, the movement of his chest almost bucking Henley off. He hissed, rubbing along his side where a black bruise stretched over the skin.

"Admit it," said Henley, poking Li in his belly before trailing down his naked chest. "I am the best secret agent *ever*."

Li snorted, rolling his eyes. "Nah. Best boyfriend ever, maybe. No one has faked my death before on a date."

Poking Li in his bruised rib, Henley lowered his mouth to his nipple, flicking the bud with his tongue and cutting off Li's laugh. "I'll take that. Now take me back to our room. I found watermelon-flavored lube, and I can't wait to eat it out of your ass."

Li moved like his ribs weren't hurting at all, leaping from the lounger with Henley in his arms and marching away from their little patch of shade. "Lead the way, old man."

Epilogue

Li

"Keep your eyes closed," said Henley, whispering against his ear before tugging him along. Li blinked behind the blindfold, squeezing Henley's hand just in case he decided to let go.

Living with Henley had been so different from their back-and-forth chase around the globe that had left them both hungry for more. Running was still a part of their daily lives, but between the two of them, they managed to cover their tracks to near perfection. They'd only had one close call and that had been…taken care of.

"Where are you taking me?" asked Li, trying to keep the laugh out of his voice as Henley shushed him.

When Henley had offered to take him on a Christmas surprise adventure, he had honestly been expecting to get tied to the bed and fucked until he couldn't remember his own name—seeing as that had been what he'd gotten for his twenty-seventh birthday surprise.

But so far, they'd gone on a puddle-jumper plane and a long enough car drive that Li had almost fallen asleep, all with the blindfold in place. And even though Henley had betrayed him before, he couldn't help but trust the ex-secret agent. He would willingly give his life for Henley to keep him safe—something that he could only say about a very few select people in the world.

"Three steps, baby," said Henley, guiding Li as they stepped onto something that creaked under his feet. *If we end up on another love boat, I swear to God —*

"Okay, blindfold off right about...now."

Li blinked against the blazing red light next to his head as he peeled the blindfold off his forehead. Henley was standing beside him, a smile on his lips as he leaned in and pushed a button. The *ding dong* that followed had Li's forehead furrowing with confusion.

They were in front of a red door, the thick green Christmas wreath decorated with tiny fake crystal snowflakes glistening in the flashing Christmas lights that alternated between yellow, red, blue and green. The wooden Santa prop next to the door, complete with red nose and fluffy beard, was even more confusing.

Looking back over his shoulder, Li spied the houses around them with the same type of decorations, their Christmas trees visible through their front windows as the families sat within. The street looked like any other in the southern part of North America, with the grass still green on Christmas day and no sign of snow on the horizon.

It was hard to tell in the dark, but the car on the asphalt driveway looked vaguely familiar, too, with a burnished bronze exterior that tickled at his memory.

The door opened and he swung back, his mouth dropping open as he came face-to-face with his big brother. He shot Henley a glare. *This is so dangerous.*

"Surprise!" Henley shouted, throwing his arms wide before turning to face Li's brother. "So nice to meet you, Jesse. I've heard so much about you. And look at you! Li never mentioned how fantastically attractive you are." Henley grabbed Jesse's hand from where it dangled at his side, shaking it furiously.

Li couldn't talk. He couldn't blink. Hell, he could hardly even breathe. He had wanted to see his brother, but he'd never dreamed of getting so close again, let alone for Christmas.

Tearing up against his will, he wiped his cheeks with the back of his hand, his smile so full that he wondered how his lips could even contain it.

"Oh, baby, don't cry." Henley whirled, rocking up on his toes before cradling Li's chin in his hands. "This was supposed to be a good surprise, not one to make you cry." He placed a kiss on Li's lips before threading their hands together and tugging him closer to Jesse.

"Listowel?"

Jesse looked to be nearly in the same state as Li, minus the tears. His big brother had never been one to show much emotion, but he looked like he was close to cracking. He eyed Henley like he had no idea what the hell he was supposed to do with him.

Li could sympathize.

"I swear that if I knew how attractive you were, I would have dragged Li back here sooner to meet you," said Henley, tugging Li through the door as Jesse finally seemed to overpower his surprise and wave them in.

The humid warmth of the house enclosed them, soaking them with the scent of turkey and stuffing and the gravy that Li could still taste in his dreams.

"Oh, and you must be Sebastian," said Henley, letting out a little cry as a handsome man peeked around the corner of the kitchen. Li blinked, looking between Sebastian and the ring on his brother's finger.

"Congratulations," said Li, his tongue sticking to the roof of his mouth as he swallowed. Henley led himself farther into the house, his voice going quiet as moved away. Sebastian followed, looking a little lost as Henley greeted everyone he came across.

Henley was probably looking for hidden weapons or wires. *Old habits die hard.*

"It's good to see you, little brother," said Jesse, pulling Li close for a hug that was all warmth and comfort. Li sagged in the hold as a few more tears fell, soaking into his brother's shirt.

"I've missed you," said Li, squeezing one last time before he pulled away. Jesse gave a little huff that betrayed his own emotions before he patted Li on the shoulder and led him into the house. "I'm sorry I didn't make it to the funeral."

The day his mother had been lost, he had been trying to escape from one of the most convoluted agencies in the world with a single microchip in his hand that had led him to freedom. He had cried in Henley's arms when he had found out.

Jesse nodded, his lips a thin line as he squeezed Li's shoulder. "I'm just glad you're here." He tilted his head toward the kitchen where Henley had donned oven mitts and was very carefully pulling the turkey from the oven. "That guy belong to you or something?"

"Or something," Li grumbled as Henley grabbed a knife, jabbing into the turkey with gusto as Sebastian looked on, seemingly mildly terrified. "Yeah, he's mine, and I'm his."

"He's...uh...interesting. I can see why you needed to figure things out," said Jesse, stepping into the kitchen and throwing an arm around Sebastian's shoulders. "Seb, I see you've met Henley, Li's boyfriend."

Li gave a wave to his aunt and uncle who he spotted seated on the couch in the living room. *God,* he hadn't seen them in...he couldn't remember how long. A hiss brought his attention back to the stove as Henley managed to touch his arm to the edge of the turkey pan.

"Seriously, Henley, the turkey has already been slaughtered. You don't have to do it twice." Li grabbed the knife, kissing Henley's cheek before nudging him to the side. He lowered his voice so that only Henley would hear. "Thank you."

Henley beamed, true joy shining back at him. He hadn't even known how broken Henley had been until he'd seen him completely free. He wondered how long Henley would have lasted if they hadn't found each other—and how long he would have made it himself without having some sort of breakdown.

"But no propositioning anyone or touching anyone's dick," said Li, giving Henley a serious glare. Henley flushed under it, biting his lip as he glanced over at Jesse and Sebastian. Then a smile flooded his face as he grinned and let out a chuckle.

"Don't worry, pup. You're the only ass for me."

Li flushed all the way to his toes, turning back to the turkey as Jesse gave him a look.

Yeah, he's mine all right.

Want to see more from this author? Here's a taster for you to enjoy!

It's a Kink Thing: Dupli-Kinked
M.C. Roth

Coming February 2023

Excerpt

Copley

The ring burned a hole through the pocket of his jeans, drawing his attention with every step. It was supposed to be a symbol of his love, which had simmered for three years and burned bright for another two. Instead, it was the sole representation of his humiliation.

He'd been so excited when he'd strolled into the jewelry store while wearing his best dress shirt and a pair of slacks that had fit him just right. He dressed well for his work, but he'd never really worn something truly expensive before.

He'd kept his jaw sewn tight as he looked at the price tags on every ring, going from glass case to glass case until he'd finally found the dismal selection targeted for men. A simple gold band had barely been within his budget, but he'd needed something. He hadn't been able to go another moment without telling Spencer how he felt about him.

They'd hardly spoken during the whispered moments at night when they had lain together in the most intimate embrace. But what was he supposed to say to someone who had started as his roommate but had stolen his heart instead?

It had all begun so innocently as a way to blow off steam. The tension had seemed to build as soon as they'd settled in as roommates, even though they'd been strangers at the time. Outside the apartment, they'd become friends who were perhaps more affectionate than most, but as soon as the apartment door had closed behind them, their walls had come down.

Spencer had been *his*. He would slip into Copley's bed and lie with him until the sun peeked through his bedroom curtains when he had to roll out and go to work with his ass aching and his lips still bruised from their kisses.

"Copley, come back to bed."

How many times had he fallen for that? How many sick days had passed with them in bed as they kissed and made love until they simply couldn't anymore?

That was why the ring had been so important, and why he'd purchased the simple gold band from the clerk, who had given him a slightly disappointed look, as if he should have spent thousands instead of hundreds.

He was in love, but he still had to eat.

His heart had been ready to pound out of his chest by the time he'd arrived home, pulling the ring from the tiny box and clutching it in his hand. He had bitten his tongue, pushing himself through the door before he could chicken out.

And everything had come crashing down.

He'd grabbed his packed bag from his side of the bed, wiping the tears from his cheeks before he'd fled the apartment with Spencer staring after him looking so confused and concerned that it had nearly broken his heart a second time.

The bag was heavy on his shoulder, thumping against his back as he took practiced steps toward the main street. He'd packed light for the second part of his would-be surprise—a camping trip just for the two of them.

The bag contained a single change of clothes with one tent and an extra-large sleeping bag that would have zipped around them just right. It was the perfect way to celebrate a new engagement.

Only he'd been wrong from the very beginning. While Copley had been falling in love for five wonderful years, Spencer hadn't felt a thing. Their stress relief had been just that and nothing more to him—which was why Spencer had introduced him to his girlfriend while Copley had clutched the ring in his hand like some clueless idiot.

Wiping his cheeks with the back of his hand, Copley looked out onto the street and the zooming traffic that was slowly starting to thin. For a gloomy fall Saturday, the road was surprisingly busy, with people rushing here and there as they prepared for winter.

It would have been near freezing in the tent on their impromptu trip, and they would have had to snuggle so close to share their bodily warmth, fogging the air as they breathed each other in.

Copley sobbed, cupping his hand over his mouth as he stumbled to the nearest bench. He sagged onto the slatted wood frame, dropping his pack as he pressed his face into his hands. A wail seeped past his lips as his chest pulled so tight that he wondered how he could still breathe.

"You okay?"

Sniffing, Copley turned to the man next to him, who looked rather startled at his new bench mate. His hair was gray, a few age spots peeking from under his waterproof cap that matched the poncho around his shoulders.

"Yeah." Copley sniffed, wiping his hands over his face to try to squish the sobs at the source. It didn't quite work, but the stranger's eyes on him stalled his tears where they were. He'd already humiliated himself enough for one day.

"I get like that on rainy days, too, sometimes." The stranger tipped his cap as he gazed up at the cloudy sky. "Not sure if it's the best weather for camping, though, son." He eyed Copley's bag and the sleeping bag nearly bursting from its packaging. "It's going to be a mighty cold one tonight, and you don't look like you're dressed for it. I can feel a storm brewing in my bones."

Copley's lips twitched in the briefest of smiles as he let out a breath. "You sound just like my mother. '*Don't forget your sweater, Copley.*'" He shook his head, pulling his arms around himself as a gust of wind stripped him of warmth. The guy was right, though. In his haste, he hadn't grabbed a jacket, and with the nightfall only a short time away, it was already starting to get chilly.

"Sounds like a wise woman, like my Nancy. I would forget my pants if my wife didn't remind me every morning." He smiled, rubbing his hand over his knobby knee and grimacing. "I'm surprised she even lets me take the bus anymore. Some days it's just nice to meet new people, but she's more of a homebody. Always was."

Smiling through the last of his tears, Copley leaned against the bench and shuddered as another wind gust swept over him. The blue and yellow bus sign blared above his head, but there were no vehicles in sight. The routes went every fifteen minutes in the city, and he could hop from one to the next with his eyes closed. He'd never even thought of having his own car before.

"Where are you headed, son? Up toward Forrest Lake? Or maybe down by the flats? We used to party there in my day. Don't tell my Nancy, but there were quite a few ladies that liked to tag along, if you know what I mean. I played football back then. Nothing like a bit of pigskin to get the fire started."

Copley blinked, chuckling awkwardly as he looked around for an escape. Listening to an old man talk about his young and straight escapades was slightly awkward, if he were honest. He didn't want to be rude, but that generation tended to be a tad…ungentlemanly to him when they found out he was attracted to men.

"I wouldn't know, actually. And as for where I'm headed…? I haven't figured that out yet." *I couldn't catch a football if it was covered in glue.*

He looked to the bus sign. Route fifteen looped around the north side of town before it hit low-income housing and some spots that he didn't dare step into while he was dressed the way he was. As much as he tried to be open-minded and non-judgmental, he clutched his keys tighter when he passed by graffiti or a few gang members on a corner.

"Well, this bus will take you to some of the best spots," said the old man, tugging his cap back over his brow as the sun peeked out one final time before clouds consumed it again. It was starting to get low in the sky, bronze blushing to pinks and reds as a few lamplights buzzed to life.

"My Nancy was raised on South Street, just next to the old inn. Not much to it now, but in its glory, it was a beautiful place. Do you know it?" He looked to Copley, his bushy eyebrows scrunching as he slowly blinked.

"I do. I was raised up that way, actually," said Copley, tugging his shirt tighter around his belly as a raindrop landed on his knee. The rain was cold, sinking straight to his skin as a second drop landed on the bench next to him.

He had been raised near Highbury Street, which was only two blocks from South, and he knew exactly why he shouldn't travel there. He remembered the noises in the night and the shouts that had kept him awake. His mother and pop had done their best to raise him and his brother and keep them safe in that neighborhood, but sometimes he wondered how he'd ever made it out.

When he'd been old enough, he'd left the neighborhood behind, and his parents had followed shortly after, only they had moved so far south that he rarely saw them in person anymore.

"My brother is still down that way, actually. He's in the old apartment building near the corner of Highbury…the one with the yellow brick and the steeples," said Copley. The brick had been all but crumbling the last time Copley had seen it, the shingles on the peaked roof barely hanging on.

"That's the old McGuire place. He used to own the old bus line in town before it went out of business. Committed suicide not long after that, and his wife went into a nunnery."

"Oh dear," said Copley, trying to keep his face blank. *Do nunneries still exist?* He used to watch *The Sound of Music* with his mother all the time, and he still knew the songs by heart. The man nodded, his mouth set into a grim line.

"We lost a lot of good men to things like that back then. Not so much now with people my age, but then, half of them aren't alive anymore, anyway. There are only two people left from my high school graduating class." He let out a long sigh, finally stilling his hand where he rubbed at his knee. "But I should be going before Nancy sends the search party out for me. I hope you find your way, son."

The old man stood with a groan, his shoulders stooped as he grabbed the cane that was sitting next to the bench. "And be careful in that part of town. There are a lot of sons of bitches out there." He walked off, slowly shuffling his feet against the sidewalk.

Copley looked to his pocket where he could still feel the ring like a blazing halo of misfortune. He wasn't close to feeling any better, but at least he had a touch of perspective.

"Well, I guess I know where I'm headed."

He grabbed his bag as the bus pulled up to the stop and parked with a burst of air brakes before the doors swung wide. Stepping inside, he clutched the strap of his pack as he paid and slipped into a seat near the front. He hadn't seen his brother in years, so he was woefully overdue. Hopefully, he had a couch that still had its cushions where Copley could sleep.

He let out a sigh as his eyes began to burn again, his tears budding afresh as he looked back to the bench and his neighborhood. *It's going to be a long night.*

About the Author

M.C. Roth lives in Canada and loves every season, even the dreaded Canadian winter. She graduated with honours from the Associate Diploma Program in Veterinary Technology at the University of Guelph before choosing a different career path.

Between caring for her young son, spending time with her husband, and feeding treats to her menagerie of animals, she still spends every spare second devoted to her passion for writing.

She loves growing peppers that are hot enough to make grown men cry, but she doesn't like spicy food herself. Her favourite thing, other than writing of course, is to find a quiet place in the wilderness and listen to the birds while dreaming about the gorgeous men in her head.

M.C. Roth loves to hear from readers. You can find her contact information, website details and author profile page at https://www.pride-publishing.com

PUBLISHING

Sign up for our newsletter and find out about all our
romance book releases, eBook sales and promotions,
sneak peeks and FREE romance books!